Dagger Quest

Dagger Quest

A USCG Cutter *Kauai* Sea Adventure by

Edward M. Hochsmann

Haldago Bay Studio

E-Book ISBN-13: 978-1-956777-99-4

Paperback ISBN-13: 978-1-956777-96-3

Edward M. Hochsmann
PO Box 286
Shalimar, Florida 32579-0286
www.edwardhochsmann.com

First Edition

Cover by SpudzArt©

Table of Contents

DEDICATION

This book is dedicated to my wife and sons, who provide the love and support that gets me through each day and every effort I face. It is also dedicated to the Coast Guard, the oldest continuous seagoing service of the United States, and its complement of supremely skilled, committed, and courageous professionals. They stand the watch and lay their lives on the line every day to save others, defend the homeland, protect the environment, and promote maritime commerce.

Semper Paratus

Main Characters

Benjamin "Ben" Wyporek, Lieutenant Junior Grade, U. S. Coast Guard. Ben is the Second-in-Command or "Executive Officer" of the Coast Guard Cutter *Kauai*. He is young for an officer, but his demeanor and experience have earned the respect of the professionals around him, and although he is firm in his job, he never lets his position go to his head.

Dr. Peter Simmons is a field agent with the Defense Intelligence Agency. He has a talent for deception, which has led to his success as a DIA field agent, but is the antithesis of Ben's ethos. Simmons also has a risk-seeking bent that borders on pathology.

Samuel "Sam" Powell, Lieutenant, U. S. Coast Guard. Sam is Ben's boss and Commanding Officer of the Coast Guard Cutter *Kauai*. Sam is one of those people who is the total package - knowledge, judgment, experience, and "people sense." He was raised in a wealthy family and was being groomed to become another Wall Street "Master of the Universe" when a clash with his father led him to abandon that path and enlist in the Coast Guard. He is over ten years older than Ben, but despite this and their different backgrounds, they are best friends.

Emilia "Hoppy" Hopkins, Operations Specialist First Class, U. S. Coast Guard. She is close in age and a lot like Sam in terms of competence and professionalism, and they have as strong a friendship as people in their respective positions can. Although a straight arrow, she is not afraid to forego convention in highly unusual circumstances.

James Drake, Chief Machinery Technician, U. S. Coast Guard. The senior enlisted member of the crew and the classic father figure among the enlisted and, to some extent, Ben. He is the quintessential "operator" and has what amounts to an underground network of fellow CPOs from whom he can acquire technical help, equipment, and "intel." His background is somewhat mysterious, but he is "connected" up to the senior officer level of the Coast Guard.

Arthur "Art" Frankle, Senior Case Officer, Defense Clandestine Service, Defense Intelligence Agency. Frankle is a veteran field officer, instructor, and mentor to many younger agents. He is approaching retirement age and considering moving from the field to a less "kinetic" post as an instructor or administrator.

Select Technical Terms

1MC	Ship's internal announcement system
252s	Transnational Criminal Organization
Afterdeck	The top deck behind the ship's superstructure
Airedale	Slang term referring to aviation personnel
Bridge	Control center for the ship
Captain	The title for a commanding officer when aboard their ship, regardless of nominal rank. Also, a Coast Guard and Navy rank at paygrade O6, equivalent to a Colonel in the Army, Air Force, and Marine Corps.
CO	Commanding Officer
Conn	Position controlling operation of the ship
Coxswain	Position controlling the operation of a small boat
DIA	Defense Intelligence Agency
EO/IR	Electro-Optical/Infrared
Foredeck	The top deck forward of the ship's superstructure
GQ	General Quarters (Emergency Stations)
Helm	Position or station controlling the ship's rudder
IC	Intelligence Community
Knots	Nautical Miles per Hour
"Light Off"	Start or activate an engine or device
Main Control	Control station for the ship's main engines
OOD	Officer of the Deck
PB	Patrol Boat
Port (side)	To the left, when facing forward aboard a ship
Puma	RQ-20 Small Unmanned Aerial Vehicle
Quarterdeck	Entry point for the ship while moored
RHIB	Rigid Hull Inflatable Boat
ROE	Rules of Engagement
SAROPS	Search and Rescue Optimal Planning System
Starboard (side)	To the right, when facing forward aboard a ship

Steerageway	The slowest speed at which the ship can be steered
Stern	The rear end of the ship
UAV	Unmanned Aerial Vehicle
WILCO	Brevity code for "Will Comply."
XO	Executive Officer—second-in-command of a ship

Prologue

It was the most dangerous period in East-West relations since the Cuban Missile Crisis in 1962. The previous decade and a half had seen the military ascendency of the Russian Federation and the renewal of its economic prospects dashed by the collapse of the oil markets. The subtle influence of so-called "Green Parties" in Germany had completely closed down the country's nuclear power capacity, making the largest consumer of energy in Europe completely dependent on Russian natural gas, not only for heating but also for electrical power generation.

The military adventures against Georgia in 2008 and Ukraine in 2014 had convinced Russia's revanchist president, Mikhail Ivanovich Platov, that NATO and the European Union were unwilling to risk war, even in the face of the most naked aggression. He began a long campaign to restore Russia to its "natural" borders, using means ranging from economic coercion to outright military threats to intimidate the smaller nations along Russia's periphery. With the West riven by political strife, he felt there would be no better time to wring out concessions to bolster Russia's military security. He would start by establishing a land corridor through Poland and Lithuania to the Russian enclave of Kaliningrad on the Baltic Sea. Kaliningrad was of enormous military and economic importance to Russia, being its only year-round ice-free seaport on the Baltic Sea. It was also vulnerable to counter-coercion from the West, as any land traffic between the enclave and Russia would have to pass through at least two other countries. That vulnerability needed to be fixed.

Platov dusted off the playbook that had worked so well before in Georgia and Ukraine. This involved fomenting unrest among the ethnic Russians toward the Polish and Lithuanian authorities, moving substantial military forces to conduct "exercises" in the Grodno region of the Russian puppet state of Belarus, and threats to curtail or cut off oil and natural gas supplies to the West. Given time, the broad front political, economic, military, and psychological pressures would force the West to shrug and deliver another bloodless victory to Russia.

This time, it did not work.

Poland and Lithuania were far more homogeneous and nationalistic than the Russia-adjacent regions of Ukraine and Georgia and, unlike those states, were governed by relatively progressive and uncorrupted regimes. Also, unlike those states, Poland and Lithuania were not unaligned countries some distance from Western military centers. These were *NATO* countries with solid internal lines of defense and communications. A trustworthy and professional military cadre might have pointed out these basic first principles and dissuaded Platov from this effort. But like his distant predecessor Josef Stalin, he had purged the officer corps of no-men, preferring the loyalty of yes-men to competence.

The governments of the West came together solidly and quietly on the issue so as not to panic their populations or trigger financial collapse. The senior military officers in the West also conveyed a strong and unequivocal message to their Russian counterparts. A single Russian aircraft, tank tread, or soldier's boot crossing the Polish or Lithuanian borders would unleash a decisive counterattack on *all* Russian conventional forces across the theater. And if they thought firing nuclear weapons was an option, the West would ensure there was nothing left of Russia but a sad story, regardless of the cost.

That threat convinced even the bellicose Platov to move toward disengagement, but there had to be a show of force for internal purposes. Russian Long-Range Aviation units carried this out. Tu-95 "Bear" bombers launched from Siberia to the edge of U.S. airspace over the Bering Sea in the West. In the East, Tu-160 "Blackjacks" flew from Caracas, Venezuela, to the U.S. Gulf Coast, and Tu-22M "Backfires" from San Antonio de los Baños Airfield southwest of Havana, Cuba, to the U.S. Southern Atlantic Coast. The Russians made no secret that these aircraft were carrying nuclear weapons—it was the purpose of the show of force. The U.S. Air Force dutifully intercepted and flew formation on the bombers with fully armed fighter aircraft. This was not the usual "poking the bear" operations, and both sides were on high alert during the bomber flights.

Formation flying carries a much higher risk of collision, particularly among tired, scared men and women flying at night around foreign aircraft with different flight procedures and communications protocols. It was not a surprise that a U.S. F-16 interceptor and a Russian Backfire "bumped" in the Air Defense Identification Zone. What was a surprise was that the collision triggered the drop of the bomber's Kh-47 Kinzhal hypersonic missile. As the crew of the bomber and the fighter's pilot fought to regain control of their respective aircraft, the missile's rocket engine ignited after it had dropped fifty meters, quickly accelerating it to its maximum speed of twelve times the speed of sound. The disabled F-16's wingman promptly fell back, locked his fire control radar on the bomber, and called his controller.

"Flash, Flash, Flash, Rondo Two, Bogie has launched, repeat strategic missile inbound!"

"Rondo Two, Plaintree, confirm strategic missile launch!"

"Plaintree, Rondo Two, confirm strategic missile launch heading Northwest! Rondo One and Bogie collided, followed by launch. I am locked on to Bogie now. Request weapons free!"

"Rondo Two, Plaintree, hold and standby!"

"Roger. Break, break. One, this is Two, come in!"

"Two, One. You've got this one. My hands are full right now.

"One, Two, roger."

"American fighter, this is bomber. Launch is accident! Missile not arm! Repeat, launch is accident, missile not arm!" It was the bomber crew calling on the UHF distress frequency.

"Bomber, maintain heading, airspeed, and altitude. If you deviate, I will destroy you. Acknowledge!" *Go ahead and try to run, you son of a bitch!*

"American fighter, this is bomber. I comply."

"Plaintree, Rondo Two, I am in contact with Bogie. They claim the launch was accidental, and the missile is unarmed. Over."

"Two, Plaintree, do you have a visual on the missile?"

"Negative, Plaintree, it's long gone."

"Rondo Two, roger. Weapons tight. Direct bogie to RTB. Follow until you hit the Cuban ADIZ. Over."

"Rondo Two, roger, out." He switched to the emergency frequency. "Russian bomber, this is the American fighter. You will execute a slow right turn to a heading of two three zero. Acknowledge."

"American fighter, I am turning right to two three zero."

The two aircraft completed a slow turn to the southwest, the F-16 trailing the larger bomber. The infuriated F-16 pilot was struggling to keep from pressing the fire switch as he listened to the steady growl of his Sidewinder missile lock-on tone. *This bastard just launched a NUCLEAR MISSILE, and we are letting him go? WTF!*

On the ground, the alert went out instantly to the Supreme Headquarters Allied Powers Europe in Mons, Belgium, North American Aerospace Defense

Command (NORAD) at Peterson Space Force Base in Colorado Springs, and Strategic Command at Offutt Air Force Base near Omaha. NORAD activated defensive systems, but it was for naught—the Kinzhal, Russian for "Dagger," flew so fast that its shock wave generated a plasma cloud that made it invisible to radar. Even if the missile could be tracked, nothing could fly fast enough to catch it.

The lack of indications and warnings of other offensive activity by the Russians lent credence to the claim that the launch had been accidental. They would know whether the missile was deliberately targeted and armed within ten minutes—the time it would take for the missile to exhaust its fuel. At that point, everyone could either breathe a sigh of relief or prepare for the next phase of the destruction of human civilization.

"A few armed vessels, judiciously stationed at the entrances of our ports, might at a small expense be made useful sentinels of the laws."

Alexander Hamilton

1

Deployment

Sailing Vessel *High Dawn*, Gulf of Mexico north of the Florida Keys
02:07 EST, 10 January

Heinrich Köhler eyed the slowly approaching beach of the island through the night vision ocular. *A few hundred meters to go, then the last turn into the wind, and we anchor. Nearly done.* He confirmed his estimate using the hand-held GPS unit—283 meters. It would be close enough to the beach for short boat trips, but not so near that an unexpected squall could put them on the beach. After coming so far, he would not be undone by a rookie blunder drawing the attention of the American Coast Guard or some other helpful do-gooder. Not with a metric ton of cocaine and one hundred kilos of fentanyl on board.

The two thousand three hundred mile trip had begun a little over two weeks earlier for Köhler. His employers dispatched him and two assistants to take charge of the *High Dawn*, a beautiful sixty-five-foot cabin sloop in Greenwich, Connecticut. The yacht's owners were a Wall Street power couple who had lately made some abysmal market choices and needed quick cash. They made the fatal mistake of contacting his organization through one of their dodgier clients in hopes of a one-and-done trip to South America and back to clear their debts with no one the wiser. They were quite adept at working the system to clean up dirty cash and carefully and completely planned that aspect of the operation. Unfortunately for them, their skills in white-collar crime did not provide them with insight into the realities of the underworld of narcotics smuggling.

Köhler could not believe his luck when the two insisted on making the trip "to keep an eye on things." He feigned a mild annoyance and then acquiescence to the demand to keep them on the hook. From his perspective, the situation could not have been better: two wealthy gay men on a Caribbean vacation on their new yacht with a dour German captain and two crewmen provided the perfect cover for the trip down. It also obviated the need to dispose of them in Connecticut, risking discovery and failure before the journey began. The men's insistence on making the trip bought them an additional week of life. Their usefulness ended after the onload and departure from La Guaira, Venezuela, when they just became another liability. Both were quickly and efficiently disposed of at sea.

The organization took a substantial risk with this trip, concentrated in a single load rather than dispersed over several vessels. Köhler had sold them on the idea a year before—use their radar masker and decoy vessels to get a single large load through at minor risk rather than accept the almost certain loss of some portion of the product in many smaller loads. Operational security was the critical factor for success. They would not go into any port or marina. Eight terminal points for the trip were selected among the less-traveled but accessible locations in the Florida Keys. All were reconnoitered just before nightfall, and the status of clear or occupied had been broadcast by radio "in the blind." Köhler himself would select the final destination and call it in once the *High Dawn* was anchored and secured.

With only a couple of minutes to go before anchoring, now was the time to go live and get things moving. After checking that Paolo was in position on the bow to release the anchor, Köhler turned the helm over to Jaime and ducked into the cabin to retrieve the satellite phone to make the call. He had to weave around the massive stacks of cargo in the cabin to get to the storage cabinet. He powered it on and verified he had a good signal link. It was the last act of his life.

Jaime and Paolo had a brief glimpse of a bright light approaching at over 3.5 kilometers per second, just long enough to turn their heads before the impact. Like Köhler working below in the cabin, they never knew what hit them.

Water, like all liquids, is virtually incompressible. A supersonic shock wave moving through the water is a solid wall for all practical purposes. This one broadsided the *High Dawn,* with the equivalent effect of dropping the boat onto a solid surface from sixty feet in the air. The three men were actually stationary at the outset of the event—the boat itself was "thrown" into them by the impact, killing them all instantly.

The *High Dawn* herself was laid waste. The shock wave crushed the starboard side of the hull. The mast stay on the port side snapped, and the mast itself was toppling over the starboard side, its attachment point to the deck shearing. Then the air shock wave hit, lifting the mast clear, snapping the starboard stay, running rigging, and the electric cable to the masker array. It was swept into the sea, along with Jaime and Paolo's bodies and anything else not fastened to the deck.

Köhler's command had become his tomb, rapidly filling with water from hundreds of cracks in the hull. Ironically, the priceless cargo was undamaged in the disaster, packaged in bales sealed in plastic and close-packed in any available space inside. The positive buoyancy of the bales would provide enough floatation to keep the boat from sinking for days as it sped off into the Gulf of Mexico with the residual momentum of the impact.

Two hours later, well past the expected time the *High Dawn* should have reported in, calls went out to the onboard satellite phones, then the crew's cell phones, and finally, first in code, then in the clear on marine band radio. When it became apparent that no answer was forthcoming, the alarm went out, and the organization began deploying resources for a covert search. Losing this cargo would be a significant hit to the bottom line. Both inside and outside the organization, those responsible would pay dearly if it could not be recovered.

USCG Cutter *Kauai*, eleven nautical miles southeast of Fort Jefferson, Florida
09:43 EST, 13 January

Ben

Benjamin "Ben" Wyporek, Lieutenant Junior Grade, U.S. Coast Guard, was coming up on the halfway point of his Officer of the Deck, or OOD, duty in the eight a.m. to noon Forenoon Watch. In that role, he supervised the watchstanders, kept the vessel on course and speed and clear of other vessels, and was the captain's representative. The workload stayed low when *Kauai* carried just enough speed to hold heading and position against the light winds and currents in the area. She held a position near a known drug smuggler rendezvous. These were locations where "mother ships" carrying sizeable amounts of cocaine and other illegal products off-loaded to small, fast vessels for the final run to shore in the Florida Keys.

The watch had been quiet so far and somewhat boring, an unfortunate characteristic of sentry operations. Ben was grateful, at least for the comfortable weather. The temperate and dry days of January were the best time to be in the Western Florida Keys, at least for a born-and-raised northerner like Ben.

Far preferable to July and August, when the only respite from the sweltering heat and humidity came from the torrential downpours of the scattered squalls that popped up during the day.

Even the seas were kind today—no swell, and the small waves stirred by the light winds gave the patrol boat a gentle rocking motion. The downside of January patrols was that weather systems often pushed down from the north with winds that stirred up moderate wave action. They were not a problem for larger vessels, but the choppy pitching and rolling they caused made even mundane activities such as eating and sleeping a challenge on smaller boats like *Kauai*.

Kauai was a Coast Guard cutter. She was an Island Class Patrol Boat (D Class), one hundred ten feet long, weighing 168 tons, with a crew of fourteen enlisted and two officers. She was old, pushing twenty-five years of age on a design intended to last only fifteen. The Coast Guard had retired many of her older sisters, but *Kauai* was still alive and serving. Ben glanced out the rear window and saw the reason: Chief Machinery Technician James Drake walking toward the cradled rigid hull inflatable boat, called "the rib" for its acronym RHIB, with a junior petty officer in tow.

Drake got the title of "Chief," being the only chief petty officer on *Kauai*, was the senior enlisted member and, at forty-four, the oldest man on the boat. He was the finest chief petty officer Ben had ever known, both for the mastery of his trade and his leadership among the crew. Unlike the more legendary members of the chief petty officer ranks, Drake never shouted at his juniors. Six-foot-four and physically imposing, he only needed to lean in on someone to command attention. Ben wondered whether the junior petty officer with Drake had committed a minor blunder or if he was just doing on-the-job training. Most of the skills Coast Guard technicians gained came from hands-on instruction on the job, and Drake took this responsibility seriously.

Drake looked after his officers as well. Occasionally, Ben had voiced a concern and soon found the problem had been corrected. He suspected Drake had dealt with many other issues before they even came to his attention. It went both ways. When Drake sensed Ben's uncertainty regarding an important decision, he often asked a respectful but pointed question. Sometimes, Drake pulled him aside and said something like, "You know XO, if I were you, I'd...." Ben always took the advice and never regretted it.

Five-foot-ten with an average build, Ben was personable and much more intelligent than his mediocre grades at the Coast Guard Academy suggested. He was among the younger members of the crew, being just past his twenty-fourth birthday. Ben had aspired to join the military since grade school, and his liking of naval history led him to apply to both the Coast Guard and Naval Academies. The Coast Guard offered an appointment first, and he accepted and never looked back.

Ben was the junior of the two officers on board, the executive officer or just "XO" by title and second in command. Besides standing the occasional watch, he oversaw the administrative needs of the cutter, including the reports, supplies, and financial accounts. Also, he preserved the crew's health, morale, and discipline, sometimes a grueling task on a surface unit as small and busy as *Kauai*. Yet, he was luckier than most officers in his position. There were no formal disciplinary actions in his year on board, and the only chronic troublemakers had rotated off to other units.

In the quiet times on patrol, such as this watch, Ben's mind often wandered back to his transfer to *Kauai*. His assignment resulted from good luck, although he wasn't sure of that at the time. Eighteen months into his first assignment on the large cutter *Dependable,* the ship's XO told him of the offer of an early rotation for the position on *Kauai*. She explained this opportunity was the perfect bird in the hand—with the number of one-tens dwindling, his chances for an XO job in his next assignment were fading fast. Needing no further encouragement, he took the job.

Lieutenant Samuel Powell greeted Ben on his arrival, having taken command two weeks earlier. The sector commander had fired their predecessors following a serious mishap, and Ben worried he was walking into a fiery mess of poor discipline and morale. Much to Ben's relief, Sam did not expect him to "whip" the crew into shape; they just needed to offer clear direction, stability, and encouragement. They set out to build *Kauai* into a successful team and shake loose the specter of failure that had brought them there. Within a few months, they had done just that.

Ben liked and appreciated Sam from the outset. An inch taller than Ben with a slim, athletic build, Sam was a Mustang—a former chief petty officer in the Operations Specialist rating who had completed Officer Candidate School and received an officer's commission. At thirty-five, he was second only to Drake in age among *Kauai*'s crew. Ben thought Sam was the most open and approachable officer he had ever met, possessing a ready, but not mean, sense of humor. He was not a pushover, and he insisted on decorum on the Bridge and in official situations. Still, Sam ensured the crew understood he stood by them if they worked hard and played by the rules.

It surprised Ben to learn later that Sam was a graduate of the University of Pennsylvania's prestigious Wharton School and came from a wealthy family. Children from that world rarely opted for the rigors of military life, particularly as enlisted personnel. He worked up the nerve to ask Sam about his choice one quiet evening when they were both on the Bridge.

Sam dropped his head for a second, then he looked up and said, "My family asked that question in shocked disbelief." After a brief pause, he said, "Let's just say I had to make a choice between two teams. One had people who'd let someone they know die just to make more money, and the other had people who risk their lives to save people they'd never met." He smiled. "The Coast Guard was the best call I ever made."

"Me too, sir," Ben had replied with complete sincerity.

Ben completed another round of scanning for targets by radar and binoculars when the alert sounded on the satellite channel used for communication with the operations center in Miami.

The message read, in plain language: "To *Kauai* from District Seven Operations Center: detach at once from the current mission and proceed to latitude 25 degrees 6 minutes north, longitude 81 degrees 8 minutes west for search and rescue on a disabled sailing vessel. The target is suspicious—a possible drug smuggler—and *Kauai* is to contact the Coast Guard maritime patrol aircraft 2303, the on-scene commander. Acknowledge."

This is more like it. Ben thought as he typed the latitude and longitude into the navigation system. *Drugs and search and rescue—buy one, get one free!* He picked up the phone to call Sam and report the development.

"Captain speaking."

"Sir, OOD here. They have detached us for SAR, disabled sailing vessel, potential drug target spotted by an HC-144. I read zero-six-seven true at one hundred-two miles. We should have comms from here if he is high enough."

"Very well. Make the turn and bring up full speed. I'm coming up now."

"Very good, sir." Ben hung up the phone and gave the orders to the helmsman. Sam entered the space a few moments later, and Ben announced, "Captain on the Bridge."

"Carry on, please." Sam returned Ben's salute. "Let's see if we can talk to them."

"Yes, sir." Ben dialed up the plane's frequency on the control console, then returned to his usual position, monitoring *Kauai*'s progress while listening to the radio conversation. "We're up now, Captain."

"Thank you." Sam picked up the handset. "Two-three-zero-three, one-three-five-one on uniform in the green, over."

After a brief pause, the Coast Guard plane responded, "One-three-five-one, zero three, roger, read you lima-charlie in the green, over."

"Zero-three, five-one, we are on the way, ETA three and a half hours. What do you have for us?"

"Roger, it's weird. We have a large cabin sloop that's a total mess. The main deck is awash with heavy damage to the deck structures, and the mast is gone—nowhere in sight. No persons on board or bodies are visible."

"Copy main deck awash—is the vessel sinking?"

"Negative, vessel is upright and stable. The hull's trashed, but something's keeping it afloat. Could be sealed contraband."

Sam paused as he pondered the plane's report. A full load of drugs in sealed plastic packages could keep a small sailing vessel afloat, even with extensive damage. But that much product was worth a fortune—the owner's abandonment of it made little sense. "Roger, can you find the cause of the damage?"

"We got as close as possible, and we have good camera footage. No apparent weapons damage, no sign of vessel collision. It could be storm damage, but I've

18

never seen it like this. It is just—weird. When you get closer, we will send the camera video to you."

"Roger that. Any other traffic nearby?"

"Negative. Radar is clear, and nothing visual to the horizon."

"Roger. Can you hang in until we arrive?"

"Affirmative. Orders are to hold here until you're on scene."

"Zero-three, five-one, roger, see you in three and a half, out." Sam replaced the handset and stepped over to Ben. "This is a helluva thing. It must be dope keeping her afloat, but it doesn't figure them abandoning it."

The problem intrigued Ben. "A storm could have washed them overboard, but there haven't been any big storms around here since last October, Captain. Maybe a waterspout or rogue wave?"

Sam stared out across the bow, rubbing his chin. "Maybe. It's strange the mast is nowhere around. The stays and running lines should've kept it nearby. Like the man said, weird. Let's go in heavy on this one, XO, full law enforcement load-out. I want Chief to go along too and give that boat a check up close before anybody sets foot on it."

"Yes, sir."

"Get Hoppy to relieve you in a couple of hours. I need your eyes on that boat with no distractions when we approach."

"Will do, sir."

"Besides, I want my best driver with the conn when we head into weirdness." Sam winked.

Operations Specialist First Class Emilia "Hoppy" Hopkins was a fast-tracker in her rating. Although that rating covered a wide range of skills, her primary responsibilities aboard *Kauai* included navigation, communications, and operational systems. She was an outstanding ship handler and the go-to OOD for any dicey situation. A thirteen-year veteran of the Coast Guard and above the cut for chief petty officer, she would pin on the coveted promotion this summer on rotation from her E6 billet aboard *Kauai* to an E7 billet elsewhere.

Hopkins was tall—about Ben's height at five-foot-ten—and a fit, thirty-three-year-old, widowed mother of eleven- and nine-year-old sons. She shared a house with her mother, who cared for the boys when she was at sea. Sam liked and felt a kindred spirit with the warmhearted and professional petty officer, but, as captain, he had to take care not to let it show. His wife Joana followed no such restraint—she and Hopkins were the closest of friends. Ben shared Sam's admiration for Hopkins and often leaned on her for help with operational issues or advice for dealing with the crew.

"Boss, I'm crushed!" Ben faked a distressed expression at the implied slight on his competence. He knew it was the right call—Sam needed him to have his full attention on the problem instead of focusing on keeping *Kauai* from running into anything. Also, he had to admit Hoppy *was* a better driver than he—hell, she could give the skipper a run for his money.

As Sam went back below, Ben returned to his OOD duties, the watch less quiet than a few minutes ago. The engines were roaring at full power, with a brisk twenty-eight knots of wind produced by the full speed run and intermittent loud thumps as *Kauai*'s hull cut through the occasional wave.

USCG Cutter *Kauai*, Gulf of Mexico, fifty-six nautical miles northeast of Key West, Florida
12:03 EST, 13 January

Ben

Right before her approach to the target vessel, *Kauai*'s crew went to Law Enforcement Stations. All topside personnel donned body armor and helmets. The gunners uncovered and loaded the fifty-caliber machine guns, and a carbine-equipped sharpshooter took position on the Flying Bridge above the main Bridge. The video downloaded from the plane did not yield any insights, just a full-round view of a wrecked boat. There was no hiding place topside, and both officers were sure the interior was uninhabitable to anyone not using scuba gear. Still, Sam did not take chances with his crew and his ship. After a slow approach from the south with all eyes on the target, Hopkins brought *Kauai* into the light westerly wind about fifty yards up sun and "parked" using throttle and rudder.

The RHIB was hoisted in position at the edge of the port main deck. Besides the coxswain driving the boat, it held the three-person boarding party led by

Boatswains Mate First Class John Bondurant and Chief Drake. Bondurant was the senior boatswain's mate, leading the deck department aboard *Kauai* and supervising the other two boatswain's mates, the gunner's mate, and the three junior seamen. He was typical for a mid-grade boatswain: an expert coxswain, competent OOD, and smart law enforcement boarding officer. In his early thirties, Bondurant was an inch shorter than Drake, but even more broad-shouldered. His duties with *Kauai* were demanding, but at least he was home with his family a lot more than on other tours on larger cutters. He was relatively new, arriving at the unit shortly after Sam and Ben took over, but he fit in nicely and liked the crew.

Although Bondurant was the senior coxswain, his tasking to lead the boarding party meant his subordinate, Boatswain's Mate Second Class Shelley Lee, had charge of the boat. Lee was also a skilled boat driver and OOD and, being the only other female aboard *Kauai*, berthing mate with Hopkins. Lee was twenty-five years old and small for a boatswain's mate, barely five-foot-three, but a superb athlete.

Once the boat crew and the boarding party had boarded the RHIB and were secure, Lee reported by radio, "*Kauai, Kauai-One*, boat ready for launch."

"Launch the boat," Sam replied. After the RHIB had lowered the remaining six feet into the water, Lee detached the hook from the lift frame and guided it clear. Firing the engine, she moved the boat smoothly away from the cutter's side.

As the RHIB arced to the left to clear *Kauai*'s stern, Sam walked back to the starboard side of the Bridge. Ben had kept his eyes on the wreck during the launch. "Nothing to report, Captain," he said, sweeping the target with his binoculars.

"Right," Sam said, then radioed, "*Kauai-One, Kauai*, circle the vessel at least once at twenty yards. If satisfied, approach and board from the south."

"*Kauai, Kauai-One*, WILCO, out," Lee replied. Although Drake and Bondurant were both senior, Lee commanded the boat and reported to the captain as coxswain. The RHIB completed a slow turn around the wreck, with no one aboard seeing anything of concern. "*Kauai, Kauai-One*, nothing seen, closing for boarding now, over."

"*Kauai-One, Kauai*, roger, out," Sam answered, not taking his eyes off the scene.

The RHIB moved alongside the wrecked sailboat, allowing the three boarding team members to jump on and spread out. After Drake boarded, Lee pulled the RHIB back to a safe observation position.

"*Kauai*, LE-One, nothing in sight, but I believe there's a dead body somewhere," Bondurant stated via his voice-activated headset. "I'm pulling the hatch now." While the team's junior member moved to a cover position with his shotgun, Bondurant lifted the hatch. "Oh, Goddammit!" he said, recoiling from the opening.

"LE-One, *Kauai*, report status, over," Sam ordered.

"Uh, *Kauai*, LE-One, sorry about that, sir. We've got a floater, pretty ripe. Standby."

Ben grimaced as he watched Bondurant don a surgical mask from his kit and add a stroke of VapoRub. "Floater" was Coast Guard slang for a human corpse made buoyant by trapped gasses generated during decomposition. This was a drawback of the operational Coast Guard: sometimes, the "R" in SAR meant recovery instead of rescue. It wasn't just the terrible smell of a decaying human corpse—it was knowing what that smell *was* that got to you. At least you can mask the odor with a pungent ointment.

Bondurant nodded when he finished, and the other team members took similar action. Drake stood back with his hand covering his mouth and nose until handed a mask and ointment container. "OK, proceeding," said Bondurant, moving back to the hatch. He stepped down through the opening and disappeared. After two minutes, he returned to the main deck.

"*Kauai*, LE-One, I have a report."

"Go ahead, One," Sam said.

"Roger. Just the one body. Lots of product down there—looks like it's the only thing keeping her afloat. The cabin's full of water. I couldn't see shit, er, excuse me, sir. I would say she took a hell of a whack. The starboard side's smashed in. I'm goin' to let Chief look around if you've no objection."

Sam paused before replying. "OK, tell Chief he can have a look if he's sure it's stable. But call the RHIB over first. If things turn bad, you guys bail immediately. Clear?"

"Roger, sir. Also, I cleared the junk hanging over the transom. The boat is the *High Dawn* out of Greenwich, Connecticut."

"Copy one, continue."

Ben called the infirmary. "Doc? XO here. There's a dead body on the boat. Please break out a body bag and stand by. Thanks. Bye."

Sam stepped inside and picked up the handset to radio the circling plane. "Zero-three, five-one, we've got it. Thanks for hanging around for us. For your records, the target's name is the *High Dawn,* and the home port is Greenwich, Connecticut. No registration numbers are visible, and documents are inaccessible at this time. Over."

"Five-one, zero-three, roger that, *laki maika'i, hoa aloha!*" The technician in the plane knew Sam from earlier encounters and that his last assignment was a patrol boat in Hawaii.

"*Mahalo hoa*, out," Sam replied with a slight smile.

After about fifteen minutes, Bondurant called again. "*Kauai*, LE-One, Chief is done. He says we might as well get off this tub. It's not safe to leave a prize crew on board."

"LE-One, *Kauai*, roger, board the RHIB and return to ship. Tell Chief to come to the Bridge as soon as he's on board."

"*Kauai*, LE-One, roger, out."

Sam turned to Ben. "Send Doc with Smitty and Lopez to recover that body. Make sure they get a thorough safety talk before they leave and have masks ready."

25

Ben saluted. "Very good, sir." He went below to arrange things. The recovery team swapped with the boarding team in the RHIB. The boat set off again, and Ben and Drake headed to the Bridge.

After exchanging salutes, Drake started his report. "Captain, I'm not sure what we can do. No point trying to dewater. The starboard side is crushed inward. You can also forget about towing her—I'm sure she'll break up if you try it."

"Crushed? The deck's intact. What do you think hit her, Chief?" Sam frowned.

"That's just it, Captain. It couldn't have been a collision. There's no dent of any kind. It's like, well, it's like the hull slammed flat against a wide stone wall, except that it didn't leave a mark."

"What?"

"I checked over the side; no scratches or mars on the paint, just cracks from the impact. It's like somebody set off a big bomb right beside her, but there's none of the scorching or residue you'd expect to see. The only time I've ever seen hull damage like this was when they tried that AirDrop of the new oil skimmer, and the chutes separated—smacked down from a thousand feet. And it gets weirder, sir." Drake paused.

"Do tell."

"The mast was yanked right off. Bolts sheared up, and the stays snapped right above the deck. That's why it's not dragging alongside. It's just gone, blown away." Drake wiped his forehead. "That body we found? I figure he was inside when it hit, or he'd been blown off too. It's too bloated to be sure, but it wouldn't surprise me if he just got smashed around inside the cabin."

Sam leaned back against the rail with a furrowed brow. "So, you're telling me you think this boat was dropped from a great height?"

"No, sir. I'm sayin' the damage looks like that other boat. I don't see how it could have happened, but that's what it looked like."

"Great." Sam shook his head. "Can't tow it. Can't just sink it because of the dope. I guess it's time to call the boss. Thanks, Chief."

"Yes, sir." Drake saluted and then turned to leave.

Sam started a "chat" on the command net with the District Operations Center in Miami to report their findings and seek further orders. By the time Health Services Technician Second Class Michael "Doc" Bryant and the two junior enlisted crew members returned with the body, he had the answer he expected:

"Standby in the vicinity of the subject vessel and await orders."

"XO, surprise, surprise. Our orders are to await orders. OOD, stay within five hundred yards of the wreck. Call me right away if anything changes. Resume the at sea watch, please."

"Yes, sir," Hopkins replied, turning to check the radar while Sam and Ben left for the afterdeck.

"Doc, you got anything for me?" Sam asked Bryant when he reached the afterdeck. Bryant provided routine medical services and was the EMT aboard *Kauai*. A slight build and bookish manner with steel-rimmed glasses hid a quiet intensity gained as an Army medic in Afghanistan before he transferred to the Coast Guard. He had good-naturedly shrugged off the "Army grunt" jokes in his first days on board. The jokes stopped when the crew saw Bryant in a tropical blue uniform with his Army Combat Medic Badge on his pocket and the Silver Star and Purple Heart topping his rows of ribbons.

Bryant replied, "Sorry, Captain, we almost needed a strainer to pull him out of the cabin. I figure he went down at least three days ago, based on decomp, but you'll need a lab to get anything definite. We ought to get him on ice, or we will have to vent the bag. Any chance we'll be heading in soon?"

Sam frowned. There was no cold storage aboard beyond two large kitchen refrigerators. "Sorry, Doc, we're to standby until further orders, and yes, I told them about the body."

"So be it, sir." He turned to Ben as Sam returned to the Bridge. "XO, I still need to do the workups for your annual. I can clean up and be ready for you in half an hour."

"Um, yeah, I'll be a bit busy for a while. Let me get back to you." Ben waved his hand dismissively, turned, and started walking forward to catch up with Sam.

"You have to let him take your measure eventually," Sam whispered.

"Sir, the best you can hope for from any physical exam is not getting fired. I'm in no hurry to take that chance."

Sam turned. "Something I should know about?"

"No, sir. Just a personal tic. I'll take care of this in the next dockside, Scout's honor." Ben grinned.

Sam returned a sad smile. "Mmmm, yeah."

2

Investigation

USCG Cutter *Kauai*, Gulf of Mexico, fifty-six nautical miles northeast of Key West, Florida
17:32 EST, 13 January

Ben

Ben returned to the Bridge twice for command net chats since completing the boarding operations on the *High Dawn*. The first entailed calling Drake up to give detailed, plain-language descriptions of the condition and damage to the hull of the wrecked sailboat. The second had good news and excellent news: the excellent news was the Clearwater Air Station had dispatched an MH-60T "Jayhawk" helicopter to pick up the body. Also, the buoy tender *Poplar* would arrive in thirty hours with specialized gear to recover the wreck. The news relieved Ben; they had already been underway for two days when diverted to the new mission. Even if refueled and restocked on-scene, a continued stay would be progressively more unpleasant. He was heading for a quick meal when Sam stepped into the room.

"Hey, Number One, we just got a secret immediate message; care to stroll up with me for a read?"

Ben grimaced. "Secret and immediate—either of those words is normally attached to 'another good deal.' I expect they mean a squared or even higher order of good deal together."

Sam chuckled. "Courage, son. That's why they pay us the big bucks!"

Secret messages were rare for *Kauai*, and the contents were astonishing. Besides picking up the body for transport ashore, the Jayhawk from Clearwater would deliver a Dr. Peter Simmons of the Defense Intelligence Agency. After the hand-off of the *High Dawn*, *Kauai* was to proceed independently and provide all services Simmons needed *as practicable* under a National Defense mission code. The message also addressed the sector command at Key West with orders to give any support *Kauai* required as a priority.

"Holy shit, Skipper!" Ben exclaimed. "Keeps getting weirder with this boat."

"You said it." Sam grinned. "What *will* they do next?" He glanced at the clock. "That Clearwater bird will be here in forty-five minutes. Brief out Bondurant and have him detail the deck crew for helicopter ops."

"Will do, sir. I suppose I'll have to room with this DIA guy."

"Yes. Sorry, Number One, but besides the VIP aspect, I don't want a spook hanging around with the crew."

"Oooo-kay. Sounds like you have some experience. Is there something you're not telling *me*, boss?"

"Me, no. But I was raised to distrust intel types, and nothing I've experienced as a blue-suiter has changed that bias." Sam finished with a neutral facial expression. "No need to worry about it, and just remember, he's no one's buddy."

"Very good, sir." Ben took the hint.

The helicopter arrived five minutes early, but the reception crew was in place and ready. Bondurant supervised the operation on the afterdeck and had been thorough in his briefing. He was pleased to see the crew members were taking safeguards against the aircraft's strong downwash of air as it moved over the deck with the DIA man lowering on the hoist cable. The man slipped out of the hoist harness on gaining footing with the deck and started walking forward. Bondurant's shouted warning to wait could not be heard over the engines and rotors. When the man crossed from directly under the helicopter, the ferocious wind struck him down like he'd been tackled from behind. Once the aircraft moved clear of the patrol boat, Bondurant crossed over and helped the man upright and then forward to the superstructure. "Are you OK?" he shouted over the aircraft noise.

"No injuries but my pride, thank you. Wow!" the man shouted back. "I have some gear coming with the litter. Should I go back and help?"

"No, you stay here. They'll be disconnecting the litter to load the body, anyway. Wait while the helo pulls back again," Bondurant received a thumbs-up from his charge. The helicopter was returning, a weighted nylon "trail line" dangling to just above deck level. The deck crew grabbed the line and kept it tight to keep the litter from swinging as it lowered. When it was under control on the cutter's deck, they disconnected the cable, allowing the helicopter to move clear again. Bondurant tapped the man's shoulder and gave a thumbs-up. The man nodded and walked over to retrieve a large canvas bag the deck crew had taken out of the litter. He then moved forward, flipping a wave at Bondurant as he passed. When he met Ben at the bottom of the ladder, Bondurant turned back to the afterdeck, shaking his head. "Dumbass!"

"Dr. Simmons, I'm Ben Wyporek, executive officer," Ben said. "Welcome aboard."

"Thank you, Lieutenant," Simmons replied. "Where can I go to get out of your way?"

Ben gestured toward a crewman standing alongside. "Petty Officer Guerrero here will escort you to my stateroom, and you'll be staying there while you're aboard. Please stay there until we finish. Then, the CO would like to chat."

"Excellent, I'll just be hanging out there then." Simmons slung his bag, and after he and Guerrero disappeared inside, Ben returned to the Bridge.

"Passenger secured, sir," Ben said when he stepped up to Sam as he watched the crew members loading the body into the litter.

"Thank you," Sam answered, keeping his eyes on the deck.

Bondurant reported the litter loaded and ready, and the helicopter returned to a hover beside *Kauai*, completing the pickup in a little over two minutes. The litter disappeared into the cabin, and the aircraft picked up speed and climbed. "Five-one, two-three, we are flight operations normal, en route Clearwater, out."

Watching the aircraft's flashing anti-collision light fading into the distance, Ben recalled the recent meeting with the Miami plane and said, "They aren't much for talking, I guess."

"Helo drivers are generally all business, the 60-drivers especially so. Not sure why," Sam replied. "OK, OOD, please, secure from flight quarters, set normal at-sea watch."

"Yes, sir," said Hopkins.

Sam turned. "Right, XO, let's grab a drink and deal with your new roommate."

****

"Welcome aboard, Doctor." Sam stood to shake Simmons's hand when he and Ben entered the cabin. "Please have a seat." They sat down in the cramped room, Sam sitting at his desk, Simmons in the spare chair, and Ben on Sam's bunk.

"Thank you, sir. I appreciate your accommodation, particularly Ben's generous sharing of his room with me," Simmons replied. Simmons was almost the quintessence of nondescript: five-foot-nine, average build, a plain face, with his brown medium-short hair and scruffy goat beard, a sharp contrast with the close-cropped and clean-shaven officers. His casual dress—a well-worn polo shirt, jeans, and topsiders—also set him apart from his hosts' dark blue utility uniforms. His age was obscure, but Ben guessed it was the early thirties.

"Not a problem. I was a little surprised to run into a DIA man called 'Doctor.' Are you an MD?"

"No, I have a Ph.D. in Astrophysics."

Sam's eyebrows raised. "Really? That's more surprising than the 'Doctor' part. OK, let's get down to business. I'm sure you know we are ordered to support you in whatever your mission is out here. Unfortunately, this is a pickup game, and we haven't received any details. I need you to explain what's going on so we can give you the best service."

Simmons rubbed his forehead and replied, "I'll do what I can, Lieutenant, you see...."

"Captain." Ben interrupted.

"I beg your pardon?" Simmons's hands froze.

"The correct address for commanding officers aboard their ships is 'Captain,' regardless of nominal rank."

After a few seconds locked in a stare with Ben, Simmons smiled and continued. "Forgive me. As I was saying, *Captain*, my work here is highly classified, and I've limited discretion on what I can share."

"I understand. Please continue," Sam said, his face devoid of expression.

"Thank you. Several research facilities detected an unusual event in this vicinity a few days ago, and we investigated. We've been on the lookout for unusual items correlating with the observations. This wreck you've discovered qualifies."

Sam leaned forward. "What sort of *event* are we talking about?"

Simmons crossed his arms and sat back. "I can't go into details on the different theories in play here. We have readings on one set of sensors that don't line up with the observations on the remaining relevant sensors. We're trying to figure out if there's an issue with the technology or if we are seeing something new and possibly dangerous. Either way, I'm sure you can understand the urgency here."

Sam leaned back. "OK, if the 'event' *is* tied to that wreck, does it pose any hazard to the crew?"

Simmons waved his hand dismissively. "No, no, no. I assure you, if we thought that was the case, you'd not be here right now. The patrol plane you relieved took a thorough scan of it with everything they had, and they'd have detected any significant chemical or radiological hazards. The final assessment pends the autopsy on that body, but we don't think we'll find anything. I've brought some field test equipment with me just to make sure. If you don't object, I'd like to examine anyone who went over there with the help of your medical technician."

"Certainly. XO, can you see to that, please?"

"Yes, sir." Ben nodded.

"I also need to visit the wreck myself as soon as possible. I've some other measurements I need to do right away," Simmons continued.

"It's dark now. I can close to twenty yards, and you can work from there. A boarding must wait until daylight. That will be…" Sam turned and consulted a piece of paper on his desk. "Zero-Six-Forty-five tomorrow morning."

Simmons frowned. "Captain, that will *not* be satisfactory. I have to take physical samples of the hull and cargo and do interior measurements—twenty yards might as well be twenty miles. It's necessary to get these readings immediately to develop a course of action."

"I'm sorry, Doctor, but it's risky enough to send a boarding party to a wrecked vessel, and I won't do it in the dark."

Simmons's eyes narrowed. "Captain, you obviously haven't gotten the memo. This is a question of national security, and I insist you put me on that vessel at once!"

Ben started to stand up, unconsciously closing his fists, before Sam rested an arm on his shoulder. Ben sat down.

Sam turned to Simmons. "Doctor, we need to get something straight right now. Only one person aboard can *insist* on anything, and you're looking at him. My orders are to act independently and cooperate with you *as practicable*. They don't relieve me of my primary responsibility for the safety of this ship and its crew. You'll need to give me a lot more than 'the pointers don't line up' before a night boarding onto a sinking vessel falls within my threshold of calculated risk. Now, anything else you care to share with me?"

"No, *Captain*, not now."

"Very well. How about you go with the XO to check our boarding crew, and we'll get you over there by first light?" Sam nodded his head toward the door and then turned back to his desk. After five seconds of Simmons sitting in astonished silence, Sam said without turning, "Was I unclear that you've been dismissed, Doctor?"

Ben stood and motioned to the door. "Sir, this way, please."

He started to follow Simmons out when Sam asked, "XO, once he's settled in with Doc, can you come back here, please?"

"Very good, sir."

Ben met Simmons in the passageway. "Please follow me, sir."

"Fine," Simmons replied coldly. "I'll need some testing equipment from my case."

"At your service, sir." Ben returned an icy grin. Simmons ducked into Ben's stateroom and returned carrying two small cases. "This way, please." Ben turned to lead him to the mess deck where Bryant, Drake, and the other personnel who had boarded the *High Dawn* had assembled.

"Guys, this is Dr. Simmons of the Defense Intelligence Agency," he began. "We're here to help him check some things that impact national security, so it's important. We think that wreck out there may be involved, so we will hang around here while he does his stuff. Now we're pretty sure there's no danger from that thing, but just to be absolutely sure, Doc here will help him run a few medical tests. Questions?"

Drake stepped forward. "Sir, it would help to know what's going on. What does a wrecked drug boat have to do with national security?" he asked, looking between Ben and Simmons.

"Chief, you said yourself there's something queer in that boat's damage. Well, you got someone's attention. As for the other stuff, I'm told it's well above our paygrade, so we'll do our jobs without knowing every detail. Not the first time, right?" He smiled at Drake.

"No, sir, I reckon not."

"Okay, it's not the preferred situation, but we'll make the best of it. Rest assured, the CO and I are on this, and we'll pass anything on when we can. Meanwhile, Dr. Simmons here is as VIP as it gets, and I expect you to treat him right and help him out whenever and however you can. Am I clear?" Ben finished, looking at Drake.

Drake smiled. "We've got this, XO."

"OK." Ben turned to Simmons. "Petty Officer Bryant here will help you. If you need anything, call me."

"Thanks," Simmons replied. "I'll see you shortly."

Ben made his way back to the cabin and sat at Sam's invitation.

Sam turned to face him. "That could have gone better. What's your impression so far?"

"He's an arrogant dick," Ben replied. "Who the hell does he think he is?"

"I understand your feelings, but I think we need to cut him some slack. I suspect he's not here for his charm and personality. It's because he can handle whatever needs to be done. Also, I can understand his agitation at having to wait. Something damned important must be happening to be diverting two cutters and laying on special flights. To sum it up, I believe he has a legitimate concern with whatever is going on here, and he's probably dead on his feet with fatigue."

Sam's response after the earlier tense meeting surprised Ben. "Sir?"

"Look at his eyes. He says this started a few days ago, and I doubt he's slept since then. That load, on no sleep, would make anybody punchy."

"I guess I missed that. I was ready to kick his ass for how he was talking to you."

Sam smiled in return. "Thanks, XO, but I can take it. I hated to take him down that way, given what I think he's going through right now, but we needed to settle who's who in this particular zoo. When we're done, I want you to take care of him. As soon as you can persuade him to get some rack time." He checked his watch. "He's got about eight hours before we can put him on the wreck. Convince him he might as well sleep as sit around and stew."

"Yes, sir, I'll try."

Sam patted him on the arm. "Stout hearts." Assuming his uncanny impression of the actor Patrick Stewart, he finished, "Make it so, Number One!"

Ben returned to the mess deck to find Simmons and Bryant processing the last crew member, and he sat to wait for them to finish. After a few minutes, Simmons started packing up his gear, and Bryant walked over to Ben.

"XO, I have *got* to get me one of those," he said, jerking his thumb toward Simmons. "Do you know it screens for 103 different toxins and can turn around the results in five minutes?"

"Doc, I expect there isn't enough money in the entire Seventh District, much less the boat's checkbook, to buy something like that, but I'll certainly ask. Thanks for taking care of this. See you later." When Bryant moved off, Simmons finished and turned to Ben.

"Lieutenant, I'm happy to report you have a slime-free crew as far as I can tell. There are still a few tests running, but I'm not expecting anything from them." Simmons rubbed his forehead and wiped his eyes.

Ben leaned in and said sympathetically, "When's the last time you've had any sleep?"

"I can't remember. A couple of days, I guess."

"Hey, there's nothing to be done until dawn, and that's eight hours off. You should try to get some rest."

"Yes, I suppose I should yield to the logic of the situation. There's no chance the captain will change his mind?"

"Not a chance in hell." Ben smiled.

"OK, the timely dew of sleep, now falling with soft slumb'rous weight inclines our eyelids," Simmons conceded as he started toward the passageway.

"What's that, Shakespeare?"

"No, friend, Milton," Simmons replied, shuffling along in trail behind Ben.

USCG Cutter *Kauai*, Gulf of Mexico, fifty-seven nautical miles northeast of Key West, Florida 06:03 EST, 14 January

Ben

"Dr. Simmons? Dr. Simmons?" Ben knocked on the locker next to his bunk, now occupied by his temporary roommate. Simmons shot upright and grasped at the location he had left his bag.

"Whoa, whoa, take a second!" Ben said. "I locked your bag up in the armory, and no one will mess with it."

Simmons's confused and desperate expression faded at once, and he put a hand to his face. "Sorry, occupational hazard," he mumbled. "How long was I out?"

Ben's heart rate was returning to normal—he had seen no one appear that wild-eyed. "A good six and a half hours. We'll be putting the RHIB over in about half an hour, and I thought you might like a bite of breakfast and coffee."

"That'd be amazing, thank you." Simmons's face twisted into a rueful smile. "I take it you saw the contents of the bag?"

"Yes, that's a lot of firepower." After seeing Simmons to his bunk earlier, Ben lifted the case, saw the pistol and Uzi submachine gun, and locked it in one of the ammunition lockers. "We can't have weapons just lying around. We'll return them to you when you leave."

"Not what I'd prefer, but I suppose it would be futile to protest, right?"

"Not even a day onboard, and you already have us figured out." Ben grinned.

"Let me splash my face for a jump-start. How's the food here?"

"It's not the jazz brunch at the Court of Two Sisters, but it'll do." Ben tossed him a towel.

"Pity, I would fancy a mimosa right now," Simmons said as he caught it.

****

Ben and Simmons arrived on the afterdeck and met Sam coming down the ladder from the Bridge. Simmons carried a smaller bag of instruments, and both he and Ben were donning flotation gear for a visit to the *High Dawn*. The wreck was visible in the pre-dawn twilight, one hundred yards away.

"Good morning, Doctor," Sam said. "I hope you had a good night's rest?"

"Indeed, Captain. And I topped it off with an excellent breakfast and coffee—your man does a splendid job." Simmons smiled.

"Outstanding. I'll pass along to Chef that his lofty Yelp score is safe." Culinary Specialist Second Class Thomas "Chef" Hebert was one of Sam's aces in the hole in terms of morale. Born and raised in New Orleans, Hebert apprenticed in a small family-owned and run restaurant in the Vieux Carré before enlisting in the Coast Guard. Sam contributed funds, and Drake scavenging to support his more "exotic" condiment and equipment needs. The result was high-end restaurant-quality meals for the crew when underway, a significant plus in the otherwise spartan existence on a patrol boat. As for Hebert, he loved the work, relished the appreciation he received, and, best of all, got to shoot a fifty-caliber machine gun in his General Quarters billet.

"He can count on four stars from me," Simmons said. "Thank you also for the loan of your XO. I can use the help with these instruments." He turned to Ben. "Although I'm afraid you might find it tedious."

"I'll live," Ben said.

After a briefing from Boatswain's Mate Third Class Jenkins, the boat coxswain, and a brief ride, Ben and Simmons boarded the *High Dawn*. When the RHIB had pulled off, Simmons commented, "That kid is into his job—the most thorough and enthusiastic safety brief EVER."

"It's his first solo sortie as a coxswain. Bondurant is leveraging a low-stress op to give him time on his own with the boat." He smiled as the RHIB pulled away to make practice approaches on *Kauai*. "He's psyched, but Bondurant is nervous—he subbed in on the OOD watch just to keep an eye on him."

Simmons paused in assembling his equipment to glance at the white-painted cutter. "Dad hands the keys over to his son. Almost sounds like a regular family."

"It is." Ben nodded. "They mess around and get on each other's nerves, but when things go crazy, nothing gets between them."

"Hmmm, must be nice." Simmons nodded, returning to his work. "Can you give me a hand here? We'll start with laying sensors...."

Ben and Simmons worked over the boat for four and a half hours, laying and moving tiny electrical sensors, cutting samples from the hull and metalwork, and measuring, measuring, measuring. Helping with the interior measurements was the worst experience in Ben's life. Crawling through the dark, flooded, and crowded cabin on a vessel on the verge of sinking evoked almost debilitating claustrophobia. This fear, combined with the revolting thought that the confined space once enclosed a rotting corpse, resulted in a struggle even to think, much less complete scientific tasks. Ben's relief at returning to the open air of the *High Dawn*'s main deck was extreme.

At last, Simmons related he had finished, and they could start gathering up the equipment. Ben inquired, "So, what's the verdict? Is this what you're looking for?"

Simmons nodded while continuing his packing. "Definitely. You are looking at the effects of a powerful shock wave that began underwater close to the surface. The hydraulic shock crushed the starboard side of the hull. This lurched the boat to the left, snapping the mast shrouds and throwing at least one guy into the scupper here, killing him instantly—there's blood and skin fragments around there." He pointed at a narrow draining channel in the deck. "The air shock wave impacted right after that. It tore away the mast and cleared anything loose off the deck." He pointed at a metal fitting on the deck. "Look at the mast step here. The pin's bent and the fork sheared to the left."

Ben eyed the twisted deck fitting, pondering the force that could do that. "It wasn't a bomb?"

Simmons paused and looked up at him. "No. Any chemical explosive close enough to do this would leave trace residue, if not actual burn scoring. A nuclear device would leave a radiation signature and heat damage. Besides, we'd detect any nuclear detonation." He looked down to finish packing his gear. "And to anticipate your next question, I know what this is, but I can't tell you about it. I *can* say we must find the event's location as soon as possible." He glanced at Ben, noting his raised eyebrow. "Hey, I know this sucks being kept in the dark, but I have my orders. I'll be reporting in right away, and I'll see if I can get them to loosen up, at least for you and your CO."

"That would be an excellent idea if you don't want this operation to turn into a major goat rope."

"I'll pass that along. When can we start back to Key West? I need to get resources organized."

Ben checked his watch. "*Poplar* should arrive in eighteen hours, figure a couple hours for the hand-off, and then four hours to motor down to Key West."

Simmons shook his head. "OK, sorry I came across as such a douche last night, but I'm not exaggerating. We can't wait another day to start on this. Can't you just leave it with a marker on it?"

This time, Ben shook his head. "No way. There could be a couple of tons of product here. On the street, that's more than a hundred million bucks. We can't leave it unattended for a second. We can try to get a patrol boat out of Key West to relieve us. That'd cut our wait time in half."

Simmons nodded. "We need to do that right away. I'll call in the request from my end as well. And I'm done here; you can call Billy Budd to come pick us up."

Ben turned away to call over the RHIB and report to *Kauai. Billy Budd? WTF?*

USCG Cutter *Kauai*, Gulf of Mexico, fifty-seven nautical miles northeast of Key West, Florida 14:27 EST, 14 January

Sam

Ben, Simmons, and Sam sat in Sam's cabin with the door closed. Not a situation the latter liked when underway. Sam had called Sector Key West and convinced an irritated senior duty officer to launch his ready patrol boat, the eighty-seven-foot cutter *Skua*. She was still more than an hour from the rendezvous, but Hopkins was on the Bridge, passing information to her captain to hasten the transfer.

Simmons shunted off to the foredeck on their return to *Kauai* to make a private call by satellite telephone while Ben briefed Sam. Simmons still could not share any information with the officers, and it was clear the limits frustrated even him.

"Captain, believe me, I'm getting sick of this situation, too. If you're in it, you should be in all the way, but they told me flat-out no deal."

Sam nodded. "I understand, and we'll continue to do the best we can. But you need to know that if we run into a critical situation, you may face a choice between following those orders or completing the mission. So, what can we do in the meantime?"

"It's been three and a half days since the event, and I imagine that wreck could drift a fair distance."

"There's a strong current in the Florida Straits, the foundation of the Gulf Stream. There's a clockwise current called the Loop in the center of the Gulf. Between the Keys and Tampa, it gets confused."

"Well, we're sure whatever happened occurred somewhere within a thirty- by sixty-mile ellipse centered about twenty miles east of Key West."

"Really? OK, you can forget Key West and Boca Chica as someone would have seen it. You can also discard anything south of the Keys. The Gulf Stream would've swept up this hulk, and it'd be off Jacksonville by now. That leaves the northern shores of the Keys. Don't you guys have any Keyhole satellites or spy planes you can search with?"

Simmons grimaced. "Believe me, everything, and I mean EVERYTHING, available has been sweeping this area for the last few days and has come up with bupkis. It seems like it'll come down to a close examination of the ground to find disturbances on the shore. Even if we had squadrons of aircraft, we don't want to draw the attention."

"From the Press?" Ben asked.

"Yes, and others. We have special unmanned aircraft we can stage locally, but they're not fast, and we need to cut down the search area. You guys are good at this search and rescue stuff; surely, you have planning tools that can help."

Sam shook his head. "We have a computer suite called the Search and Rescue Optimal Planning System, or SAROPS. It's good, but it *forecasts* the position of a target based on the time and place of the event, using known winds and currents. We can't use it to figure out where a target *was* three days ago."

"Um, Captain?" Ben interrupted.

"Yes, XO?"

"There *is* a way to use SAROPS for this. A few of us looked at an application of SAROPS for hindcasting a vessel's position at the academy. We thought it might be useful for forensic work…."

Sam leaned forward. "I'll be damned. Did it work?"

"We got an 'A,' but it didn't go anywhere as far as I know."

Simmons was now interested. "How does it work?"

Ben shifted in his seat. "The captain's right. SAROPS can only project forward, but you can pick a set of feasible launch points in the past and let SAROPS run them out to the present using historical wind and currents data. Then you can build a probability field and do a Bayesian search. We can knock down the possibilities to a workable list."

49

"I like it." Simmons beamed. "Let's start. Where is this SAROPS?"

"Um, hold on there, Doctor," Sam said. "We are a patrol boat. We don't have SAROPS here. They'll have it at the Sector Office in Key West, and we can run it there."

"Besides," Ben piped up on seeing Simmons's face fall, "There's a lot of front-end work to do, identifying potential start points and setting up the post-processing models. It'll take a good five or six hours at this end, anyway. We'll gather the information on our way down and hand it over when we moor. After a few hours of batch runs, we can drop the results into Excel, and we're done."

Sam smiled. "You believe you can do this, Ben?"

"If I can get Hoppy's help with the electronic charts, no worries, sir."

Sam clapped him on the shoulder. "Make it so then. Well done, Number One!" Ben stood and made his way past Simmons out of the compact room and closed the door. After Ben left, Sam turned to Simmons. "OK, now for the hard part, Doctor. Once we decide where to search, what are we searching *for*? If half of Space Command is bore-sighted on this area and can't find anything, what do you expect from an obsolescent Coast Guard patrol boat? You mentioned something about unmanned aircraft?"

"Yes, Captain." Simmons sat back. "I have a team equipped with two upgraded RQ-20 Puma UAVs—they have a payload package specialized for this and an associated analysis team."

"Analysis team?"

"Yes, they have advanced portable tools for image processing and analysis. They were all standing by at Homestead in case we found something. When I called in before, I directed the UAV drivers to meet us at Key West. They should be waiting when we arrive, and they can set up the aircraft to fly in an hour."

"Doctor, you're crazy; look at this boat! We don't have the space for takeoffs and landings."

"Captain, the Pumas are hand-launched and stressed and sealed for saltwater landings—no launch and recovery equipment is needed. The control antenna is shoebox-sized, and you can mount it in any clear spot. The GCS, excuse me, Ground Control Station, is a large laptop with a Bluetooth link to the antenna."

"Hand-launched? And it can carry a payload that's more effective than reconnaissance satellites? How big's a Puma?"

"It's not that small. It has a nine-foot wingspan, but a reasonably fit crew member can launch it by hand. As far as the sensors go, they wouldn't be worth a damn in low earth orbit, but from five hundred feet, they can image individual grains of sand."

Sam relaxed. "OK. We can shake out another couple of bunks. I guess I'll have to deal with two more of your guys hanging around the crew."

Simmons grinned. "Not my guys, your guys. This team is two aviation petty officers from the Coast Guard Air Station at Cape Cod."

"The hell you say! The Coast Guard's running an Intel UAV program?"

"No, Captain, the Coast Guard was researching low-cost, low-footprint, maritime surveillance technology. The Puma was an army and special ops land-based program, but the Coast Guard recognized its handiness and did research and testing up in New England. You can see its usefulness for keeping persistent surveillance on restricted areas. So, your guys provide a portable aircraft with good speed and endurance and are nearly silent in flight. My guys invest big black ops bucks to provide payload miniaturization and hardening. Voila! You have a nifty maritime tactical recon stealth bird."

"It will be a pain in the ass, but I'll admit I'm curious to see flight ops on a PB. Anything else I need to know?"

"What's your weapons status?"

Sam tensed again. "Up and running with a full ammo load. What's your interest in that? If you expect a fight, you need to tell me, regardless of security restrictions."

"Captain, I'm not gunning for a fight, and I don't expect one. But we have a wrecked sailboat with hundreds of millions of dollars worth of drugs on board. Don't you think the owners might search for that boat and maybe wait near the spot we seek?

"We won't be going in anywhere without knowing the ground—that's one reason we have the UAVs. I also have my guys back on land keeping an eye out, so I don't expect any surprises. Nevertheless, given the circumstances, I believe we can't have too much firepower."

"Doctor, you're right on the edge of my envelope without providing me the full story on this. If I get a whiff of bullshit from you, this operation ends at once. Is that clear?"

"Quite clear, Captain."

"Very well. If you'll excuse me, I need to be on the Bridge for transferring custody." They both stood up, and Sam continued, "You can follow me if you like, just stay out of the way, please."

"Captain, you'll never know I'm here." Simmons stepped out of the cabin.

"Yeah, I wish," Sam muttered under his breath as he climbed up to the Bridge.

3

Skirmish

USCG Cutter *Kauai*, Moored, Trumbo Point Annex, Naval Air Station Key West, Florida
20:36 EST, 14 January

Ben

The handoff of the *High Dawn* went without a hitch. Sam simply had to brief the *Skua*'s CO on the events to date, since the crew had removed no contraband or documents from the vessel. Within an hour of the smaller cutter's arrival, *Kauai* was charging toward Key West at her maximum continuous speed of twenty-eight knots.

It was Bondurant's turn for the mooring, and he had no difficulty bringing the cutter to rest alongside the dock. However, *Kauai* remained under quarantine until completing a drug sweep. The boarding team and Ben and Simmons's coveralls had been bagged and sealed on their return from the *High Dawn*, and the inspection team took and signed for these items. Next, a drug-sniffing dog came aboard to tour all the spaces. Except for an embarrassing moment involving Simmons's equipment bag, this too went without incident. An hour and a half after mooring, the inspectors officially "de-quarantined" *Kauai* and departed.

The UAV team, waiting on the dock since *Kauai*'s arrival, reported to the patrol boat after the inspection team left. The senior member, Avionics Electrical Technician First Class Erich "Fritz" Deffler, introduced himself and his teammate, Avionics Electrical Technician Second Class Michael "Mike" Morgan, to Ben and Drake. Then they discussed their gear and planned activities. Drake took charge of settling the newcomers, while Ben returned to the Bridge to collect the electronic files needed for the SAROPS runs. As he passed the cabin en route to his stateroom, Ben could hear Sam on the phone with his wife, Joana. He poked his head in, waved, and mouthed, "Hi, Jo!"

Sam held up a finger to wait. "Pardon me, my dear, but the executive officer has interrupted to respectfully offer his greetings to the captain's spouse. Yes. Very well." Sam held the phone down. "The captain's spouse sends her compliments and suggests the executive officer should find a nice girl and settle down."

Ben grinned. "My respects to the captain's spouse, and if she can find someone as classy as her to introduce to the executive officer, he would commence ring-shopping forthwith."

Sam relayed the message and received a response. He held the phone down again and said, "The captain's spouse's response is: 'Awwww!'"

Ben flipped a casual salute and continued to his stateroom. The exchange was only half-joking—Ben thought Jo Powell was one of the finest women he knew. A freelance computer graphics artist working from home, she was smart, gracious, funny, and drop-dead gorgeous. She was the perfect match for Sam, and despite his reserved demeanor, he was obviously crazy about her. Social events with a CO were usually an ordeal. Dinners and cookouts with the Powells were relaxing and pleasurable. They and their two kids, who Ben also adored, were like his family.

Jo shared their story with Ben during the first of those gatherings. The couple's fateful meeting took place while Sam attended Officer Candidate School in New London, Connecticut. He had befriended a young University of Connecticut graduate named Eduardo Mendez and mentored him through the rough spots of officer candidate training. In gratitude, "Eddie" invited him to dinner with his parents and sister Joana in Gales Ferry on their first liberty. His sister, a few years his senior, lived at home while attending Eastern Connecticut State after completing an enlistment as a Navy Mass Communications Specialist. Jo said Eddie related later that Sam had smelled a setup and tried to beg off, but Eddie managed to guilt him into attending.

Sam was hooked about halfway into that first dinner. At least, that's what he told Jo. Jo claimed it took two dates before she was all in. Jo said she was ready to swap vows upon Sam's completion of OCS. However, they agreed to put it off for a year to finish her degree, and Sam could find his feet as a commissioned officer. He was lucky enough to hook a billet on a large cutter based in Boston for his first post-graduation assignment and be nearby for those rare occasions the ship was in its homeport. They married in her family's church a year later, with Eddie standing up as Sam's best man.

Reaching his stateroom broke him from his reverie, and he stepped in to grab Simmons. "I'm heading over to the sector office now. Care to tag along?"

"You know I do. How'd it go with your girlfriend?"

Ben's jaw clenched, "If you are referring to Petty Officer Hopkins, please say 'Petty Officer Hopkins' or 'Hopkins' or 'Hoppy' or even 'Emilia.' Never refer to her as 'girlfriend' or 'girl' anything again to anyone here, especially me, clear?"

"Shit, I'm sorry," Simmons was genuinely embarrassed. "I swear I didn't mean any disrespect. Far from it. She's one of the most professional people I've ever met."

"OK, OK. Come on, let's roll."

Once off the ship and walking toward the sector building, Ben said, "About your ill-phrased question, we did well. We have twenty-three potential spots where a boat like that could anchor and be within reasonable reach of an offload point."

"Is twenty-three good?"

"It's a good start."

"What's well begun is half done."

"More Milton?" Ben asked.

"No, Horace. I thought I'd spare you the Latin version."

"Thanks for that. If you'll pardon me, I'm a little surprised hearing all this poetry talk from an astrophysicist. I thought you guys were all about quarks and comic books."

Simmons smiled in the darkness. "I'd like to take offense, but I was at Princeton with several guys who were exactly like that. It's actually a question of biology."

"Biology?"

"Yes. You see, if you'd like to have a second date with a pretty English Lit grad student, you better bring more to the conversation than Stress-Energy Tensors and Stan Lee."

Ben laughed. "That's all right. Did it work? Did you get a second date?"

"Yup."

"Care to elaborate?"

"Nope. You have a clearance, but no 'Need to Know,' sorry."

Ben chuckled again. "Touché." When they stepped into the sector building, he said, "OK, let's see how much pushback we get from the watch supervisor." After passing through security, the watch supervisor, a chief operations specialist, shuttled them to a room with several workstations. A man in civilian clothes greeted them when they entered, and the chief introduced him as Jim Rossetti, a civilian employee and the sector's resident SAROPS expert. Ben put him in the picture with a brief explanation of the problem.

"We can run five separate threads of SAROPS simultaneously," Rossetti explained. "But I have to hold one open in case we get a search mission."

"You do?" asked Simmons. "On a weeknight like this?"

Rossetti glanced at Ben and rolled his eyes. "Doctor, we have more than a thousand response cases per year in this sector alone. We're actively working two now, and a dozen are open. I'd say it's almost certain that we'll have at least one more new one before morning."

"Sorry, I'm new to this."

"Perfectly OK. Hey, at least it's not Miami—they have more than double our load."

"So, best case," Ben interjected. "We've six cycles of runs plus set up time. When do you think it'll wrap up?"

"I already have a batching macro setup. Figure about sixty to ninety minutes per cycle, end to end. I think we can have the last runs complete by 05:30, 06:30 at the latest."

"OK, let's get on it," Ben said, handing him the disk. "Everything's in one file."

"Thanks. Hang around for a minute while I get this loaded and make sure there are no hiccups, then I can cut you loose." After a few minutes of typing, he said, "OK, everything looks good. You got a number I can call when they finish?"

Ben jotted down *Kauai*'s in-port number and handed it to Rossetti. "We'll see you later." He turned to

Simmons. "I'm heading back to catch some z's. You coming?"

"No, I'll hang here and catch up with the outside world." To Rossetti, he said, "Can you spare an office with a landline?"

"Sure, right out the door, then second door on the right."

"Thanks." Waving to Ben. "See you later, friend."

Ben returned the wave. "See you back here at 5:30-ish." He then excused himself to return to his ship. After a brief walk, Ben arrived at *Kauai* to the familiar odor of diesel fuel. Drake never procrastinated with the readiness of the engineering department, always setting up refueling first. Ben waited for him to look over from whatever he was supervising, then asked, "How's it going, Chief?"

"Halfway through, sir," Drake replied. "I have the Cape Cod guys billeted. I put Deffler with Joe and John and Morgan with the non-rates."

"Good. Thanks for that. Anything else going on?"

"Nothing to hold up sailing, sir."

"Roger that," Ben said and then walked on board. After taking a quick turn around the decks to check things, he stopped by Sam's cabin. "Captain, the SAROPS runs are working, probably be wrapping up around 05:30."

"Fine," Sam said. "Is our new aviation detachment settling in OK?"

"Yes, sir. Chief put the first class in with Williams and Bondurant. Unfortunately, his buddy will slum with the non-rates."

"Them's the breaks." Sam nodded. "OK, I know you're tired, but I'd like to hold a strategy meeting as soon as possible. Can you get the department leads together, please? Make sure Williams, Guerrero, and the aviation lead attend too."

"Will do, Captain."

About fifteen minutes later, Sam strode into the mess deck after being called down by Ben for the meeting. The assembled crew stood up, and Sam waved his hand. "Relax, please." After they resumed sitting, Sam sat at the head of the small table. "OK, guys, it's late, but we need to get a plan together for tomorrow. Oh, and the inconvenience of this extended patrol will be reflected as usual in your pay." The group chuckled, and Sam looked over at Drake. "Chief, what have you got?"

"We are topping off with fuel and water now. I'm replacing the generator air filters. Should be wrapped up in a couple of hours. Ready for sea, sir."

"Thanks, Chief." Sam turned to Bondurant next. "Boats, what say you?"

"Captain, Connally just left on Emergency Leave with his dad's passing, but we're solid in spite of that, and we have no equipment casualties."

"Thanks, Boats. Hoppy, what's up in Ops?"

"Captain, I have just loaded the latest SeaWatch software patch, and I'm running a diagnostic right now. The radar and comms gear are all up and available."

"Thank you, and I have good news: I'm doubling the size of your department. If anyone here hasn't heard, we've picked up our own aviation detachment: two Aviation Electronics Technicians from Cape Cod and their pair of UAVs. Petty Officer Erich Deffler here is the senior, and he'll be reporting to Hoppy. Petty Officer Deffler, welcome aboard. Do you go by Erich?"

"Thank you, Captain. Most people call me Fritz."

"Great, I'll ask you to tell us a little about your aircraft shortly. XO, how are we doing?"

"Captain, I've just been over to the sector office, and our SAROPS runs are proceeding. They'll wrap up by 0530, and I'll have a good list of investigation sites an hour later. Chef and Junior are out getting dry stores and the refrigerators restocked. I'm sorry, but we had to go on the economy for this one—I didn't want to wait for the commissary to open tomorrow."

"Can't be helped," Sam said. "I'll sign whatever exigency forms you need."

"Thank you, sir. The crew's in good shape, with no medical issues. As Bondurant mentioned, we sent Connally off to help his family. Chief's been collecting for flowers from the crew." He nodded to Drake.

"Hit me up when we're done, Chief," Sam said.

"Right, sir."

Ben continued, "We'll be turned around and ready for sea in about three and a half hours, sir."

"First rate. OK, everybody, I know you're wondering what the hell is going on here. Mr. Wyporek and I are in the dark too. What I *do* know is this: that boat we boarded took a huge whack from something that landed right next to it. They sent an astrophysicist, so I'm guessing it must be some sort of rare meteorite. It lit off plenty of screens, and they all point somewhere between here and fifty miles east. Now XO and Hoppy churned through the charts and came up with a list of every spot in this general area that boat could have anchored when 'the event,' as our passenger calls it, happened a few days ago. We are using the SAROPS computer software to.... What's the word, XO?"

"Hindcast, Captain."

"Thank you. 'Hindcast' to ditch the impossible spots and rank the ones left. If you want a detailed explanation of the geeky-mathy stuff that makes it work, I'll refer you to the XO. Anyway, we'll use that list to guide our search. Fritz, I'm told your UAVs have the latest gear and should be very helpful to us for this job.

"Now, the bad side. As you also know, that wreck is chock full of dope. A street value of a hundred million plus is likely, and you can't get that much product without investing lots of cash. I think you can see where I'm going here. The owners are not likely to be satisfied just writing it off on their taxes. In fact, they might look right where we'll be searching for that space rock."

Sam let that set, watching the assembled crew exchange concerned glances. "I don't think they'll be foolish enough to take a crack at us. But better safe than sorry. Gunner," he looked at Gunner's Mate Second Class Guerrero. "We will exercise the main gun and fifties tomorrow, with live rounds, if we can get clearance in the warning area. Sound good?"

"Hell, yes, Captain!" Guerrero grinned.

"Sweet. Hoppy, after we break up, I want you to see if you can get us one of the warning areas for at least four hours starting about 13:00 tomorrow."

"Yes, sir."

"OK. It's easier said than done, but try not to worry about this. We'll have eyes in the sky to prevent surprises, and we can beat anybody dumb enough to try taking us on. I'm sharing this because you deserve to know the risks. When I get anything, I'll pass it along. Any questions?" He scanned the table, and, getting no response, continued. "OK, Fritz, tell us about our new air force, and, by the way, we're pleased to have you here."

Erich Deffler was a thirteen-year veteran and an experienced crew member on all Coast Guard fixed-wing aircraft types. He had jumped on the opportunity to pilot UAVs. After a rigorous training course, he was among the first in the Coast Guard to pass the FAA examination for Small UAV pilot. He took part in the flight testing the Coast Guard's Research and Development Center conducted at Air Station Cape Cod and on several cutters. This was his first independent deployment, and he was psyched. In his mid-thirties, he was six-foot-one and thin with thick, slightly graying black hair, deep blue eyes, and an angular face.

"Not as pleased as we are, sir." Deffler smiled. "We're in the season at the Cape with only two kinds of weather: butt-ass cold alternating with snow!" He paused while a few of the attendees chuckled. "We have two new Pumas with us. They have a special electronics payload that I've trained on but never operated. Since you're heading out to the warning area tomorrow, can I ask for the opportunity to launch one of the birds? I need to check for glitches with the payload and antenna blind spots."

"You read my mind." Sam nodded. "I was going to ask you for a show."

"Yes, sir. It is amazing hardware. The resolution is wicked good on the camera, and we have a laser designator built-in. It's hand-launched and sealed for saltwater recovery. I'm sorry to say we haven't come up with a practical way to recover aboard a patrol boat yet, so we'll need your small boat to do the pickup."

"Not a problem. Will you want your man in the boat, or are you OK with one of us knuckle-draggers doing the pickup?"

The phrasing of the question startled Deffler, but he quickly recovered. "Captain, we can do it whichever way you want."

Sam smiled. "We'll let him show us how, at least the first few times."

"Righto, sir," Deffler continued. "In theory, we can launch from any clear space on the weather decks, but I recommend the main deck forward of the gun. It has the best aspect clearance and, likely, the best relative wind. I'll need to mount the antenna in a prominent place. It has a Bluetooth connection to the control station, so I won't need to run any cabling if it's within fifty feet."

"I'll see to the antenna placement, Captain," Drake said.

"Great. We'll try putting the control station on the chart table for now," Sam said. "How much space will you need, Fritz?"

"Oh, not much at all, sir. It's just a laptop and a USB joystick."

"OK, it seems like we can make it work. What can it do for us?"

Deffler beamed. "Sir, the camera is hi-res with a hyperspectral imaging capacity. We can scout locations as well as having eyes-on. Sometimes it's even better because the hyperspectral can pick up traces we wouldn't normally see. We can get into a narrow waterway or cove and save you a risky transit or long small boat ride. We can even provide target designation for the gun."

Sam noted Williams's impassive face and folded arms. Williams was the Electronics Technician on *Kauai*—he worked and maintained the fire control station for the main gun and was territorial on this subject. "We'll check it out tomorrow, but it sounds good. Anything else we need to know?"

"No, sir. That covers it."

"Right, anyone else?" Sam looked around the table. "OK, let's plan on stations manned by 11:45 and underway at noon tomorrow. Thanks everybody, and good night." They all stood when Sam rose and left the room, with Ben a few steps behind him.

Hopkins stepped over to Deffler, hand outstretched. "Fritz, I'm Emilia or 'Hoppy' if you like."

Deffler shook her hand and smiled. "Glad to meet you."

"Likewise." Hopkins smiled back. "I'd like to meet on the Bridge at 08:30, and we can go over placing your equipment and do some dry runs. I'd also like to chat about tactics."

"I'll be there." He nodded.

USCG Cutter *Kauai*, Moored, Trumbo Point Annex, Naval Air Station Key West, Florida
05:43 EST, 15 January

Ben

"XO, XO?"

"Yes?" Ben opened his eyes to see Pickins, a non-rated watchstander, leaning over him.

"You have a phone call, sir, line two."

"Thank you." Ben swung his legs off the bunk and reached for the phone on his mini-desk. "Wyporek here."

"Hi Lieutenant, Jim Rossetti. Your runs completed successfully, and I saved the output for you."

"Outstanding. Is Dr. Simmons there?"

"Uh-huh. He's wearing a ditch in the carpet waiting for you."

"I'll be there in ten."

After a quick electric shave and comb, Ben jogged over to the building and the analysis office. "Good morning, Doctor, Jim. Shall we work some Bayesian magic?"

"When did morning ever break, And find such beaming eyes awake? Dazzle us with your analytical wonders, Lieutenant," Simmons smirked.

Rossetti stared at Simmons, then turned to Ben with a tired "Is this for real?" look before holding out an external data drive. "Here is the output you requested. Mind if I watch you work through this?"

"No problem." Ben sat down at the workstation. "I'll explain as we go."

After cranking the data through formulas on Microsoft Excel, Ben eliminated eleven possibilities and divided the remaining twelve between "more likely" and "less likely" candidates. After more work, he identified the best search plan based on the SAROPS data. "... And you see here, the remaining probabilities update as we eliminate each candidate."

"Very nice." Rossetti nodded. "Can I keep copies of those spreadsheets?"

"Sure. I'd appreciate it if you could print out a copy for me while we're here."

"No problem."

The day was bustling on the Coast Guard base when Ben and Simmons walked to *Kauai*'s mooring. "So, get any sleep last night?" Ben asked.

"A couple hours head down in between phone calls. Interesting developments have occurred, both in my dark domain and yours of sunlight and truth."

"For instance?"

"I got a report on the body you guys found. The cause of death is 'Generalized Acceleration Trauma,' meaning his injuries were consistent with a hundred-foot fall onto a pile of rocks. The time of death is unknown, but the decomp suggests it's contemporaneous with the event. No ID from CODIS, but we're still working it through Interpol."

"OK, not unexpected. Anything else?"

"Yes, I have arranged for us to access the highway camera recordings on U.S. 1 between here and Key Biscayne. Unfortunately, the only place we can view them right now is the Monroe County Sheriff's Office downtown."

"Ah, what's this 'us' and 'we' shit? *Kauai* will sail in a few hours for workups on the guns and those toy airplanes of yours. The executive officer isn't just sitting around when operational preps are underway."

"Understood, but this could be an important piece of the puzzle. I'm sure your captain wants all the information he can get."

"What's so interesting about highway footage?"

"Presuming this boat is linked to the event, we might see some evidence that can help us narrow down the location further."

Ben stopped and turned toward Simmons. "Alright, maybe I'm a bit slow here. What exactly do you hope to see on the camera footage? Some kind of vehicle?"

Simmons frowned and said, "No, something else."

Ben put his hands on his hips. "OK, Doc. You have to do better than that. The CO will ask me why I need to take the time to go downtown and stare at video footage when I should be helping with sailing preps. Right now, I don't have a good enough answer."

"Very well. The, um, *effect* that we are looking for generates a bright light. If it passes one of those cameras, we should see a brief illumination of the highway. Hopefully, we can follow the effect from camera to camera until it does not present anymore. That should help narrow the search."

"Interesting. I'm not sure you'll be able to convince the CO."

"Ye of little faith. I can be very persuasive, you know." Simmons winked and smiled.

Ben shook his head. "Dude, you're on your own."

Sam

The pair's return to the patrol boat elicited a mixture of reactions. The success of the SAROPS analysis pleased Sam, and he directed Ben to meet with Hopkins to plan the sequence of exploratory visits. Simmons's requisitioning of his executive officer for investigative work was another matter. After dispatching Ben, Sam took Simmons for a private talk in his cabin. "I don't like coughing up my XO when we're prepping for a hazardous operation, Doctor. You must have other assets here you can call."

"Captain, we keep a light footprint on the ground for operations this classified. We roll in the FBI and the rest, and we'll blow the lid off the entire thing. Ben's levelheaded and smart—I'm sure he'll be fine. Besides, wouldn't you rather have Ben with eyes on than me skulking around on my own?" Simmons smiled slyly.

Sam *did* prefer having one of his people monitoring Simmons's activities. Still, he could not comprehend Simmons's sense of urgency for a matter that seemed trivial and irrelevant to their mission. Also, something hidden behind the too-pat story and the agent's maddening expression worried him, so he temporized. "Tell me, if this thing is so damn secret, how will you keep a lid on it, flashing a DIA badge?"

Simmons nodded. "Yes, that would normally be a problem. Fortunately, besides being DIA guy Dr. Peter Simmons, I'm also Investigator Douglas Pearson of the Florida Department of Law Enforcement. My people handled the groundwork with the locals to reduce curiosity."

"What about Ben?"

"We don't have time to build a legend around him, so he goes in clean. The cover is there's a maritime element that needs Coast Guard involvement."

This whole deal put Sam on edge. He wanted to put an end to it, but his thoughts returned to his orders: *provide all services he needed as practicable*. He knew Ben would have front-loaded any pre-sailing tasks requiring his direct attention, so Simmons's demand was *practicable*.

Sam relented despite his misgivings, made worse by the reptilian smile he wanted to wipe off the agent's face. "Very well. We sail in…." he glanced at his desk clock. "Four and a half hours. I want you both back on board in four. You can take the government vehicle. But Doctor, I don't like this. If you haven't picked up on it already, let me speak plainly here. Besides being an indispensable part of this crew, Ben's a close friend of mine. If anything happens to him because of you, I'm likely to react *irrationally*."

Simmons's smile faded to a blank expression. "Yes, Captain, I'm familiar with your personal history."

Sam's face darkened. "That will be all, Doctor. I'll see you here within four hours."

Monroe County Sheriff's Office, 5525 College Road, Key West, Florida
08:28 EST, 15 January

Ben

Getting access to the camera footage involved the usual appeasement of officious clerks in the different departments governing interagency cooperation, information technology, and security in the main office. Afterward, they had to drive to a second office that actually housed the archive. It took the better part of two hours to get into the technology center and in front of the console where the archived footage could be retrieved and viewed.

A clearly bored technician sat next to them and operated the viewing equipment. "Anything in particular you guys want to see?" he asked around a wad of gum he was chewing.

"Yes, I would like to start at the first camera on U.S. 1 south of Key Biscayne, then work our way south.

We're looking for the footage recorded between one-thirty and two a.m. on the 10th of January."

"OK," the technician said, then went to work on his keyboard. After a minute, he said, "KB-South is coming up now." He nodded toward the screen that showed a darkened highway bridge with the lights of passing vehicles every few minutes.

After about ten minutes of staring at what was essentially an unchanging picture, Ben asked, "Is there any way to speed this playback?"

Before the technician could answer, Simmons said, "No. The effect will only last a few seconds, and we can't afford to miss it. Once we get a good time reference, we can narrow down the time frame on the other cameras."

"Right," Ben replied, trying to keep the irritation out of his voice. The passive watching continued for another five minutes, then a sudden flash of light briefly lit up the scene. "Whoa! Did you see that?"

"Pause it!" Simmons said. After the technician hit the pause button, he added, "OK, run it back thirty seconds, then forward at one-quarter speed, please."

"OK," the technician said as he worked the playback controls.

The scene repeated, and Ben could see on the slower playback that the illumination was not the general flash it appeared to be at full speed, but a progressive brightening and then darkening, moving toward and passing the camera. Ben glanced at Simmons, who was grinning while jotting down the time.

"Now, we're in business," Simmons said. "Let's see the next camera south, same date, start at one-forty-eight."

They carefully reviewed the footage of the thirteen cameras between Key Biscayne and Boca Chica, noting the passing effect on the first seven. After screening the last one, Simmons stood and said to the technician, "That'll do-er. Thanks, friend."

"Yup," the technician said between pops of his wad of gum.

Ben and Simmons turned their visitor badges in at the front desk and walked to the car. After they were seated, Simmons asked, "OK, Lootenant. So we know now that there is no need to look at Marathon or points east."

"That helps some."

"Yes, indeed. Feel like breakfast on me? I haven't eaten since last night."

"There's a Denny's on Roosevelt."

"Excellent! We should have plenty of time for the best of American fare."

"Right," Ben started the car.

A short time later, the two men finished their coffee at the restaurant, and Simmons gave Ben a hard look. "How much experience have you had with tactical driving?"

Ben choked on a small mouthful of coffee. "What?"

"It's a simple question. Have you had any training in tactical driving?"

"No. Why?"

"I need to get something together. Did you notice the four-door following us?"

"No. Since the base?"

"Since the sheriff's office, actually. I wasn't sure at first, but after the second stop, I knew for certain. Don't worry. We will make this work. I need you to walk to the restroom and hang out while I work through the checkout line. When I'm number two in the queue, you step out to the car and bring it up front. Once I get in, just do as you're told, and we'll be fine. OK?"

Ben nodded, stood up, and strolled to the washroom. After two minutes, he peeked out and saw Simmons stepping into the second position in the checkout line. Ben strode through the restaurant and scanned the parking area while walking to the car in the bright sunlight. Again, nothing stood out, and he wondered if his companion was seeing things. He pulled the car up and parked in front of the restaurant. Half a minute later, Simmons emerged and sat down in the passenger's seat. Putting on his seatbelt and pulling his sidearm, he said, "OK, let's move. As you leave the parking lot, take a right on Roosevelt. Nice and easy, just like before."

"OK," Ben nervously glanced at the drawn pistol. After turning on Roosevelt, he noticed another car emerging a discreet distance behind them. "That them?"

"Yep. Now, bear left and follow Roosevelt. When we make the curve to the right, get in the left turn lane for Overseas Highway, like we are going to continue on U.S. 1. Remember, nice and steady, just like we don't have a care in the world."

Ben complied, rolling to a stop in the turn lane behind two other turning cars.

"OK, now for the interesting part. When the light changes, creep up, and when you have a clear path, head straight at the intersection and floor it. Start sounding the horn and keep pumping it. You will want to shift right as soon as possible—you'll be hanging a right on Flagler. You got all that?"

"Yes."

"Now take it easy. We will be fine. I want you to slow down before the turn on Flagler. We can't afford to roll this thing, OK?"

"OK." Ben nodded stiffly. The light changed to a left turn only, and when the car ahead cleared their path, Ben jammed the accelerator and swerved right to pass through the intersection. Their tail jogged out of the turn lane in pursuit two seconds later.

"Horn! Hit the horn!" Simmons shouted, his head turned to track the pursuing vehicle, and Ben complied. "OK, OK, slow down for the turn."

Ben slowed and veered right onto Flagler with a screaming of tires and modest fishtailing as he straightened on the new path. Their pursuers also swung in behind them from Roosevelt a few seconds later.

"Floor it! We'll be hanging a right on Tenth in ten blocks, same tactic. Keep hitting that horn!"

Ben stayed on the horn, dodging through traffic at speeds approaching fifty miles per hour.

"Counting down," Simmons said, "Fourteenth, Thirteenth, twelfth, Eleventh, slow down and prepare to hang a right, NOW!"

Ben executed another tire-squealing turn and straightened out, heading north on Tenth, gunning the engine and leaning on the horn.

"Stand by to hit the brakes!" Simmons shouted. "Steady, steady, NOW, hit the brakes!"

Ben stood on the brake pedal, tires shrieked, and the anti-lock braking chattered. After skidding to a stop in the middle of the street next to a large lagoon, Simmons shouted, "Get down!" He opened both doors on his side of the car, using the rear door for cover.

Ben dropped behind the seat as their pursuer began screeching to a stop. Suddenly, there was a tremendous crash with the sound of tearing metal and followed by a large splash. Simmons shut the doors and said in a normal tone, "OK, let's roll. Back to the base, nice and easy."

Ben shot up and saw several figures in combat gear with guns drawn running forward from an SUV stopped in the middle of Tenth Street. The car chasing them was coming to rest upside down in the lagoon. "WHAT—THE—HELL!" he shouted at Simmons.

"Come on, friend, we need to move it. It's handled. We're clear now, so stay law-abiding all the way, please."

Ben stared at him for a few seconds, then pressed the accelerator. The engine raced briefly, and then, with shaking hands, Ben shifted into Drive.

"See, you're a natural," Simmons said with a smile. "You didn't even realize you shifted into Park."

4

Revelation

Secure Compartmented Information Facility, Coast Guard Sector Key West, Key West, Florida
11:17 EST, 15 January

Ben

Ben sat silently next to Sam, looking straight ahead while stealing the occasional furtive glance at him. Sam sat quietly, also staring straight ahead, drumming his fingers on the table. They had been waiting in this state in the dim, windowless room for about two minutes while the Sector Security Watch fetched Simmons from the office he was using. Ben's hands had finally stopped shaking; it relieved him to see. They had still been shaking rather noticeably when he had reported to Sam aboard the ship on their return from Key West town. It was his first experience with post-adrenaline surge effects.

Sam had listened to the report without comment, then brought both hands down on his legs with a jarring slap. "Right. Let's go." They left the ship, pausing at the quarterdeck to reserve the sector's Secure Compartmented Information Facility. Sam's gaze fixed forward in steely determination on the silent walk over. Ben had not seen this side of his friend before, but he knew there were times he should keep his yap shut, and this was one.

After a knock, Simmons entered with the security watch. Sam nodded to the petty officer. "Thank you, that's all."

"Yes, sir," the petty officer mumbled as he exited and closed the door.

"Sit down, Doctor," Sam said. Sam leaned forward after the other man had complied, fixing Simmons's expressionless gaze with his own. "I will recap the morning's activities for you, Doctor, based on the report I received from my XO and some personal inferences," Sam began with a stiff formality. "After you left this base, you went to the Sheriff's office to gather information. You detected unknown persons trailing your car at some point in that journey. Is that correct?"

"Yes, it is."

"You withheld this information from my officer until you had completed a leisurely breakfast. After that, you had my officer lead those individuals on a high-speed car chase, ending with their vehicle being upside down in a lagoon off 10th Street. Is THAT correct?"

"Essentially correct, yes."

"You know what I think, Doctor? I think this entire exercise was a setup. I think you found out someone pretty bad was lurking around here, and you decided to take them out. This investigative mission was a bullshit pretense to go on the hunt. You dragged your coat around until they picked up on you. Then you took in a meal. Not because you wanted breakfast and coffee, but to give your thugs time to set up their thugs in an ambush. What do you think of my hypothesis?" Sam glared across the table at the agent.

"The investigative mission was not a ruse. I needed to see those archives. I didn't know the opposition was here, but when I picked up on the tail, I recognized an opportunity to change the gameboard, and I took it. That's my job."

Sam's face flushed with anger. "Doctor, you dragged my officer, unarmed, without his permission or even knowledge, into a life-threatening situation. Instead of calling in law enforcement, you forced him into violations of the law and put his and innocent civilian lives at risk. You had your sidearm out at the end. You were expecting a gunfight if your little bumper car ploy didn't work, weren't you?"

"Yes, but that was an unlikely possibility. This isn't our first rodeo, Captain. We practice and execute these tactics regularly, although not domestically. You should get hold of yourself here."

"I told you what to expect if you needlessly put my people in harm's way!"

"Aw, come on, Captain. It was well-controlled and successful. Your man came to no harm. In fact, he did well. He's a military officer who signed up to take risks, not your little sister."

Sam's mouth clamped shut, and he stood up. Ben followed and said, "Captain?" When Sam shoved the chair backward, closed his hands into fists, and started around the table, Ben grasped his arm and held him back. "Sam!"

Sam turned and blinked at his name, seemingly seeing Ben for the first time. He gave Simmons one last glare, then yanked the chair forward and sat down firmly. He took a breath to steady down and said, "Doctor, you just crossed the last line with me. You are out one patrol boat."

Simmons's smug smile continued. "Perhaps true for you, *Lieutenant*, not me. It seems you've forgotten I'm in charge of this operation. One phone call from me, and you'll be on the beach."

"Perhaps, but I don't think so. Anyway, *Kauai* will be out of it."

"Nonsense. They'll just move up your copilot here. I have a national security priority...."

"You obviously don't have a good grasp of what it means to command a military vessel," Sam interrupted. "Sure, if we were in the middle of a critical operation and I dropped dead, Ben would succeed to command. The operational commander would weigh the risks and then decide whether to continue or abort the mission. But, one thing is certain: after the first mooring line goes over, *Kauai* will be offline until a new CO is appointed and installed. Make your phone call. Whether I'm in or out, the result will be the same."

Simmons's smug smile faded when he realized his poker hand was not as strong as he thought. "OK, stalemate. How do we move on?"

Sam sat back and cocked his head slightly. "You have one chance here: build trust by coming clean. We're in this SCIF to give you cover to spill on the whole scenario without compromising security. You give me the whole story on this, convince me it's complete and truthful to the last nit-noid detail, and maybe, MAYBE, you can also convince me to continue this excellent adventure. Otherwise, you might as well start packing."

The "stalemate," as Simmons described it, lasted another sixty seconds. He and Sam glared at each other, with Ben wishing he were *anywhere* else right then. Finally, Simmons blinked. "Fine, I hope you guys can keep this between us because I will be in deep trouble just sharing it with you."

"I understand," Sam said. "You have our word that nothing you say here will go any further. Right, XO?"

"Understood, Captain."

"Gentlemen, I am reluctantly reading you in on a top-secret operation under code word JUBILEE. Are you familiar with the term 'Broken Arrow'?"

Sam leaned forward. "If memory serves, that refers to a lost nuclear weapon. Please tell me I'm wrong."

"Alas, no," Simmons replied with a completely blank expression. "That is the correct reference to what we are dealing with here."

Ben felt a sudden icy chill and gaped at Sam, who returned a similar look of disbelief. "Bullshit!" was all Sam could say.

"Captain, I get I'm in a hole with you guys credibility-wise, but this is not a ploy or a cover story or any other weaselly spy trick." Simmons looked from Ben to Sam. "This is the real deal."

"OK," Sam began. "Let's pretend we would believe anything you tell us right now. And, by the way, that's a stretch, given you have consistently denied we were facing any radiological hazard. Where did this nuke come from?"

"To begin, we are not sure there is a nuclear weapon."

Sam snorted with disgust. "There is, or there isn't. How can you not be sure either way?"

"Because the weapon is Russian. We *are* sure they launched the weapon. We just don't know if it was carrying a conventional or a nuclear warhead."

"I don't believe it," Sam said. "The Russians attacked the United States? How could they cover up something like that?"

"It was an accident, Captain, not an attack." Simmons looked at Ben and asked, "You are aware of the current tensions in the Baltic?"

"The Russians are hammering the EU for a land corridor to Kaliningrad again. So what? Belarus may be a Russian puppet, but no one thinks Poland or Lithuania will cough up any territory. This is not Georgia or Crimea—Poland and Lithuania are both

NATO. Any incursion by the Russians would trigger World War III."

"True, but it does not preclude some good old-fashioned saber-rattling. Here, a combination of Russian exercises in Grodno, Belarus, just over the Lithuanian and Polish borders, and some provocative flybys of our Air Defense Identification Zone in the Southeast by their Long-Range Aviation assets staging out of Cuba and Venezuela. One of their Backfire bombers got a little too close and triggered an intercept by F-16s out of Homestead. One thing led to another, there was a bump, and then an uncommanded launch of one of their Kinzhal hypersonic missiles."

"Holy Shit!" Ben exclaimed. "How did they keep that out of the news?"

"The missile did not hit any targets, on land anyway. There would be no hiding that—the vehicle's kinetic energy alone has the impact of a four-ton bomb, even if the warhead doesn't detonate."

Sam interrupted. "Take that kind of impact, a launch from a target we were not only tracking on radar but had eyes on, and the best you can do for a position estimate is a thirty-by-sixty-mile ellipse? What the hell?"

"Our pilots lost sight of it a few seconds after launch, and there's no way to track a Kinzhal on radar. The missile flies so fast that it generates a plasma cloud that absorbs radar energy," Simmons explained. "That's what caused the bright light we saw on the traffic cameras. Our non-radar sensor coverage is very sparse in the Keys. From Ben's and my efforts at the sheriff's office, we know it passed Marathon, but did not reach Boca Chica."

For Ben, the chill was passing. "OK, no explosion, no global nuclear war, and the missile vaporized on impact. What are we doing here?"

"That's the thing," Simmons answered. "The *vehicle* likely shattered, but the warhead has to survive the impact to operate correctly—it is almost certainly intact. Which leaves a live bomb packing an explosive power somewhere between one thousand pounds and five hundred thousand *tons* of TNT waiting to get tangled in someone's fishing trawl or anchor chain."

"OK, Doctor." Sam leaned back, folding his arms. "Let's say I believe what you have just told me. Answer me this: why us? Why isn't this place crawling with Army and Marines or the sky dark with search aircraft? Who thinks an aging Coast Guard patrol boat with a couple of toy airplanes is the right tool for this job?"

"Good question. You can't sortie forces like that on a moment's notice when everyone is already bore-sighted on Europe. Even if we could, we'd just draw attention to something we must keep quiet at all costs.

"From whom?" Ben asked.

"From everyone. Imagine the panic that would result if it got out that the U.S. government was hunting a lost nuclear weapon in the Florida Keys. Or the outrage when the public got wind of the Russians launching a nuke our way, even if we could prove it was an accident. This isn't the early 1960s, when the President could ask the publishers and network heads to help calm things down. They'll be stoking the viewers for ratings and mouse clicks until we declare war or have an insurrection. It's difficult to see how we *don't* end up in a nuclear exchange.

"You can see why you're ideal for this. You guys have a low-key footprint, and your presence where we will search is not considered unusual. Also, by all accounts, your crew is very sharp."

"What do you mean, 'by all accounts'?" Sam asked.

"You are highly regarded by the authorities. When we contacted the Coast Guard and asked for high-quality patrol boat support, they stuck with you."

Sam smiled ruefully. "Has it occurred to you we just might be the most expendable?"

Simmons feigned a distressed expression. "Good Heavens, I never thought of that!"

"And who were the guys who chased us? Russian agents?" Ben asked.

Simmons's smile faded. "No, those guys aren't with the Russians, and their presence is real bad news."

"Huh?" Sam said. "You're telling me a potential live nuke in our backyard is not the *worst* news? Who are we talking about here?"

"It's my day job at the agency. In short, they're the owners of the dope you interdicted. As you said, that amount of product would be worth a fortune. When that load dropped out of sight, the bad guys started searching hard. No mention of a large bust in the news media convinced them some rival organization must have snatched it. According to my sources, they've combed every harbor and marina within five hundred miles searching for it. I'm sure they had people keeping watch on every law enforcement group—federal, state, and local—and they're probably rolling up a big body count of their rivals gathering intel. Unfortunately, their watch at the Sheriff's office must have spotted me—I'm proud to say that I'm well-known to them for good reason. They've put together we have the boat, and something unusual is happening if I'm poking around. That little set-to this morning was a ham-fisted try by their local B-Teamers to grab and squeeze me for information. It didn't work out well for them."

"Drug cartel?" Sam asked.

"More of a transnational criminal organization. They informally call themselves the '252 Syndicate,' from February 25th, 1991, the date the Warsaw Pact fell. Founded by the worst the KGB, Stasi, Securitate, Sigurimi, and other Warsaw Pact secret police goon squads had and staffed with ex-agents and mercenaries with no wars to fight. They fund themselves through drug smuggling, human and weapons trafficking, extortion, and anything else that produces large profit margins. This mob's smart, well-equipped, and absolutely ruthless. That's another reason we wanted you guys, the Coast Guard, I mean. The Navy doesn't do law enforcement, and it may come to that before we finish."

Both officers sat in silence, processing what they had just been told. Sam finally broke the silence. "So, you have assets in the area, but I guess you have to presume that they'll draw in the TCO forces if they're observed."

"Yes, that's about it. We can flail around on a hard-target ground search, but we'd lead the 252s right to our target. As you can imagine, the last thing we want is for them to get hold of a nuclear weapon."

"So," Sam continued. "It's our job to prowl offshore with the UAVs and appear conventional."

"Yes, but we'll probably need a close look at some locations with your RHIB."

Sam leaned forward, putting his hands on the table. "And if we run into these guys, we can expect a fight?"

"Not necessarily. They don't want to start a war with the U.S. government. Bad for business, you know. However, if we corner them or get between them and something they want, they won't hesitate to shoot it out with us."

Sam sat back. "Is our operational commander aware of all this?"

"Select Coast Guard individuals are read-in, your Commandant, the Area Commander, and the Seventh District Commander and Response Chief."

"Forgive me, Doctor," Sam said. "I'll need to verify my chain of command is OK with things as they stand now. Since Captain Mercier is read-in, I'll get on a secure line with her."

"If you must, but remember, the details are compartmented information, and you can't discuss that on an ordinary secure telephone."

"Understood." Sam turned to Ben. "XO, can you call down to the District and arrange for a secure phone call with Captain Mercier, please?"

"Yes, sir," Ben replied, rising and heading out the door. Captain Jane Mercier was the officer in charge of response for the Seventh Coast Guard District. She handled the better-known Coast Guard missions of search and rescue and law enforcement in South Carolina, Georgia, most of Florida, the Bahamas, and Puerto Rico. For now, she was also Sam's boss, and his and Ben's fates rested in her hands.

It was a short walk to an empty desk and phone. After logging on to the computer, Ben looked up Captain Mercier's number in the global directory and dialed her number. She answered after three rings.

"Response, Captain Mercier."

"Good morning, ma'am. This is Lieutenant J.G. Ben Wyporek, XO of *Kauai*."

"Good morning, Ben. What can I do for you?"

"Ma'am, we are in Key West and have hit a sticky part in our mission. My CO, Lieutenant Powell, requests an opportunity to get some clarification over the STE."

"No problem. Give me five minutes to close up and get down to a secure space. I'll call you. I presume you'll be in the SCIF?"

"Yes, ma'am."

"All good. Talk to you in five."

"Thank you, ma'am," Ben said, then hung up and returned to the SCIF.

"I talked to Captain Mercier, sir," Ben said as he sat in front of the STE telephone. "She'll call us here as soon as she gets to her STE."

"Good. Now, Doctor, would you mind giving us the room, please?" His expression conveyed: *this is not a request.*

Simmons stared at Sam in astonishment. "Very well." He stood and walked out without another word.

After the door closed, Ben asked, "Sir?"

"I expect an 'inside baseball' talk with the captain. I don't want her holding back because our favorite spook is in the room."

"Yes, sir." Ben nodded.

"What do you think of this, really?"

"I don't know, sir. I can see the argument for staying lean for the sake of operations security. But just us? That's cut to the friggin' bone!"

"I agree. It's possible, I guess, but I need a lot more than a professional liar's word before I believe enough to continue on this one."

"I'm sure the captain will clear it up for us, skipper."

"Maybe. I wouldn't count on it, though."

The secure phone rang after a few minutes, and Sam activated the speakerphone. "Sector Key West, Lieutenant Powell speaking."

"Good morning, Sam. Jane Mercier here. What can I do for you this morning?"

"Yes, good morning, ma'am. You're on speaker with just my XO and me in the room. I'm sorry to bother you, but I need to verify that you are up to speed on developments before continuing the operation."

"OK, please go ahead."

"Ma'am, Dr. Simmons has told us about something related to this mission he claims I can't discuss over an

STE. I'll just refer to it as 'X.' Do you know what I'm referring to, ma'am?"

"Yes, I do."

"Ma'am, I'm unsure how to put this. Is it for real?" After a few seconds of silence, Sam asked, "Captain, are you there?"

"Yes, Lieutenant, I'm here. I'm trying to figure out the best way to answer your question. Let's just say that several highly placed people believe it's real enough and issued orders accordingly. You are at the tail end of that chain of orders. Do you understand me?"

"Yes, ma'am."

"Good," Mercier said. "Was there anything else?"

"Yes, ma'am. It gets worse. A TCO has gotten involved, and they took a shot at grabbing Simmons and my XO this morning."

"Shit! Are you all right, Ben?"

"No worries, ma'am," Ben replied.

"They're both fine, ma'am," Sam interjected. "Simmons's people negated the immediate threat, and we are safe for now."

"I'm relieved to hear that."

"Ma'am, these guys don't screw around, and there's a genuine possibility of high-caliber use-of-force if we tangle with them. I'm sure there won't be time to get a Statement of No Objection when that happens."

"So, you're asking me for a blanket SNO? You know I can't give you that."

"No, ma'am, I'm not asking for a blank check, but you need to understand I will do whatever I need to do to protect my crew. Given that, should I continue this operation?"

"Your orders stand, Sam. All the 'But, sirs' have been said, believe me. I appreciate this is not what you wanted to hear, but I expect you and your crew to do your duty. In this case, that means you cooperate with Dr. Simmons to the maximum extent possible within the current rules of engagement until further notice. Clear enough?"

"Yes, ma'am. Sorry again to bother you, but I needed to be sure I understood the expectations. Thank you, ma'am."

"Not a problem. I understand your concern, given the new players. Keep your crew and ship safe. If there's nothing else, I'll wish you good luck."

"Thank you, ma'am. Goodbye." After turning off the phone, he turned to Ben. "Your thoughts?"

Ben's head swam at the implications of the conversation. "My God, Skipper! She thinks it's bullshit, too!"

"Mmm. And yet, we have our orders. Can you invite the good doctor back in, please?"

"Yes, sir." Ben blinked and then stood up to retrieve their passenger.

After Ben returned with Simmons and sat down, Simmons gazed at Sam. "Well?"

"Standard rules of engagement apply. We need a Statement of No Objection for the use of force unless it's self-defense. That means, Doctor, if your bad guys do not present an immediate and credible threat of lethal force, we need to get permission to shoot first. Is that understood?"

"You mean to say that given what I told you about these creeps, you will give them the first shot?" Simmons was aghast.

"No, what I'm saying is if they're not offering an immediate threat, I will call it in. If they come after us or pull out a weapon of any kind, I'll blow them right out of their socks."

"That works for me." Simmons nodded.

"I'm delighted to hear it. OK, XO, let's thank our hosts and get going before I come to my senses."

5

Workups

USCG Cutter *Kauai*, Gulf of Mexico, fifteen nautical miles northwest of Key West, Florida 14:08 EST, 15 January

Sam

Sam had put the shakedown of the Puma system first on the list after they reached the weapons exercise area off Key West known as W-174. Sam had seen testing of the larger ScanEagle unmanned aircraft system on the large National Security Cutter he served on before he attended officer candidate school. The ScanEagle needed a catapult for launch and a catch wire system for recovery that occupied a significant part of the cutter's flight deck. That experience had led to his doubt any UAV system could work on a unit as small as a patrol boat.

Thus, Sam continued to expect Deffler's junior counterpart Morgan to set up some sort of launcher on

Kauai's foredeck. Morgan assembled the aircraft while Deffler ran through control checks on the GCS. Ben was on the foredeck, observing the setup and launch. Finally, Deffler announced, "Pre-flight checklist complete. Request Green Deck for UAV launch."

Sam looked at Bondurant, who had the OOD, and received a shrug in return. He made a mental note to work out a formal procedure later. "Very well, Green Deck, launch when ready."

Deffler spoke to Morgan through the headset. "Green Deck, Mike. Let me know when you're ready for the count."

Sam glanced down and watched Morgan pick up the UAV by its fuselage just under the wing. At his ready report, Deffler activated the battery-powered engine into idle and began his countdown. "Launch in three, two, one, now!"

To Sam's astonishment, at the count of two, Morgan drew his arm back like a javelin thrower and threw the aircraft into the air, releasing on "Now!" with the engine coming up to the loud buzz of full power. The aircraft arced downward slightly when it cleared the rail on *Kauai*, then started a slow climb over the water.

Sam shook his head in amazement as the small aircraft continued its ascent. The ScanEagle had cost millions of dollars in ship alterations and had mostly disabled the flight deck of the cutter when operating. The Puma took two crewmen for the launch, and Morgan had already picked up his gear and left the foredeck. Deffler started his planned flight pattern to check for any communications blind spots caused by the ship's superstructure and radar interference.

Deffler "mapped" signal strength and quality in every direction for about an hour and noted the dicey locations. Afterward, Deffler brought the aircraft back to put the cameras through their paces. Bondurant delighted in bringing *Kauai* up to a brisk twenty-four knots and putting her through a series of quick turns and reversals. The Puma remained in a steady orbit through it all, its camera doggedly locked onto the gyrating patrol boat.

The quality of the images sent from the aircraft impressed Sam. Even from one thousand feet of altitude, the resolution was sharp enough to read the quarter-inch lettering on the warning labels of the life raft canister. "Deffler, you need any more dedicated time? I would like to get going on the gun shoot before we lose the light."

"All set, Captain. If you don't object, I'd like to keep the bird up to do shot spotting."

"Good, I'd like to see that too." Sam nodded. "How much endurance do you have left?"

Deffler smiled. "Oh, a good four hours if we're frugal, maybe three if we get fancy."

Sam pondered what "get fancy" meant, but put it aside for the moment. "OK, OOD, let's set Condition One for gunnery exercise, please."

"Yes, sir," Bondurant replied. He picked up the microphone for *Kauai*'s public-address system and announced, "Now, General Quarters, General Quarters, set Condition One for gunnery exercise." He then pulled the handle on the GQ alarm, starting a twenty-second repeating gong sound. Crew members began moving briskly to their GQ stations, putting on helmets and survival gear and, with the topside personnel, light body armor. Ben quickly appeared and relieved Bondurant as OOD, allowing him to leave for his GQ station on the boat deck.

Sam watched the quick transition of his cutter from peacetime cruising to combat-ready with satisfaction. He hid a smile while he saw Hopkins patiently helping Deffler get into his battle gear. Simmons had brought his own body armor but wore a loaner helmet and survival vest. Typically, during GQ, Sam would not have had visitors on the already crowded Bridge. However, he wanted Simmons to have a good understanding of *Kauai's* combat capability, and Deffler was piloting the airborne Puma.

"OOD," Sam called over as Ben settled in and completed a radar check and circle round with the binoculars. "When the fantail station reports manned and ready, have them launch targets at two-minute intervals."

"Very good, sir."

The targets Sam referred to were small wooden boxes containing an inflated beach ball and rigged with a stone weight on one side and a plastic flag on the other. The ball would hold the box afloat even with leaks, and the weight would keep the flag upright, improving the target's visibility. Drake supervised the construction of a dozen targets this morning to prepare for the shoot.

"Captain, the first target is away," Ben announced after the deck crew dropped the first target buoy off the stern of the boat.

"Thank you. Hold this course until the last one goes over, then give me a wide turn course reversal to starboard. Put us about five hundred yards off, parallel to the target line at five knots. We'll take the first six with the twenty-five-millimeter. Then close to one hundred yards to finish off the others with the fifties and small arms."

"Very good, sir."

Sam glanced across to see Hopkins huddled with Deffler at the UAV control station while the latter tracked the targets with the Puma. "XO, a word, please," Sam called as he stepped out onto the bridge wing.

"Yes, sir?" Ben said when he caught up.

"XO, I'd like you to get in some shooting with an M4 and pistol, at least two mags each."

"Very good, sir. May I ask why?"

"Our guest implied we would need to go ashore, despite our newfound air capability. When that happens, I'll need you to keep an eye on him, but you'll be properly equipped this time. I think it's been about six months since you've been to the range?"

"More like eight."

"Ever shoot the M4 on automatic?"

"No, sir, the range monkeys wouldn't have it."

"Do it today." Sam nodded. "I want you comfortable with that weapon in all modes."

"Yes, sir." Ben grinned. "This secret agent gig has perks."

"Before you get too giddy, think beyond the sale a bit."

"Sir?"

Sam fixed on Ben's eyes. "I'm making sure you're ready to use them because your life may depend on it."

"Yes, sir."

****

"Surface action starboard," Sam declared. "Target is the floating buoy bearing zero-eight-five relative."

Kauai armament included the latest model twenty-five-millimeter chain gun—a testbed installation of the new versions fitted to the latest ships. Williams controlled *Kauai's* main gun from a compact control station on the Bridge. Its electro-optical and infrared gun sights and gyro-stabilization made it deadly even in rough weather.

"Target identified, target confirmed, on target and tracking," Williams announced, with the gun's electro-optical gun sight centered on the target buoy. Although challenging to see with the naked eye from five hundred yards, Williams had no problem tracking the target with the gun sight.

"OOD, is the range clear?" Sam called over to Ben.

"Affirmative, Captain, no surface or air contacts."

"Deffler, is the UAV clear?"

"Affirmative Captain, the UAV is overhead." Deffler locked the aircraft's camera on the target buoy.

"Very well. Batteries release, commence fire."

"Firing," Williams toggled off the safety and tapped the trigger. The gun responded with a sharp BANG, followed by the clank of the chain loader and the rattle of the spent cartridge ejecting on the deck. Williams pitched the first shot short, as he used a "walking up" technique with three single shots, then a "fire for effect" quick burst of three rounds of high-explosive incendiary shells, all of which detonated on impact.

"Damn!" Deffler exclaimed when the target on his screen exploded in a bright flash. The others on the Bridge turned to look at him, and he said, "Sorry, sir!"

Williams shook his head and turned back to his screen. "Airedales!" He declared under his breath before, more loudly, "Target destroyed."

"Check fire," Sam declared. "OK, let's make sure it's not a fluke. Shift target to next target float bearing zero-eight-zero relative."

Williams slewed the gun sight to the left to acquire the new target and then activated the target lock. On the foredeck, the gun barrel traversed a few degrees to the left and then crept up and down as its gyro stabilizers compensated for *Kauai*'s gentle pitching and rolling. "Target identified, target confirmed, on target and tracking."

"Commence fire," Sam repeated, and six rounds later, another target disintegrated. "Check fire. OK, I'm a believer. Williams, let's try infrared targeting only on the next two."

"Yes, sir." Williams brought up the infrared targeting system, but struggled at once. The infrared sight keyed on differences in temperature and the overcast skies and time since the launch had rendered the target almost indistinguishable from the surrounding water. Finally, Williams settled and locked the sight on a barely discernable smudge, announcing, "Target identified, target confirmed, on target and tracking."

Sam had noted his fire control expert's difficulty with a bit of concern. "Commence fire."

Williams tried the same technique as before, pitching the first round into the water about fifty feet short. Unfortunately, the hot incendiary tail and explosion from the round distracted the infrared gun sight and broke its lock on the target. "Crap! Oh, sorry, sir, target track lost, reacquiring." After a few seconds of jiggling, he brought the smudge representing the buoy into target lock again. "Target reacquired." This time, he aimed for a direct hit. "Firing." Another bang and another target lock break. "Target track lost, shot unobserved," Williams reported with discouragement.

"Shot fall five meters right and twenty long," Deffler reported from the chart table. Again, all heads turned to him. "Captain, recommend illuminating the target with the UAV—it's tuned to the Mark 38's infrared gun sight."

Sam looked from Williams to Deffler and then replied, "Why not? Permission granted. Let's see if it works."

Deffler worked his console, announcing, "Unmasking, target illuminated."

Williams noted a bright dot on the infrared screen and locked on it. "Target identified, target confirmed, on target and tracking."

"Commence fire."

Williams selected a three-round burst on this try. "Firing." The three shots within 1.5 seconds were followed almost at once by the detonation of the target.

"Target destroyed," Williams and Deffler announced simultaneously.

"Check fire," Sam ordered. "Very nice. Let's use the designator on the next two. Shift target to the next buoy bearing zero-eight-five relative. UAV, illuminate the target."

Deffler slewed the Puma's camera to the next target, locked on, and activated the illuminator. "Target illuminated."

Williams noted and locked on to the bright spot, selecting another three-round burst. "Target identified, target confirmed, on target and tracking."

Sam noted the briskness of the acquisition and ordered, "Commence fire." Three more quick shots were followed by another "target destroyed" announcement from the two technicians. After they repeated the process on the next target, Sam ordered, "Ceasefire." He glanced at his technicians. "OK, now we know we can use the infrared sight against a relatively cool target if we can illuminate it. We'll need a standard procedure for that. Hopkins, will you coordinate that in the follow-up, please?"

"Will do, Captain," Hopkins replied.

"OK, secure the twenty-five," Sam ordered. "Let's close to twenty-five yards for the rest of the shoot, please."

"Very good, sir," Ben replied, then issued the orders to the helmsman.

The boarding team members blazed away at the targets with carbines and pistols for about an hour. Hopkins relieved Ben as OOD to allow him to join in for the last twenty minutes. The targets still afloat were dispatched with the fifty-caliber machine guns to give Seaman Lopez and Hebert some experience. Although not as impressive as the main gun, the fifties still made quick work of the target buoys.

Sam secured the shoot at 17:15 to give the shooters a chance to gather the spent cartridges from the decks and help the gunner's mate clean the weapons. In the meantime, Sam directed the RHIB launch to recover the Puma. The RHIB sat idling off *Kauai*'s starboard quarter as Deffler brought the aircraft down, cut the engine, and flared it for a gentle splashdown between the two vessels. The RHIB motored to the Puma within a few seconds, and Morgan carefully lifted and secured the aircraft in the boat.

As the RHIB returned for recovery aboard *Kauai*, Ben turned and picked up his weapons and "sack o-brass" and headed out toward the main deck. When he passed Simmons, the latter asked, "Got a minute? We need to review tomorrow's plans."

Ben held up the weapons. "I got clean-ups. I'll be with you in about half an hour."

Simmons frowned. "You don't have people for that?"

Ben stared coldly in return. "I suppose I can order one of these guys to clean my weapons—if I was a complete *dick,* that is. Excuse me." Ben continued down the ladder as Simmons turned to see Sam had watched the exchange.

"Your officer is quite the egalitarian," Simmons remarked.

"That's what makes him effective. Field-stripping and cleaning your weapon after a shoot, tedious as it may be, is an important part of maintaining familiarity and qualifications. Ben knows that officers shirking their duty negatively affects the crew and wouldn't do so unless he had a damn good reason. I've seen plenty of JOs who believe their shit doesn't stink and wouldn't think twice about dumping this work on the junior crew. None of them made a difference to the unit or the mission like Ben has."

"Yes, I see." Simmons smirked. "I hope he can find time for other 'duties' soon."

"Don't worry, Doctor," Sam turned to leave. "He handles all pains-in-the-ass with equal diligence."

USCG Cutter *Kauai*, Gulf of Mexico, fifteen nautical miles northeast of Key West, Florida
20:17 EST, 15 January

Ben

"XO, got a minute?" Sam called out as Ben walked by the cabin.

"Yes, sir." Ben stepped aside as Hopkins moved out.

"Thanks, Hoppy," Sam said. "I appreciate you getting that turned out so quick."

"Not a problem, Captain. Goodnight," the petty officer replied, nodding to each man as she walked off.

Sam looked at Ben. "She came up with standard language for the UAV launch and gunfire spotting. We won't stumble around next time."

Ben glanced out the door sadly. "Figures she'd nail that. It will suck to lose her."

"Tell me about it." Sam shook his head equally sadly. "I won't have her turning down chief, though."

"Damn straight." Ben nodded. "You wanted something, sir?"

"Yes, yes. I wanted to ask what our guest is cooking up for us."

"Oh, he just wanted to go over the visit sequence."

"Right. And how's it going with you two?"

Ben sat back. "Skipper, I'm trying my best. But every time I warm up to him, he pitches another 'Asshat, Esq.' card, and I want to kick his ass. Or step aside and let you kick his ass." He finished with a slight smile.

Sam closed his eyes and shook his head. "Not my finest moment. Sorry to drop you in the middle of that."

"It's OK, sir. Although the last thing I expected after our adventure this morning was to be compared to a little girl."

"Oh, he wasn't doing that. He aimed that shot squarely at me. I owe you an explanation. Please close the door."

Ben complied and then sat down. "Captain, you don't owe me any explanations."

"Maybe, but you will get one, anyway. You've been curious about my background and patient enough not to ask questions, and this morning's lunatic episode provides an excuse to come clean with you. So, sit back, relax, and let me sate your curiosity."

In the close quiet of the cabin, Sam began describing his early adolescence as the elder child of a Wall Street financial "Master of the Universe." His home was a mansion twenty miles from Manhattan in Essex Fells, New Jersey. Private schools, tutors, and lavish parties dominated his memories when he and his sister Gabrielle, three years his junior, grew up with their devoted mother, Danielle. His father, James, typical of the financial class, spent his weeknights at an apartment close to work downtown and returned to his family on the weekends. Although not close to his father, he was aligned with him in affection for his mother. Her death in a car accident when he was twelve blew both their worlds to pieces. His father coped by throwing himself into his work with increasing devotion, while Sam turned to his sister and a family friend, a retired Navy SEAL named Robert "Bobby" Moore.

James hired Moore to protect the family when Russian organized crime elements put the squeeze on some of his colleagues. Moore did not come cheap, but he brought a retinue of supremely skilled and dedicated former special forces acquaintances who quickly "negated" the threat. When Sam asked him how he managed it much later, Moore responded he had explained the situation to them in a language a Russian could understand and left it at that. Sam's father discovered Moore possessed many valuable skills beyond physical security and kept him on to help manage his personal life. Moore stepped readily into the void created by the death of Sam's mother. He became a multi-hatted head of security, household majordomo, and general "fixer," keeping things running while the family coped with and eventually overcame the grief of their loss.

With time and nearness, Sam and Moore forged a strong personal attachment. Moore admired Sam's quick mind, innate sense of duty, and the fundamental goodness of character fostered by his mother, and Sam was in awe of the older man's experience and talents. Both shared an exasperated affection for Sam's sister Gabby, whose charm and blossoming beauty matched the independent streak often found in a family's younger child. Under the distant oversight of his father and close mentoring by Moore, Sam matured into an outstanding student, both academically and athletically.

After high school graduation, Sam entered Wharton's Financial Engineering program. Sam thrived there from the intellectual challenge, despite the conflict between the intensely competitive culture and his natural tendency to team up with people. He finished at the top of his class and was accepted into the MBA program. He was moving inexorably toward following his father into the family firm when he confronted the event that changed his outlook and purpose in life.

As Sam progressed through undergraduate studies at Wharton, Gabby matured into a beautiful, social young woman. Intelligent in her own right, she had no intention of following her brother into the family business and opted for a fine arts track at Princeton. She met and fell in with Paul Griffith, a scion of the family of one of her father's business competitors and classmate of Sam at Wharton. Paul was popular, handsome, and rich, and Sam had run into him periodically since they were young children. Growing up, Sam grew aware something was "off" about Paul, gradually distancing himself despite their shared background. By the time they completed their undergraduate work together at Wharton, Sam had seen enough inside and outside the classroom to conclude Paul was an undiagnosed sociopath.

Sam was appalled by Gabby keeping company with someone he regarded as a toxic, if not dangerous, personality and made no secret of it. Gabby, tired of living in her big brother's shadow, was having none of it. Paul sensed the conflict and played on it. He lacked any genuine interest in Gabby, but she was socially useful, and the knowledge he twisted up "straight-arrow" Sam by staying with her made it a win-win. Even Moore couldn't shake the hold Paul had on the young woman—he had to settle for suggesting he would not take it lightly if anything happened to her. The implied menace had no effect on the privileged young man.

The event Sam and Moore dreaded came to pass on a late fall weekend as Paul and Gabby were driving home from a party. He indulged heavily in alcohol and party drugs, and even Gabby was terrified as they sped through the night. Unsurprisingly, he missed a turn and rolled his Porsche down an embankment and into a tributary of the Raritan River. Paul glanced at his unconscious companion as the car filled with water and then bailed.

By an incredible stroke of luck, the accident happened in front of two off-duty Coast Guard petty officers on their way home from a unit gathering, who pulled off and immediately sprang into action. Passing Paul as he climbed the embankment, the two men paused briefly to ask if anyone remained in the car. Not getting a response when the young man fled, one plunged into the freezing water to get to the vehicle, while the other called 911, then waded in to help extract the young woman. Both performed CPR until relieved by paramedics, who transported the unconscious but living victim to the local emergency room.

A thoroughly alarmed Bobby Moore roused Sam, and the two sped to the hospital, James joining them from Manhattan an hour later. The three men sat together in frightened silence in the waiting room for over four hours while the neurosurgery team did their evaluation and response. When the doctor emerged, he reported they had put Gabby into a medically induced coma until her brain swelling went down, but the prognosis was good. Near weeping in relief, the men agreed to take shifts standing by, with Sam remaining for the first watch while Moore escorted his father home.

Gabby's youth and good health paid off. Within a day and a half, she regained consciousness and went home in three. Although reasonably fit, she had no memory of the accident or even the party. After seeing her safely home with temporary live-in medical care, Sam and Moore began inquiries into the accident and the actions law enforcement intended to take.

Paul vanished for several days, then reappeared, completed unscathed. Sam was convinced he hid out to make sure whatever party drugs he had taken were clear of his system before encountering the police. A cursory investigation resulted in misdemeanor reckless driving charges for Paul, and he escaped with a fine. It was rumored Paul's father had dealt with issues like this before and had contacts in the local police and district attorney's office. Paul's father quietly made right on Gabby's medical costs, and, as far as he and James were concerned, the matter was closed.

Sam was furious at this result. He had taken the time to visit the Coast Guard station where the two petty officers were stationed to thank them and offer them a reward, which they politely refused. They told Sam of the events that night, including the driver fleeing the scene. After learning they had contacted the police the following day to offer statements and been summarily rebuffed, Sam was convinced the fix was in.

His anger only increased after a confrontation with his father. Sam was astounded he would go along with a slap on the wrist for the man who had recklessly put his daughter in mortal danger and then abandoned her to die. James was not unfeeling about the incident. But, in his view, more significant business issues were at stake, and he told Sam to put the matter behind him. He then left the task of calming down his son to his trusted adviser Moore and returned to work, a decision that only added more strain to a fragile relationship between father and son.

The situation simmered for several weeks. Sam and Paul returned to their studies at Wharton, but did not share any classes where they would cross paths. Finally, a chance meeting occurred outside the library. Sam nodded at Paul in passing, and Paul took it as a sign of acceptance and submission—an enormous mistake. Sam couldn't remember what Paul had said, only that after he said it, his world went red. By the time Sam was pulled off, Paul was on his way to the hospital with two broken ribs, among other injuries.

It took all the "fixer" juice Moore had to keep Sam clear of a felony assault charge. Paul and his father agreed not to file charges after Moore arranged the payment of Paul's medical bills and made subtle threats about Paul's known drug use and other activities.

On the other hand, James was apoplectic at his son's behavior and the threat to the family business. In a showdown shortly afterward, he told his son in no uncertain terms to "get with the program" or get out.

The ultimatum proved the final straw for Sam. He hated the cutthroat environment of high finance presented by his father and school, but strove to succeed out of a sense of duty to his family. This incident made it clear to Sam that business came first and family was a distant second in this world. He often thought of the two men who saved Gabby's life after the accident. They hadn't hesitated a second to plunge into a freezing river to rescue a young woman they'd never met from a sinking car. *That* was the world Sam wanted to join.

After a sleepless night and a long talk with Bobby Moore that didn't dissuade him, Sam visited the Coast Guard Recruiting Office in Philadelphia. He completed the required entry forms and tests and signed up to report to recruit training at Cape May the following January. The recruiter could not believe what he had in hand between Sam's aptitude test scores and top-of-the-line undergraduate degree. He frankly explained that Sam would have an excellent chance of acceptance to OCS or even a direct commission as a finance officer if he were to apply. He just followed protocol in this, as highly educated recruits could be problematic when they found enlisted life less intellectually challenging. Sam insisted, and the recruiter accepted his application for enlistment and administered the oath. Sam chose Operations Specialist for his desired rating. His test scores and background qualified him to go straight to the Operations Specialist A-school on graduation from boot camp without the usual period as an apprentice seaman.

January came, and the farewell was a hard one. James failed to appear, refusing to talk to Sam until he told Moore, "he returns to sanity." The thought of not having Sam close at hand depressed Gabby. They had grown closer since the accident and his fight with Paul. Although fully recovered physically and getting back in rhythm at school, she still had mild post-traumatic stress and occasionally leaned on him for support. Sam assured her he would keep in touch and that Moore could get word to him in any emergency.

Bobby Moore was another hard farewell. Moore did his best to talk Sam out of joining at James's request. However, he was privately relieved he failed, and proud the boy he had helped raise was stepping up for service. He assured Sam that Gabby would be looked after, and he'd work on his father as best he could, providing Sam relief that at least the home front was well-covered. Moore drove Sam and Gabby down to Cape May on that fateful day. There, the young man joined a sizable group of apprehensive young people making tearful goodbyes from their families and moving to a new phase in life.

Gabby turned out all right. She finished school, met and married a decent man, and set up a successful art studio in Manhattan with her father's financial help. Sam had to give his father credit: he really stepped up to become more engaged and supportive of his daughter after Sam's departure. Moore continued in his role as Sam's surrogate father and family overwatch. He remained a close and most trusted friend to this day. In fact, Jo and Sam named their first child after him, Robert Eduardo Powell.

****

Ben sat back in wonder as Sam finished the story, deeply moved by his friend's trust in sharing some truly private parts of his life. He found it difficult to think of something to say that didn't sound trivial by comparison. After a brief pause, he asked, "Whatever happened to Paul? Did he stir up any more trouble?"

Sam smiled grimly. "Bobby went harder at him on the second try and applied some 'Russian grade' menace. He stayed well clear of Gabby and me since then. The big merger planned with Griffith's company fell through, which pissed Dad off even more. But it worked out better in the end since their company tanked in the subprime lending catastrophe. The last I heard, Paul and his father fled the country with a bag of cash and the Securities and Exchange Commission hot on their heels. Good riddance."

Ben nodded and scratched his head. "Sir, it sounds like everything worked out great. So, what's the continued beef between you and your father?"

Sam shook his head. "No beef on this end. Dad's been invited to every event, and we tried to let him know he's welcome in our lives. His prime beef is he can't accept that someone of my 'breeding' and education would want a job among hoi polloi, making a hundredth of what I can working for him. I think there's a bit of grudge nursing too since, in his view, I told him where to stick it right after he went to the mat to keep my ass out of jail." He smiled ruefully. "I'd agree he had a legitimate gripe back then. Pride can be an ugly thing sometimes, and I don't exclude myself from that indictment. Bobby is still hard at it. Maybe someday he can get us back together."

"Amazing, and what about Gabby?"

This time, Sam looked down sadly. "Things have cooled off with Gabby. She's still part of that world, and she and Jo never took to each other. They put on a brave show for my sake, but it's a strain on both of them when they're together, and we try to avoid it."

"Sorry, sir." Ben frowned in sympathy.

"That's the way it goes. You can see how that's still an open wound for me. The good doctor surprised me enough this morning to generate a psychotic break." He smiled maniacally. "But I'm much better now!"

Ben rocked his head back and laughed. "Roger that, sir. I'll put your Prozac dose back in the safe then. I'll keep Doc Simmons's on hand for a while, though." He winked, then stood and extended his hand. "Thanks for sharing all this, sir."

Sam stood and grasped Ben's hand in a firm shake. "It was easier than I thought. Thanks for hanging in there while I bared my soul. Trust is vital for us, Ben, particularly now. I want you focused on the job and not worrying that I will go postal and throw our guest overboard."

As Ben turned and stepped out, he said, "Yeah, get in line, Boss."

6

Seizure

USCG Cutter *Kauai*, Gulf of Mexico, nineteen nautical miles northeast of Key West, Florida
07:01 EST, 16 January

Ben

"All hands, set Flight Quarters Condition One, clear the foredeck for UAV launch," Ben announced through the ship. Flight quarters on *Kauai* proved to be a low-key operation compared to his previous ship. On *Dependable*, the activities associated with launching a helicopter and standing by in case of crash and fire tied up dozens of crew members for hours. Ben watched as Morgan walked out with his toolbox, one seaman following with the separated Puma fuselage and wing. Turning aft, he saw the ready boat crew moving to stand by the RHIB if the immediate recovery of the aircraft was needed. He turned back inside when Deffler arrived from his check of the ground control antenna and set up the control station.

Ben pulled and reviewed the laminated card Hopkins had prepared the previous night and completed the pre-flight checklist. Ben put the card back in its holder and picked up his binoculars to make his final survey of the area around the boat. Returning inside, he called Sam to let him know checks were complete for launch.

"Very well, OOD, carry on," Sam said.

"Very good, sir," Ben replied. Simmons had arrived and pulled up a stool next to Deffler for the flight. The two consulted using the annotated chart extract Hopkins had provided, showing the likely anchorages on the first two targets. After a brief time, Deffler paused and touched his earpiece.

"OOD, Flight Control, pre-flight checks complete, request Green Deck for UAV launch," he announced.

"Very well, Green Deck."

"Yes, sir. Green Deck, Mike," Deffler spoke into the headset. "Let me know when you're ready for the count." He activated the battery-powered engine. "Standby, three, two, one, launch." The Puma arced over the side and began its climb. "Flight operations normal, camera operating, climbing to three hundred."

About forty minutes later, Bondurant appeared on the Bridge to make his rounds in preparation to relieve Ben of the OOD for the Forenoon Watch. When satisfied with his understanding of the current situation, he stepped up to Ben. "XO, I'm ready to relieve you. Do you have anything to pass?"

"No, Boats. Just monitor our aviation detachment there. Expect they'll bring the bird back about 11:00."

"Got it. I relieve you, sir," Bondurant stated with a smart salute.

Ben walked over to the chart table, where Simmons and Deffler gazed at the video displays. Simmons looked up after a moment. "Heading down for some sleep, friend?"

"I wish. Hopefully, I can coax Chef to turn out one last breakfast ration. Then it's on to my three least favorite things: paperwork, paperwork, and paperwork. Will you be sitting there watching the screen all day?"

"From time to time. Frankly, I don't expect to discover anything this way. The previous searches would have picked up whatever we see. We'll have a better chance letting the analysis team's machine learning algorithms paw through the imagery. They will process the visual and hyperspectral in half-hour blocks."

"You don't have machine learning on the earlier stuff?"

Simmons shook his head. "No, the resolution's too low, and the atmospherics are problematic. The clouds and junk in the air confuse the algorithms."

"Right. How do you plan to get the imagery to the analysts? You have satellite comms through that thing?"

"Not exactly," Simmons replied, his voice dropping. "Also very hush-hush, please. We have a High-Altitude UAV doing communications relay throughout this operation, and they are getting the imagery at the same time we are through high-bandwidth UHF."

"Wow. OK, I'm off. Can I send anything up for you guys? Coffee?"

"No, I'm good," Simmons turned to Deffler. "Fritz?" and received a head shake in reply as the airman concentrated on the screen. "Thanks anyway, friend. See you later."

"Later," Ben replied, turning to leave.

A couple of hours afterward, Ben and Sam were going over the drafts of operational reports in the cabin when the phone rang, and Sam hit the speaker button. "Captain."

"Captain, OOD here, could you come to the Bridge, please, sir?" Bondurant's voice came from the speaker.

"On the way." Sam hit the hang-up button, and he and Ben stood up to make their way to the Bridge. Half a minute later, they arrived and walked over to Bondurant.

"Captain on the Bridge," Bondurant announced.

"Carry on. What have you got, OOD?"

"We have a visual on a surface contact heading slowly in this general direction, sir. It appears to be a sloop under sail, but it is not showing up on radar."

Sam frowned. "Show me."

Bondurant led the two officers to the SeaWatch console and pointed at the screens. "Lookout picked it up first. Then we locked on with the camera. You can see it's definitely under sail and hull-up. I would say nine thousand yards right now. But check out the radar plot: nothing. And nothing's wrong with the radar. You can see we have a good trace on Snipe Point here." He pointed at the screen.

Sam picked up his binoculars and trained them on the bearing. After a brief search, he picked up on the distant object, barely visible through the haze, a small vessel under sail. "Can they see us, you think?"

"If they have radar, yes, sir. Otherwise, I doubt it in this haze."

"Hmmm. XO, what do you think?" Sam whispered, keeping his eyes on the boat through the binoculars.

"Captain, a few days ago, I would have shrugged and said, let's check it out. After yesterday's adventure, I'd rather send the UAV in first."

"Agreed. Doctor, could you come here, please?" Sam called across the Bridge.

"Yes, Captain?" Simmons said when he stepped up.

"Doctor, take a look." Sam handed him the binoculars. "We have a large sailboat that's not showing up on radar. Do you know anything about this?"

As he peered through the binoculars, Simmons replied, "Definitely not." He handed back the glasses and looked Sam in the eye. "I presume you'd like the UAV to go investigate before we close on it."

"I would indeed, Doctor. Can you break off the survey, or do we need to launch the other bird?"

"We're at a good breakpoint. Fritz, what's the fuel state?" he called over.

"One plus five-five."

"OK, bring her up to one thousand and head her back this way. Get the Ghost ready."

"Cool! Turning to three-three-five, leaving three hundred for one thousand."

"Ghost?" Ben asked.

"Compass Ghost System. It's one of our spook add-ons to the basic aircraft. I'll wait until it's almost overhead to switch on so you can get the full effect."

"OK, I'm breathless in anticipation," Sam said wryly. "OOD, let's keep a parallel course and match speed with the target as best you can. Put the radar on standby. Except for the UAV, full emissions control—I'd like to stay undetected for now."

"Yes, sir." Bondurant issued the orders to the helmsman and selected the settings on the console.

The three men stood outside a few minutes later, watching the UAV approach from the southeast. The nine-foot wide aircraft was small but very visible against the cloudy sky at one thousand feet. Simmons turned to Deffler, "Stand by, Fritz. OK, gentlemen, you have the little bird in sight?" Seeing nods in return, Simmons said, "Now, Fritz."

Suddenly, the aircraft vanished before their eyes. "Damn!" Ben exclaimed, and Sam startled and then brought the binoculars up to his eyes.

"Wait, OK, I can just barely make it out. XO, still not seeing it?"

"No, Captain," Ben said in wonder. He glanced at Deffler, now smiling at the three men.

"Welcome to Compass Ghost," Simmons stated. "There are sensors on top connected through a processor to LED projectors on the wings and lower fuselage. It eliminates the underside shadow with an approximate representation of the sky's color and brightness. It's not invisibility, but it's close. Under these conditions, with a solid overcast, performance is optimal. It's still pretty good against a clear sky, but it's not as effective when there are scattered clouds."

"Doctor, I'm impressed," Sam admitted. "Does it affect the performance of the aircraft?"

"It knocks about ten percent off the maximum airspeed and maybe twenty percent off the endurance if we leave it on for the entire flight. The cameras and designator are unaffected."

"Wow!" was all Ben could say.

"Captain, if I may?" Simmons asked Sam, receiving a nod in return. "Fritz, your contact is about two-seven-five degrees at four-point-five, but that's an estimate. We need a distant, then close survey," he directed.

"Roger that, going wide."

"Doctor, even if it's made of fiberglass or composites, we should be able to get a primary radar return on that sailboat from this distance," Sam began. "Do the people you tangled with yesterday have a, well, whatever the correct scientific term for a radar cloaking device would be?"

"Captain, I have never seen anything like this, but I'm not in on everything. I do agree with you. It's far more likely this one is a non-Russian. If you'll allow me to send a burst transmission through the VHA-UAV antenna, there's a chance I could get some useful info from my guys."

"Very well, you may go ahead, Doctor. I expect you to share everything you get back."

"Absolutely, Captain!" Simmons smiled and ducked back inside.

"Should we set the LE Bill or GQ?" Ben asked.

Sam shook his head. "Neither. Let's check out this guy first. We've plenty of time either way, and I'd hate to call one, then jump to the other." He turned to Ben and smiled. "It'd make me appear indecisive."

"Sir, the UAV has the target," Bondurant said, poking his head out the door.

"Thanks, OOD, I'm coming," Sam replied, and he and Ben turned to enter the Bridge.

Ben and Sam stood behind the seated Deffler and Simmons, the former working the flight controls and the other controlling the camera.

"Still about two miles out," Simmons said. "We're powering down to slow flight now to reduce the noise signature. They should be unaware it's up there."

The vessel was a large, black-hulled sloop under a single jib and mainsail, making about three knots in the light wind, with no one visible.

"Remarkable," Sam replied. "Get a read on the crew first, followed by a close examination of the mast and deck. Whatever they're using to mask their return, I'd like eyes-on before they figure out we're here. Any chance you can scan for crew or weapons?"

"Only visually."

"That'd still be useful. I don't suppose you heard back on your inquiry."

"No, I'm afraid not."

Sam turned back to the screen. "Let's see what the bird finds. OOD, can you come over here, please?"

"Yes, sir." Bondurant walked over to the UAV station. He glanced at the screen and nodded approvingly. "Marlow Hunter 50AC. That's a sweet ride. Captain, that's at least half a million dollars' worth of boat. There should be plenty of information available if we call it in."

Sam nodded. "Agreed, but I still want a good look before canceling emissions control. How big a crew do you need to handle one of these?"

Bondurant was puzzled by his CO's caution, but shrugged and went along. "It can be handled solo, sir. That's a Marlow Hunter specialty, but it's a handful for just one."

"Coming around port side, sir," Deffler interrupted. "There's a name on the aft quarter."

"Zooming in," Simmons added. "Okay, it's the *Sunrise Surprise II*. Homeport Clearwater. One person is visible in the cockpit, and no weapons or contraband are visible.

"Examining the mast now. Normal, Furuno radar. Wait a sec. Hello there!" He zoomed in on an egg-shaped object mounted on top of the mast. "I don't believe this comes with the standard package."

Sam and Ben both joined Simmons in gazing at the object. Finally, Sam broke the silence. "Assuming that's what's obscuring the radar image, how would it work?"

"I can think of several possibilities, Captain, but it's hard to figure anything that small containing the hardware needed. Suggest we file that one under 'maybe' and move on."

"Very well, complete the survey, please."

"Yes, sir." Simmons returned to the screen. After a few minutes, he called out again, "Survey complete, Captain. We have good imaging of everything. Still only one person visible, a white male, age appears to be early twenties. No weapons visible."

"Very well. OOD, discontinue emissions control, take the radar off standby, and set an intercept course at ten knots. Who's up for Boarding Officer today?"

"Guerrero, sir."

"OOD, let's set the LE Bill, but I believe I'll let the XO earn some of his pay today. Once Hopkins relieves you, I want you to hang around and get a feel for the risk based on the pre-board interview. If you think you need to bump Lee and take the boat, I'll approve it."

"I'm sure she'll be fine, Captain."

"Thanks, carry on, please." Sam turned to the chart table. "Deffler, keep your eyes on that boat, sing out if anything changes. XO, Doctor, come with me, please." Sam led the way out to the bridge wing, and Bondurant announced setting Law Enforcement stations over the PA system.

Turning around after closing the door, Sam addressed Simmons first. "Doctor, I am convinced that there's more to this boat than meets the eye. If he is carrying a load of drugs like the other boat, what's the probability your hyperspectral camera would pick up something?"

"Pretty much one hundred percent, Captain. Even sealed, the camera would pick up a trace. If a dog can smell it, the camera will see it."

"So, if they are not carrying a load, they would have no reason to mount a vigorous defense if we try to board them, correct?"

"It would be foolish of them, Captain. They know that you've reported in. Even if they took us out, they'd lose big time. We'd slap a terrorist label on them and anyone they associated with and, best case, that'd be game over for most of their revenue stream. Worst case, they know we have a history of pursuing cop-killers to the ends of the Earth. There's a remote chance this is some psycho they don't have a handle on, but that's unlikely. No, I believe this might be a pickup boat for moving product off the *High Dawn*. That presupposes this *is* their boat and not another rich kid out to get laid."

"Very well." Sam turned to Ben. "XO, I want you to take this one because you're up to speed on everything, and I need someone who can think on his feet. I want a thorough look inside, but I don't want this to get ugly. I wish we had a way to check for hidden compartments without knocking a bunch of holes in her."

"You've got it," Simmons interrupted. "I have a hand-held X-ray backscatter recorder among my gear I can lend Ben here."

"Doctor!" Sam smiled. "I may revise my opinion of you yet. Can you train this young man on its use in the next fifteen minutes?"

"It's switch-on, then point and shoot. You get the image in real-time, and it records." Simmons grinned. "Even an Ops Research grad can handle it."

Ben rolled his eyes. "Thanks, Doc."

"Don't mention it." Simmons winked. "Just don't drop it overboard, please. You wouldn't believe how expensive it is!"

"All right, XO, gear up, please." Sam nodded.

"Very good, sir. OK, Doc, let's get some tech on."

Sam

Hopkins had relieved Bondurant after *Kauai* had completed the turn toward the sailboat and came off of emissions control. Williams manned radar and communications during law enforcement operations, allowing the OOD to focus on ship handling and safety. After a few minutes, a radar target track coinciding with the sailboat's bearing and range popped up on the SeaWatch system.

"Captain, OOD, they appear to have shut down their masker," Williams commented. "Range sixty-eight fifty and bearing consistent with the visual target."

"Very well. Now we know."

"Captain, I have a second POB coming up into the cockpit," Deffler called. "Appears to be female based on dress or <ahem> lack thereof. I, uh, do you want me to continue scanning and recording, sir?" he added, glancing at Hopkins and shifting on his stool.

Sam observed Hopkins turning away to hide an amused grin and suppressed one himself. "Yes, Deffler.

They know we're here and watching. Your job is to maintain situational awareness—keep it so."

"WILCO, sir." Deffler was clearly wondering where the boundary between close observation and leering lay.

Sam caught Hopkins's eye and nodded to the starboard bridge wing. Once out of sight and earshot, he turned to her and smiled. "I appreciate you're enjoying the hell out of this, but I need him on the top of his game. In a minute or so, wander over and reassure him he's not looking at a sexual harassment violation."

Hopkins affected a downcast expression. "Aw gee, Captain, I never get to have any fun!"

Sam turned back and raised his binoculars to watch the sailboat. "Yes, it's the monstrous burden of command, so get used to it, Chief-to-be. Carry on, please."

"Yes, sir." Hopkins smiled and turned back inside.

****

After a briefing and instruction on the operation of the x-ray scanner, Ben and Simmons returned to the Bridge, the former wearing his boarding equipment and the latter in his personal body armor. They went straight to the chart table to check the UAV feed. The picture invoked a "Yowsa!" from Simmons and a stoic silence from Ben. There were still only two people visible on the boat: the male handling the wheel and the bikini-clad female lounging on the foredeck. *Kauai* had come around and was now paralleling the sailboat's course about two hundred yards distant.

"Any changes besides the fresh face?" Ben asked Deffler.

"No, sir. And I've had eyes on since you left."

"I bet you have!" Simmons quipped, drawing scowls from both men. After two seconds, he continued, "She's a bit underdressed, don't you think?"

"All right, knock it off," Ben said with irritation.

"No, I'm serious. It's cloudy and cool right now. Why walk around quasi-nude like that when she knows we're here?"

"Because she's a tease? How would I know?" Ben said.

"Think about it. The radar masker switches off, and she pops up on deck looking like a centerfold right afterward. The 'evade detection' plan didn't work, so it's on to Plan B. Be very careful over there, friend."

Ben gazed at Simmons's face and saw actual human concern. "I get what you mean. Thanks."

Ben turned and walked over to Sam. "Captain, I'm ready to begin the interview."

"Very well, XO. Carry on, please."

"Yes, sir." After setting the radio frequency to Maritime Channel 16, he picked up the handset. "Sailing Vessel *Sunrise Surprise II*, this is the United States Coast Guard, Channel 16, over." No response. Ben repeated the call with the same result. After two more unsuccessful attempts at contact, Ben hung up the handset. "No joy, Captain. Recommend close to one hundred yards and use the loudhailer."

"Very well. OOD, close to and maintain one hundred yards from the target vessel."

"Yes, sir," Hopkins replied and gave the orders. After they had closed the distance, she said, "Holding at one hundred yards, Captain."

"Very well," Sam replied and nodded to Ben.

Ben activated the loudspeakers. "Sailing Vessel *Sunrise Surprise II*, this is the United States Coast Guard. Contact me on VHF-FM Channel 16 immediately." After a brief pause, Ben repeated the hail and finally saw movement in the sailboat's cockpit.

"Coast Guard, *Sunrise Surprise*, what do you want?" said a male voice on the radio.

"*Sunrise Surprise II*. This is the Coast Guard. Reply with last port of call and next port of call, please," Ben said into the radio handset, keeping his eyes on the vessel through his binoculars.

"And how is that any of your business, Coast Guard?"

Ben grimaced. "*Sunrise Surprise II*. This is the Coast Guard. You are a U.S. vessel sailing on the High Seas. The Coast Guard may make inquiries, examinations, and inspections and enforce federal law on all U.S. vessels on the High Seas. Now I'll ask again, and you will reply. What are your last and next ports of call? Over."

"Fine. We are out of Clearwater, heading for Key West."

"*Sunrise Surprise II*. This is the Coast Guard. Thank you. How many people do you have onboard? Over."

"That's it, Coast Guard, inquire into this!" said the voice with an accompanying gesture from the man in the sailboat cockpit.

Ben turned to Sam. "Captain?"

Sam nodded in return. "That's it, indeed. Pull him over, XO." He turned to Williams at his SeaWatch station. "Williams, start a Command Net chat with the Ops Center. Tell them we are preparing to board a less than-fully compliant US-flagged sailboat named *Sunrise Surprise II*, homeport Clearwater, FL, and give our position."

"Yes, sir."

Ben turned back and activated the blue flashing "law enforcement light," turned the siren on for ten seconds, then returned to the radio. "*Sunrise Surprise II*. This is the United States Coast Guard. You will stop your vessel immediately for boarding and inspection. Acknowledge, please, over."

After a pause, the voice replied, just as angrily, "I don't think I have to do that, Coast Guard!"

Ben took a breath, straightened up, and keyed the headset. "Captain, this is a lawful order, not a request. You will stop your vessel immediately and prepare to be boarded. Failure to comply violates U.S. law, which will make you subject to arrest and your vessel to seizure. Acknowledge, please."

Through the binoculars, Ben watched the woman on the foredeck jump up, sprint aft, and engage the man in a lively discussion. When Ben saw the man pull his arm back as if to strike her, he transmitted, "This is the Coast Guard. Acknowledge my last transmission!"

The man hesitated, then lowered his arm. "Fine, Coast Guard, I'm taking in the sails, but I'm also going to contact my lawyer over this!"

Ben turned to Sam. "Did you see that, sir?" Receiving a nod in return, Ben continued, "If you've no objection, I'd like Lee in the boarding party."

"Great minds, XO. By all means. Bondurant, I want you on Coxswain, please. You OK with Jenkins handling the crane for this one?"

"Absolutely, sir."

"Excellent. I think we're about done here. Go get your people ready." Bondurant saluted and departed, and Sam turned to Ben. "XO, this one will be tough. After seeing what that guy did, I get how you feel, but I'm sending you because I know I can count on you to keep hold of the big picture." Ben nodded, and Sam continued, "I'll back you whatever you decide to do, but make it solid. Don't let him goad you into a mistake. OK?"

"Captain, prepare for some world-class 'counting to ten' unless he makes another move at that woman or one of our people."

"Just right. Off you go—play it cool and play it safe."

"Very good, sir." Ben saluted and left.

Sam turned to see Simmons watching him from across the Bridge. When their eyes met, Simmons nodded, then returned to his work with the UAV. Sam returned to the window with his binoculars and addressed Hopkins, "Status please, OOD."

Hopkins recognized the heightened concern Sam hid and replied in a quiet voice, "Captain, the target vessel has heaved to with sails furled. We are maintaining position one hundred yards north. The ship is at LE stations, awaiting launch request from the boat deck. UAV is performing covert overwatch at one thousand feet. District operations center has been advised and is standing by on Command Net chat." She gave a slight, sympathetic smile. "You have everything covered, sir."

Sam turned to Hopkins and smiled. "Thanks, Hoppy."

Ben

"Hey, XO, you slumming with the little people today?" Seaman Lopez joked. Another recent addition to the crew, Juan "Lope" Lopez was the senior among the non-rated crewman of the cutter's deck force. He was a Southern California native, hardworking, reliable, intelligent, and somewhat quiet, except for the occasional joke. Lopez was waiting for a slot to open at the Maritime Law Enforcement Specialist School in Charleston, South Carolina, to fulfill his dream of becoming a full-fledged law enforcement officer.

"Well, Lope, I occasionally venture down to the nether reaches to see how the other 'haff' is getting by," Ben responded in his best upper-crust accent. After waiting for the chuckles to subside, he snapped into professional mode. "OK, guys, here's the deal. No weapons or contraband in sight, but keep your eyes open. As far as we know, only two people are on board, one male and one female. I've got this boarding because the master has a bug up his ass about stopping, much more than usual. We're still checking for safety and compliance, but I consider this a medium threat, so stay sharp. I think we will get a lot of abuse over there, but I want you to keep your cool and let me take it for you." He nodded toward Lee. "Shelley, the reason you're along instead of driving the RHIB is I think the female POB may be taking some physical abuse. I don't know for sure, but it looked close to that during the approach. I want you to evaluate and, if necessary, find out if she wants us to take her off."

"You've got it, sir." Lee nodded with a grim expression.

"Good. Don't push it. We're not relationship counselors, but if it seems like there's an actual problem, give me the high sign, and we'll deal with it. Finally, the female is wearing very brief swimwear. Do NOT get distracted," He gave Seaman Smith, the fourth boarding party member, and Lopez his sternest expression. "Copy?"

"Yes, sir," both men answered with slight smiles.

"Anybody have questions?" Ben asked.

"Yes, sir," Lee piped up, smiling now. "What's with the bag?"

"Ah, yes. Dr. Simmons has loaned me one of his toys. It's good at seeing through walls, so I can get a peek without drilling holes if there are any hidden compartments. Let's keep that to ourselves, please. I don't want to stir this guy up any more than he already is. Any other questions?" Seeing nothing but shaking heads, Ben concluded, "OK, let's do it. Remember, stay cool and see something say something." He turned to Bondurant. "Boats, we're ready when you are."

"OK, XO, everybody, follow me," Bondurant said, stepping into RHIB alongside the rail and up to the center console. The rest of the boat's crew and the boarding party followed, and when they were secure, Bondurant gave a thumbs-up to Jenkins at the boat crane control and announced, "Ready for launch."

"Bridge, Boat Deck, RHIB is manned and ready for launch," Jenkins said into his headset. After a moment, he said, "Cleared for launch, swinging out." After moving the boat clear of the side, he lowered it to the water. He watched Bondurant start the engine and then veer off toward the sailboat. "Boat away, Boat OK," Jenkins transmitted as he recovered the cable.

Bondurant brought the RHIB around the sailboat, with everyone onboard alert for anything suspicious. The sailboat's two occupants were sitting on the deck forward of the cockpit, having mustered reluctantly at Ben's request over the radio. Satisfied, Bondurant looked at Ben, "Looks OK, XO."

"Right. We'll board on the stern steps aft of the cockpit. Smith, you're first. Get on board and cover the rest of us. Lee, you're second. Head to the bow and cover from there. I'll go next, and you bring up the rear, Lopez. I'll do the standard walkabout to check the lights and stuff, and then I'll head below with the camera. Lopez, I'll have my hands full with that, so I want you to stay in sight and cover me. Silent routine, everybody, unless you see something. Let's get a discreet radio check, please. Lee?" Lee responded by clicking her transmitter twice <click, click>. "Smith?" <click, click>. "Lopez?" <click, click>. "OK, Boats, we're ready to go in."

Bondurant swung the RHIB in a wide loop and brought it to a stop with the center console, even with the boarding step. Ben said, "Now." All four boarding team members were on board and moving to their positions within five seconds, and Bondurant backed the RHIB out to a safety and cover station. Ben stepped up to the male passenger and announced, "Captain, I am Lieutenant Junior Grade Benjamin Wyporek of the United States Coast Guard. I am here to conduct a safety and compliance inspection. Thank you for your cooperation, and we hope to have you on your way shortly. Before we start, I need to confirm that you two are the only ones on board, correct?"

"Correct," came the curt reply.

"Thank you. Are either of you carrying any weapons right now? Sir?" The male shook his head in response, and Ben turned to the woman. "Ma'am?" The woman looked up and shook her head. The expressionless face behind narrow sunglasses and the absence of any marks on what was a mostly uncovered body made Ben question his original concerns about abuse. He looked at Lee, who arched an eyebrow, shook her head slightly, and then turned back to watch the woman. "Thank you. Sir, I'll need to check your registration and your IDs. Where might I find them, please?"

"They're all in the Nav drawer. I'll show you...." The man started to get up.

"Sir," Ben held up his hand. "I need you to stay where you are, please. I can find them if you tell me where to look."

"Fine. In the drawer under the main panel."

"Thank you. Wait here, please." Ben ducked into the cockpit, found the drawer under a panel of switches, and located the boat's registration certificate and two driver's licenses. He noted the registration lined up with the description and display numbers on the boat and passed the names, addresses, and driver's license numbers to Williams to check out, although they appeared correct. Several life jackets were sitting beside the door to the main cabin. Check. Ben found the switch labeled "NAV LTS" on the panel, flipped them on, and then popped back out of the cockpit. Once on deck with an unobstructed view of the subjects, Ben nodded to Lee. "Lee, can you check the nav lights, please?"

Lee nodded in reply and glanced at the boat's navigation lights. "Port nav light on and correct, starboard nav light on and correct, sir."

Ben checked the functionality of the stern light himself, then flipped the switch off. Check. Popping up to the deck, he addressed the man, "I will need to go down into the cabin to check your sanitation device and test for fuel vapors, sir. Are there any hazards I should beware of, slippery decks, that sort of thing?"

"You're not going to be poking around our stuff without me down there," the man said with increasing menace.

"Sir, I will need you to stay on deck here while I complete the check for your safety and mine."

"Like hell, you fucking fascist!" The man jumped up and stepped forward.

Ben stepped backward, putting his right hand on his sidearm, holding up his left hand, and announcing, "Stop there, sir!" He noted that the other boarding party members had drawn their Tasers and held them behind their backs. "Now stay exactly where you are, please," he continued. Ben locked eyes with the man, who had stopped, his hands shaking at his sides. "Hey, I get this isn't how you want to spend your day, but when I step aboard a vessel, my duty is to conduct a complete inspection. This includes checking for safety and sanitation compliance, for which I *will* need to go down below. Mister, I will do my duty. While that's going on, you can sit quietly right there or sit in restraints on board that big white boat. What's it going to be?"

The man stood silently for a few more moments, holding Ben's gaze with clear hatred. Then the woman made a throat-clearing sound. The man glanced at her briefly and sat down. "Fine, but you'll be hearing from my lawyer."

"That is your prerogative, sir, and thank you again for your cooperation." He scanned at the other boarding party members and gave the "hold in place" signal, receiving a nod from each. Ben returned to the cockpit and picked up the bag, waiting until he was out of sight to pull out the backscatter scanner. After a brief tour around the cabin, he activated the device and recorder as Simmons had shown him and began scanning the bulkheads and decks. He spent a few minutes going through mundane items like stored clothing and foodstuffs, then came upon an image of an oddly shaped electronic device behind a forward panel. Several circuit panels and other solid-state components were visible, along with a cable leading to the mast. He directed the scan beneath the device, looking for other components and connections, and his heart nearly stopped.

The image on the screen showed, below and disconnected from the device, four brick-shaped objects connected by wires to a smaller, cell-phone-sized object. Pretty much how you would expect a bomb to appear.

Ben shut down the scanner and took a few deep breaths. If this was a bomb, it could explode when he opened a panel or disturbed something else in the cabin. It could also have a remote trigger worked by a sailboat crewmember or be on a timer running down right now. Ben carefully retraced his steps to the after part of the cabin and keyed his microphone. "Everybody stay real steady and silent and take a breath." He paused briefly. "There appears to be an explosive device fixed to the hull. We will do a coordinated takedown of both POBs in case one of them has a remote detonator. I need Smith to step behind the male POB and Lee to stay where you are behind the female. When I step out of the cabin and get their attention, bring up your Tasers. If either of them so much as twitches before I get them cuffed, you tase them immediately. Lee, you take the female. Acknowledge silently, please."

Two clicks sounded in his headset.

"Smith, you stay on the male, acknowledge," Ben said, receiving two clicks.

"Lopez, I want you to step down into the cockpit and draw your sidearm, but keep it at your side and out of sight. If a POB gets away from a tasing, you take them down, acknowledge."

"Click, click." Through the open cabin door, he watched Lopez step down slowly into the cockpit, then draw and charge his pistol, careful to keep it low and beyond the view of the main deck. "OK, guys, I'm coming up now. Standby." Ben secured the scanner in its bag, then stepped into the cockpit to Lopez's left. He gathered himself, stepped up onto the main deck, and announced, "Ma'am, Sir, I need your attention, please." Both turned to him, and he paused briefly while Lee and Smith brought their Tasers to the ready. "I am sorry, but I have to place you under arrest for...."

At this moment, the woman growled and lunged forward, the move followed instantly by the pop and buzz of Lee's Taser and the woman crying out. The man's arms shot over his head. "Don't shoot! Please don't shoot!"

Lee was already fastening handcuffs on the stunned woman, and Ben did the same for the now-crying man while Smith covered him with the Taser. Ben nodded at Lopez, who holstered his pistol and came up to take over. Satisfied the two people were safely subdued, Ben keyed his microphone. "*Kauai-One*, LE-One, return at once for pickup of six. Break, Break, *Kauai*, LE-One, over."

"LE-One, *Kauai*, report," Sam's voice responded.

"*Kauai*, LE-One, I have detected what I believe is an explosive device concealed in the hull. I have placed the POBs under arrest, and we are evacuating now. I had to order non-lethal on the female POB, over."

"LE-One, *Kauai-One*, this is *Kauai* actual, do not acknowledge, cease all transmissions, carry out evacuation, and return to ship."

"Radios off, everybody, and don't touch anything," Ben ordered, turning to see the RHIB approaching the sailboat's stern. "Smith, you go in first and keep overwatch. Grab the scanner bag on the way and treat it *carefully*, please. Lopez, you help Lee with her prisoner and board next. I'll follow with this man. Board as soon as it's safe."

"Don't hurt me, please!" The man's voice was pleading and markedly different from the arrogant prick of minutes before. "It's her, not me. I was just hired to drive the boat! It's her, man!"

Ben shook his arm, "Quiet! I'll hear what you have to say when we get aboard the cutter. Zip it until then!"

When Bondurant nudged the RHIB to the cockpit steps, Smith jumped aboard with the scanner bag, followed by Lee and Lopez carrying the semi-conscious, handcuffed woman between them. Ben tugged the cuffed man to his feet and led him to the RHIB, holding him upright as he stumbled on board. "OK, Boats, let's go," Ben said and sat down next to his prisoner.

Bondurant nodded and eased the engine control back, pulling the RHIB away from the sailboat. He slammed the control forward at twenty-five feet of distance, turning toward the cutter as the boat picked up speed. After half a minute, he pulled alongside *Kauai*, preparing for the hoist back on board.

Sam stood at the base of the ladder, arms folded when the RHIB hoisted even with the main deck. "Well done, XO!" He clapped Ben on his shoulder. "You and your people OK?" Sam's expression showed deep concern.

"My heartbeat is back below a hundred, I'm happy to say, and the rest are fine." Ben smiled. "How do we handle these two, sir?"

Sam's face relaxed, and he whispered to Ben, "Let's split them up. I want them both under armed guard and manacled at all times. Doc is standing by in female berthing to check the woman out, after which I want her strip-searched. Have Lee do that. I'll have Bondurant relieve Hoppy so she can help."

"Yes, sir. I'll have Smith take the other one to non-rate berthing with Guerrero to do the same. Our tough guy here crapped himself when I mentioned the bomb on board so that the strip search won't be fun."

Sam grinned back. "It'll be excellent practice for when they have their own kids."

"Yuk, and you can quote me on that, sir," Ben stepped aside when Lee and Lopez approached with the still-staggering female. "I guess we won't need your counseling skills after all, Shelley."

"Ya think, sir?" she puffed as they stumbled past.

After they passed, Sam asked, "Now, what did you see?"

144

"I'm pretty sure I saw the masker, or whatever you call it. It's behind the paneling in the berthing area. Didn't see much, a general shape and features that make it appear electronic with a cable leading to the mast. The bomb is right under it. It looks like four M112s strung together with a small box that I'm guessing is the detonator. There might be others. I beat-feet when I saw that one."

"Good call—five pounds of C4 would have done the job for sure. Simmons put in a call for their bomb disposal team on alert up at MacDill Air Force Base and a relief prize crew to take custody of the boat afterward. The sector folks will bring them out in a Medium Response Boat as soon as they get down here. In the meantime, we standby at a safe distance. We're back on emissions control until we get a safe signal from the bomb techs. Let's get the interrogations done ASAP. I want to offload the prisoners on the sector boat."

"Yes, sir. You want me to handle both?"

"Yes, but break off when the boat arrives. You'll need to brief the bomb techs on what you found and where."

"Yes, sir." Ben looked down. "About that, sir, it could have gone badly without the scanner the Doc loaned us." His head came up eye-to-eye with Sam. "He didn't have to, you know. I don't imagine his bosses would be too keen over him sharing the details on that thing, much less letting me haul it around on a chancy boarding."

"Yes, I get that," Sam said with a wry grin. "I find myself on the horns of a dilemma—deeply grateful to him you're safe, while I'd personally get a big lift out of throwing his ass overboard. I suppose I must lean on the net positive and try to tolerate him for the sake of the mission."

"You remain an unyielding source of strength and inspiration to me, Captain. I'll do my best to keep him out of your hair."

"Do that." Sam turned back to the ladder to head up to the Bridge.

7

Defusing

USCG Cutter *Kauai*, Gulf of Mexico, nineteen nautical miles northeast of Key West, Florida
12:02 EST, 16 January

Ben

As Ben approached the Female Berthing room, Bryant pulled him aside. "I completed the check over of the female detainee, sir. She's not showing any aftereffects of the tasing, a couple of bruises when she went down, but nothing actionable. However...."

"However?" Ben asked with raised eyebrows.

"However, we need to be very careful with this one, and by careful, I mean armed guard out of reach. I've seen this type before in Iraq and Afghanistan."

"Suicide bomber? Must be one hell of a bomb vest."

"No, sir." Bryant shook his head. "This is the type that recruits and launches suicide bombers, smiles at you until you turn your back, and then...," He drew his finger across his throat. "I got these out of her hair and a fake scar on her hip." He held up an evidence bag with two needle-like metal objects.

"A *fake* scar? No way!"

"Way. New one for me too, believe it or not. Fortunately, Doc Simmons briefed me on what to watch for before I started. I hope you don't mind, sir, but I told Shelley and Hoppy to hold off on the strip search. She might be hiding stuff where I can't go, and honestly, they're not trained to find what she might have. I promise you she's not secreting explosives or a detonator anywhere, and that should do until she's ashore with the intel guys. In the meantime, she's double-cuffed, wrists and ankles around the bed frame, and I strongly recommend you NOT uncuff her before the Marshals arrive."

"OK, thanks Doc." Ben shook his head. "Between bombs and spies, this place is getting hazardous to my health."

"On that subject, XO, when are you coming down for your prelims?" Bryant asked, his face empty of expression.

"All this, and you're still hung up on my physical?"

"Yup. This is what I do, sir."

"OK, OK, let's set it up during the next home port stop."

"OK, sir. But I *will* hold you to that," Bryant said, turning away.

Ben turned to the door of the berthing area and knocked, announcing, "XO."

Hopkins opened the door and stood aside as Ben entered the small room. The female detainee sat on the bottom bunk, arms and legs encircling the corner post with her hands and ankles zip-tied. She now wore a set of prisoner coveralls over her brief swimwear and canvas shoes. She was stunningly beautiful and turned to Ben with long dark brown hair and deep blue, almond-shaped eyes that should have been attractive, but chilled him to the bone. The moment reminded him of a tiger he once shared a staredown with through a zoo window. Hopkins and Lee stood in opposite corners of the room, out of reach of the prisoner. Ben looked at Hopkins. "Anything?" Receiving a head shake in return, he turned to Lee. "Lee?"

"Nothing that I would share in mixed company, sir," Lee replied, keeping her eyes on the prisoner.

"OK. Miss," He glanced at the ID taken from the sailboat—Laura Treblinsky. "Treblinsky. Did I pronounce that right?" Ben paused, received the same cold, silent glare, and continued reading from the "Miranda Crib Card" boarding officers carried with them. "Ms. Treblinsky, I have placed you under arrest on suspicion of violating Title 18, United States Code, Section 844. You have the right to remain silent. If you give up that right, anything you say can and will be used against you in a court of law. You have a right to an attorney and have them present whenever you are questioned. If you cannot afford to hire an attorney, one will be appointed to represent you before questioning if you wish. You may decide at any time to exercise these rights and not answer any questions or make any statements. Do you understand these rights I have explained to you?" Silence. "Having these rights in mind, would you wish to talk to me about these charges?"

The woman's icy stare remained fixed. "Lawyer."

Ben returned the blankest expression he could muster. "Am I to understand that you do not want to answer questions or make a statement without an attorney present?"

A half-smile appeared on the woman's face. "You're not as stupid as you appear, *Lieutenant Junior Grade*. Now, why don't you just fuck off and take the dykes with you? I don't like how the short one is undressing me with her eyes."

Ben turned toward Lee with a raised eyebrow. "My goodness, Petty Officer Lee! You aren't undressing the prisoner with your eyes, are you?"

"Definitely not, sir," Lee smiled, patting her Taser. "Just hoping for a reason to give her another zap."

Ben turned back to the woman. "See, no offense meant. Ms. Treblinsky, I regret our efforts do not seem to rise to your expectations, but you'll be glad to know that your stay with us will end shortly. I'll be stepping out to interview your companion, but if you change your mind about talking, one of these petty officers can fetch me."

The smile on the woman's face became broader and, if possible, colder. "Not happening, *dick!*"

Ben smiled, nodded to the petty officers, then turned to the prisoner. "Good afternoon, ma'am," he said, then turned and stepped through the door, closing it behind him. Simmons waited out of sight beyond the door. Ben looked at him and shook his head. "Holy Shit, Doc! What the hell is *that?*"

"Friend, my educated guess is *that* is a Next-Generation Sparrow, formerly of the Russian SVR, now working either freelance or full time for our TCO foes. You can bet on that ID being bogus. We'll see if her biometrics pop when we get her back ashore." He glanced back at the door to the berthing area. "Will your people be OK in there?"

"Worry about her," Ben replied as they turned toward the mess deck. "They both understand the situation, and if she makes a move or does anything off-key...." He snapped his fingers. "They'll take her down or out, as needed. Like I said, family."

"Gotcha. You know, my people would just keep her knocked out until we had her in a secure facility."

"Must be nice. We still have to play by the rules here."

Simmons smiled back sadly. "Yes, I don't envy you guys. I watched your CO having to send you in with one hand tied behind your back this morning—it was eating him up."

Ben stopped and faced him. "Good. Keep that in mind. Doc, I get that you have an important mission, and you're focused on that. I'm grateful to you for sharing the scanner. It probably saved our lives. But you're still in the hole with me for the crap you pulled on him yesterday. He's the best man I've ever known.

Get it? We're the good guys here. Make us want to trust you."

"Touché. I'm genuinely sorry about that. I was furious at him for being so obstinate without considering that he did not understand the stakes— very poor judgment on my part. At least now you guys are in on everything, and I can stop being so cagey. May I ask the favor of a clean slate?"

"I'll grant it, but that's just me, and it doesn't automatically extend to the captain. He's down with the mission, but I'd keep my distance when possible if I were you."

"Thanks for the consideration and advice." Simmons nodded, extending a hand that Ben shook. "I'll try to keep on the undark side of the force. OK, let's interrogate the Cowardly Lion."

Clarence "Hawk" Rodin, the male detainee, was as effusive in his interview as "Laura" was reticent in hers. Ben had to threaten to gag him to enable reading his rights and offered him the Miranda Waiver, which he readily signed. Rodin was an itinerant deckhand on yachts in the Tampa area. The most beautiful woman he had ever seen approached him and paid a fantastic amount of money to captain the *Sunrise Surprise II* wherever she needed. When they sighted the approaching Coast Guard cutter, she had offered him a fifty percent bonus on top of non-monetary benefits to make like one of the rich assholes who typically hired him. She hoped he would intimidate the boarding officer into moving along without thoroughly searching the boat. He insisted the display of the physical threat during the interview was part of the scam. Knowing they weren't carrying any drugs—he'd checked, and who carries drugs *south*, anyway—he jumped at the opportunity.

Ben wrapped up the interview when the word passed the Sector Key West boat had arrived. As Ben and Simmons moved toward the main deck, Simmons asked, "What do you think?"

Ben shook his head. "He's either the greatest actor of our times or a complete doofus. They might charge him with accessory on 844, but it'd be a stretch to prove. He keeps cooperating, and he'll probably walk."

Simmons nodded. "That was my sense, perfect patsy."

"I guess we'll see. I'm not sure of anything on this crazy mission." They walked out on the main deck as the sector boat moored alongside *Kauai*. Within two minutes, the bomb disposal team leader climbed the ladder onto the main deck, followed by his deputy. He recognized Simmons and crossed over with a smile and hand outstretched.

"Pete, goddammit, I might have known you were hip deep in this one!" he said as they shook hands.

"Chief, it's great to see you; sorry it's about work." Simmons smiled back. He gestured to Ben. "Matt Kemper, Chief EOD Technician, U.S. Navy, Retired, this is Lieutenant J.G. Ben Wyporek. He's XO here and found the bomb."

Kemper shook Ben's hand. "Glad to meet you, sir, and that you're still in one piece." He turned to his subordinate. "This is Ken Davis, my deputy, and the man who'll be going after the device if we take it on."

As they finished shaking hands with Davis, Simmons asked, "Matt, you guys got on the scene in a hurry. Were you down here already?"

"No, a stroke of luck. The Coasties had a Herc in the training pattern at MacDill when the call came. They full-stopped on the next landing to pick us up. An hour later, we're rolling off at Boca Chica. You must have juice. It would have taken a week to get a lift from the Transportation Command."

"Yeah, we're saving the world, one sailboat at a time."

"Dedication, very inspiring." Kemper nodded. "Now, tell me about this bomb."

The four men retired to the mess deck. Simmons replayed the video capture from the scanner, and Ben described the sailboat's interior in detail. Kemper nodded and asked the occasional question. He pulled up his laptop and opened two files. "We got these plan views from Marlow Hunter, showing the basic design of the boat and some options. Lieutenant, which one looks closest to you?"

Ben scrutinized the three plans, trying to translate the lines on the screen to what he remembered seeing on the boat. Finally, he pointed at one drawing. "That one is closest."

Kemper nodded. "Alrighty then. The robot can't complete the disarm. We'd need the big one, and there isn't room to maneuver it. I'll send the mini in to drill holes and get a good peek with the camera. Then we can weigh the risks." He turned to Simmons. "Pete, I gotta tell you I will need powerful persuadin' before sending one of my guys in that box to clip wires."

Simmons nodded. "Chief, we're sure that rig's a self-destruct for some new stealth technology that we really need to get our hands on. We've seen it work—that boat was invisible to this cutter's radar until they switched it off."

Kemper whistled and shared a glance with Davis. "OK, you're on. If it looks like we can take it after the close inspection, we'll try it. Now, Lieutenant, you said the woman was making a move when you took her down. Did it seem like she was going for a detonator?"

"I thought so. She could have been reaching for a weapon or taking a shot at knocking me overboard for all we know. By that point, I didn't want my people sitting on top of a bomb while I went searching for answers."

"Definitely the right call, sir." Kemper nodded. "We will send Wally the robot in for a scan around the top deck to find what she was so eager to grab. Pete, I like this scanner of yours, and we will have one of those 'tater-to-taters' about that when we finish here. Howsomever, I would like to use it for a top to bottom on that boat before we go. Are you down for that?"

"I'll even run it for you if you're sure it won't set the thing off."

"Naw, if it was sensitive, the Lieutenant would've set it off." Kemper winked at Ben and smiled. "These things are a compromise between doing the job and making sure it doesn't trip on you before you need it to do the job. That means they're rarely that sensitive. The last thing these guys want is for this gizmo to self-detonate when the boat bumps into a buoy or sails past a destroyer with the fire-control radar energized."

The four men continued the discussion for another twenty minutes. They completed a plan of action, after which the two bomb technicians made their way back to the sector boat. Simmons and Ben walked forward to exchange some gear. While they walked, Ben inquired, "Doc, I'm at a loss, but I didn't want to come across as a newbie. What's a 'tater-to-tater'?"

Simmons chuckled. "Matt Kemper is not just one of the best bomb disposal experts in the world. He can spin eggcorns and malaprops that would put Yogi Berra to shame. He meant 'tête-à-tête.'"

Ben laughed as much from the release of tension as the joke. "That one's going into the hall of fame!"

****

Much to the relief of Hopkins, Lee, and Sam, the sector boat also brought three members of the Marshal's Service to take custody of the prisoners. Once they were signed over, the women returned to work.

Shortly afterward, Sam and Ben stood together on the bridge wing, watching the RHIB maneuver slowly around the *Sunrise Surprise II,* while Simmons and the two bomb technicians performed x-ray scans in the preliminary survey. Sam preferred not to expose any of his crew, but the response boat was as large as the sailboat and too heavy for the close work needed. Ben glanced at the afterdeck to see Bondurant watching the operation intently. Bondurant had been preparing to take the sortie himself when Lee walked up and reminded him *she* was supposed to be coxswain today. The sight of the diminutive Lee standing on her toes to press home her point to her full-foot-taller superior had evoked a broad smile from Ben. Lee's blood was up after a two-hour faceoff with the hostile and dangerous prisoner, and she was not settling for standing around quietly afterward. Bondurant eventually raised his hands in surrender and stepped back with a smile as Lee donned her helmet and led the crew and three passengers aboard the RHIB.

"*Kauai, Kauai-One*, external scanning complete, no other devices visible. Request approach outboard of response boat for passenger transfer. Over," Lee's voice came over the radio. Sam turned to Hopkins and nodded.

"*Kauai-One, Kauai*, cleared for approach and moor outboard of response boat," Hopkins responded.

"*Kauai, Kauai-One*, roger, out." The RHIB swung away from the sailboat and settled on a course back to the Coast Guard boats. A short distance away, Lee turned the RHIB's heading almost parallel to the two connected vessels and then slowed it to a soft bump and stop against the sector boat. The boat seaman and engineer fastened lines to the larger vessel's deck cleats, after which Lee turned to Simmons and the two bomb technicians and said, "Go!" After the three men had scrambled onto the sector boat, Lee shouted, "Let go!"

Her two crewmen unhitched and retrieved the lines. A brief thirty-five seconds after contacting the sector boat, the RHIB swung clear to take up its rescue station between the cutter and the sailboat.

Simmons and Kemper shook hands with Davis aboard the sector boat and then climbed the ladder to *Kauai*'s main deck while the latter remained behind. After dropping off the scanner, they walked to the Bridge to confer with Ben and Sam. The sector boat headed for the sailboat with Davis and the robot.

Kemper set up his laptop on the chart table, opened his communication module, and set it to speaker mode. "Okay, Ken, we're set up. Light off when ready."

"Roger, Boss, coming on now."

Two windows popped on the laptop screen. "Gentlemen, welcome to Wally-vision," Kemper announced. "The top screen is the wide-angle scanning camera, the lower left is the fore/aft chassis cameras, and the lower right is for the scope camera." He leaned over the comms module and said, "Long view looks good, Ken. Let's check the close in."

The wide-angle camera was obscured, then quickly refocused on Davis's comically twisted face. "How's this?"

Kemper smiled. "Good resolution of some major butt-ugly. Make it stop, please!" The picture returned to a distant view of the sailboat. "Ah, much better." He hit the mute button. "For luck, we like to start all our ops with a little levitation." Sam's mouth opened and closed silently, Ben turned away to hide a smile, and Simmons stared back, completely poker-faced.

The picture became jerky as the sector boat pulled alongside the sailboat, and Davis and one of the boat crewmen lifted the robot aboard. "Wally's onboard. We're pulling back fifty meters," Davis called through the comms module. "OK, in position, beginning wide scan."

The plan had the robot survey the top deck of the sailboat and secure anything resembling a detonator. Davis would return briefly to move the robot down to the sailboat's cabin since it couldn't "climb down" independently. After a close inspection of the bomb with the robot's cameras, Kemper would decide whether Davis could risk a hands-on disarm.

The robot's pass on the top deck found a canvas bag with objects resembling a pen and a cellphone. Kemper held his breath as these were deposited in the robot's lead-lined steel holding box. If either was broadcasting a continuous signal, the box would interrupt it and detonate the bomb. The box snapped shut. "No boom. I guess we're still in business." Kemper smiled. "OK, Ken, move in for repositioning."

The sector boat returned to the sailboat, and Davis and the seaman carried the robot down to the cabin level. The sector boat had pulled back to a safe distance, and the robot repeated the inspection process in the cabin.

Finally, the moment of truth arrived, and the robot stopped in front of the panel concealing the bomb. Davis had the robot drill a hole in the panel and insert the articulating camera to look inside. After a thorough interior inspection of the entire panel and seams for booby traps, Davis turned the camera on the bomb.

"Boss, it seems like they're playing it safe with this one—nothing hinky in sight. I am OK doing the clip."

"Stand by, Ken." Kemper selected mute on the comms module and turned to Simmons. "Pete, you and I know Ken can't work in there in the Bomb Suit. We'll be mopping him up with a sponge if this goes south. I need convincin' this is a no-shit national security deal and not some egghead science project."

Simmons locked eyes with Kemper. "Matt, I've been there. I know what I'm asking Ken to do, and I'd do the job myself if I could handle it. It's a big ask, but we've got to get hold of that masker."

Kemper held the stare for another ten seconds, then turned back to the comm module. "Ken, you are cleared to go. If anything goes one nanometer out of whack, you run like hell, clear?"

"Roger, Boss. You don't have to tell me twice. See you later."

"Not if I see you first. Good luck, whackjob." Kemper punched the mute button again. "We'll be going radio silent until he's done, just to play it extra safe. Nothing left but sit back and listen to the noise in my brain," Kemper said with a wry smile. As if on cue, the video feed from the robot cut off.

"Can we bring you up a mug of coffee or something, Chief?" Sam asked.

"No, thanks, Captain." Kemper stood up and closed the laptop. "I may take you up on that later. Excuse me, please, sir." He picked up the comms module and walked out onto the bridge wing to watch the operation.

Ben asked Simmons, "On the other side? You've done this yourself?"

"Yes, I have a few times." Simmons nodded. "In the field, sometimes you're your own bomb disposal. I'm still breathing because Matt was talking me through the other end of the phone. I'd rather be the one working the bomb than have his job." He nodded toward Sam and started outside to join Kemper. "Your CO knows what it's like, I'm sure." He walked out silently to stand by Kemper and put his hand on his friend's shoulder.

Ben and Sam shared a look and followed.

****

"All safe, Boss," Davis's voice came over the comms module. "And I did another sweep. No surprises."

Holding the rail, Kemper put his head down for a few seconds, then stood up straight and pressed the transmit button. "Roger, pack it up. First one at Willie T's is on me." He turned to Simmons. "Your show now, brother."

"Thanks, Matt. Next time we catch up, I'm buying for everybody."

"You better believe it." Kemper nodded and turned to Sam. "Captain, that coffee offer still good?"

"Definitely." Sam offered his hand. "Dr. Simmons can show you to the mess deck. I need to stick around here, so I'll bid you a safe journey now."

Kemper shook his hand firmly. "Thanks, Captain. You've got a wonderful ship and crew here." He turned and followed Simmons down.

Sam turned to Hopkins. "OOD, recall the RHIB, please. We might as well get it stowed before the sector boat comes back."

"Yes, sir," Hopkins responded and continued inside the Bridge.

Within an hour, the makeshift conclave broke up. In the freshening westerly breeze, the *Sunrise Surprise II* was under sail, heading north for MacDill Air Force Base in Tampa. The sector boat with the prisoners and bomb disposal team motored down to Key West. *Kauai* headed southeast for the next round of reconnaissance. Sam had agreed to launch the Puma for a short sortie and quick surveillance of Resolution Key, the next on their list.

The aircraft returned a little before sunset, and Simmons had asked for a meeting with Sam and Ben afterward. The three men retired to Sam's cabin and gathered around Simmons's laptop for the discussion. "Captain, I need to ask if we can go ashore on Resolution Key tomorrow morning."

"I don't see that as a problem, Doctor. As I recall, there's good water to the west of the island's northern tip. Did the Puma turn up something?"

"It's probably nothing, but there appears to be human activity up there—a small shack with signs of recent habitation. If someone is there, I'd like to talk to them."

"Um, don't you think if somebody is there and they saw something, they would report it?" Ben asked.

"Think about someone who would live in those conditions and ask yourself if you believe they might fit that old cliché of 'because you didn't ask.' It's a long shot, but we need to check all the boxes on this."

"I agree, Doctor." Sam nodded. "Plan on taking the XO and Seaman Lopez with you. I want the Puma to do a security sweep and then maintain an overwatch while you are ashore. I don't expect trouble, but I'm into playing it safe these days. Once you're done, it can continue the recon. When we break up here, please sit down with Hoppy and Fritz and gin up one of your geeky-mathy optimized Op Plans for tomorrow. I'm sure the Doctor here would appreciate our trying to make up some time we lost today."

"That I would. Thank you, sir." Simmons smiled.

"Okay, this was quite a day." Sam sat back, scratching his close-cropped hair. "XO, before you get head-down with Ops and Air, I'd like you to do a wellness check of the rest of your boarding party. The adrenaline's worn off by now, and they might be a touch wound up. I'd do it, but the only answer I can get when I ask how someone's doing is 'Awesome, sir!' I figure they'll be a little franker with you than they'd be with the Old Man."

"Yes, sir." Ben nodded.

"Holler if I need to pitch in."

"Awesome, sir!"

"Dismissed, wiseass!" Sam threw a crumpled ball of paper in Ben's direction as he and a grinning Simmons stepped out the cabin door.

8

Reconnaissance—Sea

USCG Cutter *Kauai*, Gulf of Mexico, Off Resolution Key, Florida
07:56 EST, 17 January

Ben

Kauai idled a quarter-mile off the northern tip of Resolution Key, with Lee putting in a turn as the OOD. This morning, the driving was dull, occasionally goosing the idling engines to hold position and heading in the calm air and slow current. A small shack and a beat-up old pickup truck were visible on their arrival. An older man in a straw hat had emerged carrying fishing gear when the Puma completed its circuit and assumed overwatch. The man waved on seeing the cutter, then began fishing on the chair. Satisfied there was no apparent hazard, Sam had green-lighted the launch of the RHIB to put Ben, Simmons, and Lopez ashore for an investigation.

Bondurant was the coxswain of record this morning, but Jenkins was breaking in for landing operations. Landing operations could be tricky, and Bondurant would never pass up an opportunity to give his junior boatswain hands-on training. Ben, Simmons, and Lopez were sitting forward, ready to jump off when it nudged the shore. They were landing one hundred yards from the shack to avoid disrupting its resident's fishing and get a look at the ground. Bondurant whispered coaching instructions as Jenkins steered into a soft bump when the prow touched bottom. The three passengers turned and, getting a thumbs up from Jenkins, jumped into the shallow water. The boat floated free, and Jenkins backed it off the beach.

As they waded ashore, Simmons said, "Your man is settling down nicely. That was only the second most thorough safety brief I've ever had."

As both the coastguardsmen smiled, Ben replied, "Yes, we're riding the asymptote down to the 'Yeah, blah-blah, don't get hurt' version."

Simmons chuckled and then stopped, scanning the sand inland of the high tide ridge. "Hang on a minute, guys. Check out these impressions." He crouched down and peered hard, tilting his head back and forth. "What do you think?"

Ben shrugged silently, but Lopez spoke, "The track is too wide for that Toyota." He nodded toward the pickup truck. "More like a big SUV or Hummer. They dismounted there and walked to the tide line. From the tracks, I'd say two, maybe three guys."

"Yes, indeed!" Simmons responded with Ben looking at Lopez in surprise. "Notice the vehicle tracks move inland instead of toward the shack. Let's file that one away." He turned and continued toward the shack, Ben and Lopez following.

"Lope, I never considered you the Sherlock Holmes type," Ben said.

"You should update yourself, XO. Doyle's great, but Deaver and Cornwell are the thing for modern detecting. Back in LA, a police detective and his wife took me on in the foster program. He turned me on to the books and took me on some ride-alongs. It stuck."

"Steer me to some good ones when we get back to Miami." Ben looked over at the shack as they started toward it. The old gentleman was seated in a beach chair under a canopy extending from the front. He had his straw hat off in the shade, and Ben guessed his age to be between sixty-five and seventy, with long, scraggly gray-white hair and an equally pale walrus mustache. The older man saw his gaze and waved, which Ben and Lopez returned.

"Gud'day fellers!" the old man said with a smile as they approached. "Whadda y'at?"

"Um, good morning, sir," Ben began as he tried to place the accent he heard. "I'm Lieutenant Junior Grade Ben Wyporek, U.S. Coast Guard, and these are my associates: Seaman Juan Lopez and Investigator Doug Pearson. We're investigating a boat accident around here a week ago and wondered if you might have seen anything."

"Oh, I bin round since just after Boxing Day." The older man nodded. "I always come down dis time a'year to warm up in me pally's place here. Pally and me swap—he comes up for a break in me cabin when it's burnin' hot down here, and I come down when it's cold enough to skin ya up home. Yup, I was out here a week back, didn't see nuttin'. A few fish cops come round in a big SUV, but dem's the only folk I seen. No boats, no time except yours dare," he said, nodding toward *Kauai*.

"Sir, you're from Canada, I take it?"

"*Newfoundland*, 'Olyrood." The man huffed up.

"Sorry, sir, no offense meant. Do you mind if I see your passport, please?"

"It's on de cuddy inside de door." The man pointed. "I hopes you don want my arse outta dis nice chair right now?"

"No, sir, if you don't mind, Seaman Lopez will peek in and grab it for you." Ben nodded at Lopez. He ducked into the shack, returned with the booklet, and handed it to Ben. The photo inside was a cleaner, slightly younger version of the older man. Ben read aloud, "William Witson, 23 MacKenzie Ave, Holyrood, Newfoundland and Labrador. Did I say that correctly, sir?"

"That's Newfound-LAND, son, spot-on wi tother."

"Thanks, Mr. Witson. Is that truck a rental or on loan from your friend?" Ben noted the entry stamp in the passport dated December 27th.

"Ya can call me Bill if ya like. Dat's my pally's truck. He loans it t'me when I comes down. Ya can look round it if ya likes."

"You don't mind?" At his nod, Simmons turned and walked toward the vehicle.

"Naw, anyting for the law." Turning toward Lopez, he continued. "I'm 'bout to have an eye-opener, son. Care to join in?" He reached for a beer in the cooler beside the chair.

"Thank you, sir, but it's a little early for me." Lopez smiled back. "Besides, I don't want to be drinking in front of the lieutenant." He winked conspiratorially.

"Ha! I dies at you. Where you from, son?"

"East Los Angeles, sir."

"Cally-fornia? I bet it never gets cold dare."

"Not like Newfound-*Land*."

The light conversation continued while Simmons searched through the truck and shack. He caught Ben's eye and shook his head almost imperceptibly as he returned. Ben nodded equally subtly and then brought the conversation to a close. "Sir, thank you very much for your time and cooperation. I wish you a pleasant visit and good luck with the fish."

"Tanks, Leftenant." Witson smiled and nodded. "You take care, and long may your big jib draw."

Ben called for the RHIB as they walked down toward the pickup point, and it nosed in as they arrived. Lopez held the bow just short of grounding while the other men climbed in, then he pushed off and swung up. Jenkins backed the boat off, turned, and headed for *Kauai*. Ben turned to Simmons, speaking loudly over the engine. "Wow, that was some accent. I could barely make him out. I usually have more trouble telling someone's Canadian." He waved when he noticed the older man watching them.

Simmons smiled. "They're rather insular in Newfoundland. It wasn't even part of Canada until 1949. Still, you probably wouldn't have noticed with someone younger."

"Nothing interesting with the pickup or shack?"

"Nothing I could see. The truck is registered in Hialeah. It's big enough to carry survey gear, but there's no evidence of it—only some receipts for food and beer. I got the registration information and VIN. Only clothes and junk in the shack."

"I'll send that and the passport info in and see if we get any hits, but it looks like a bust."

"Perhaps." Simmons paused and glanced back at the shack receding in the distance. "Still, I'm keeping this one in my pocket while we check on the others."

Old Bill watched the RHIB make its way toward the patrol boat and raised his beer exaggeratingly in return for the wave from the young lieutenant in the shade of his makeshift porch. He smiled again and returned to fishing.

USCG Cutter *Kauai,* Gulf of Mexico, twenty-four nautical miles east-northeast of Key West, Florida 17:32 EST, 17 January

Ben

Kauai sped westbound for a return to Key West for refueling. The remaining survey areas were completed by launching both Pumas on independent flight plans with staggered launches and recoveries. Simmons and Deffler had worked a double shift, pre-processing the data for the image analysis to follow.

The crew cycled through an exquisite meal by patrol boat standards of mahi-mahi with coconut rice and mango salsa prepared by Hebert as the day's catch. During the Puma sorties, the lookout spotted a floating raft of seaweed, and Bondurant recognized the opportunity and persuaded Sam to stop for an impromptu fish call. As Bondurant expected, the area under the seaweed raft teemed with dolphinfish that began a feeding frenzy when the first line hit the water. Hebert had a dozen large specimens within thirty minutes and began planning the feast.

Ben sat across the table from Drake and Simmons, the latter shaking his head in wonderment. "My God, this is incredible. How do you keep this man? I couldn't get a meal like this for under a hundred bucks back home."

"In a big, fancy restaurant, he'd just be another guy at the stove, working under a puffed-up asshole. Here, he's the king and gets to work a machine gun in his spare time. The skipper and Chief keep him fixed up with all the fancy spices and tools he needs," Ben said, holding up a piece of the fish. "He's also seriously appreciated."

"He damn well better be!" Simmons responded. Catching Hebert's attention, he said, "*C'est fameux, Maître Cuisinier. Je me regale!*"

"*Merci beaucoups, Monsieur Professeur!*" Hebert mocked a sword salute with his spatula.

Simmons renewed his attack on the helpless fish. Ben glanced at the other end of the table where Hopkins, Deffler, Lee, and Williams were dining and sharing relaxed conversation. Williams, as usual, expounded on a perceived atrocity of modern government, with Lee nodding and Hopkins patiently waiting for her chance for rebuttal. Deffler sat quietly and seemed to focus more on Hopkins than the conversation going on around him.

"Now, Hoppy. I think providing free school meals, that is, taxpayer-funded meals encourages poor behavior. I mean, if you're not held responsible for providing for your own kids, where does it stop?" Williams said.

Hopkins shook her head sadly, as she often did during similar table debates. "Joe, it isn't a question of trying to hold parents responsible. I doubt the decision would affect someone like that either way. You have to think if they're letting their kids go hungry, it's because they can't do anything about it, or they don't care. The government won't change that behavior by withholding food. It comes down to stopping children from going hungry. I'm sorry, but I just can't get worked up against stopping that."

"Aw, c'mon, Hoppy." Williams turned to Deffler. "Hey Fritz, help me out here."

Deffler smiled but continued gazing at Hopkins. "Sorry, sailor, can't help you outta this one. A guest like me should maintain a strict non-interference policy regarding the hosts."

"Airedales!" Williams scoffed, shaking his head.

Ben chuckled and returned to his conversation. He looked across at Drake and asked, "Chief, what happens with you, I mean, after we decommission? Are you going to move on to the Fast Response Cutters?" He referred to the new class of patrol boats replacing the one-tens.

"No, XO. I'm a PB guy to my bones. Not interested in Mini-Me's."

Ben's fork paused halfway to his mouth. "Mini-Me? Where'd that come from?"

Drake sat back, signaling the delivery of some deck-plate philosophy. "Think about that boat—four officers, so full of electronics and other gear, you can't even turn around. They jammed everything electronic you'd find on a two-seventy into a hull half the size—like they were going for a miniature Medium Endurance Cutter. Thus, Mini-Me."

Ben guffawed. "Chief, is it that bad? Wouldn't you like not needing to grind out replacement parts after every patrol? You'd have more than three guys working for you and not have all the EO paperwork."

"XO, I enjoy having a nice tight engine room crew I can run. And as for paperwork, that's why I have *you*, sir!" He paused while the other two men chuckled, then continued. "Naw, this is my twilight tour. I reckon I'll go out with the old girl and maybe hire on at a marine repair shop."

"Yeah, I don't doubt it. Just don't bail before I move along, please. You know, it's all about me."

"Don't I know it, sir." He turned to Simmons. "So Doc, any luck with finding the space rock?"

Simmons swallowed. "Alas, no, the quest for the Holy Grail continues, and I'm hoping this last batch of imagery will bear fruit for us."

"I don't get it. A rock ginormous enough to cave in a boat ought to be easy to see."

"On the contrary, Chief. The impactor is likely quite small. Remember, speed is the big part of the kinetic energy of an object. An impactor ten feet across, hitting the Earth at a typical meteor's speed, would produce an explosion comparable to the Hiroshima atomic bomb. We're lucky most burn up in the atmosphere. I believe the water kept it from vaporizing, but whatever was left probably shattered. No, we're searching more for the effects of the impact, breaks in the patterns of the shore and seabed. That's why we crank the imagery through computer algorithms. They can pick up on anomalies too subtle for humans to see."

Ben hated the deception Simmons perpetrated on Drake, despite complete understanding and agreement of the necessity. Still, he had to admire the skill

Simmons displayed in his almost casual obscuration of the genuine nature of their mission. Ben tried not to think of how the crew would react if they learned the truth. He glanced at his watch. "Sorry, guys, gotta shove off for the entering-port brief."

Simmons turned to him. "As many times as you've been to Key West, you still need detailed briefings?"

"Doc, every mooring is unique. Tides, currents, and lighting effects can change daily or hourly. Try figuring things out while bearing down on the dock, and you add another dent on the hull. Chief wouldn't like that." He nodded to Drake.

"No, that wouldn't make my day." The look Drake gave told Ben the older man knew he was not hearing the truth, at least the *whole* truth. Ben kept his face impassive and nodded to Hopkins, inducing her to excuse herself from the table and follow him forward.

****

Having wrapped up the brief, Ben had started his usual mental preparation for the ship-handling effort to come in two hours when Sam beckoned him over. "Our guest has requested a confidential meeting to discuss the next steps. Meet you in the cabin in five minutes?"

"Yes, sir."

A few minutes later, Sam, Ben, and Simmons were sitting in their usual places in Sam's cabin with the door closed. Sam looked at Simmons and said, "OK, Doctor, you have the floor."

Simmons nodded. "Thank you, Captain. Image processing is continuing, but we have done all the seaborne reconnaissance we can. I need to get with my people to coordinate some deeper dives on land. If you don't object, I'll be moving ashore when we return to Key West."

Sam glanced at Ben, then back to Simmons. "Am I to infer that our role in this mission is ending?"

"No, sir. We know that warhead landed in the water, not ashore. Until it is located, there's still an important maritime part to this effort. I have to ask you to stay nearby and be available."

"Very well, Doctor. Until our orders change, we'll continue on the mission. What do you envision us doing?"

"I need you to be the maritime response force in the event we locate the target. It'll mean being underway in a standby position north of the Keys, and we can work out a geographic point that would allow the best average response time."

Sam nodded. "That's doable, provided you remember, this is a patrol boat, not a large cutter, and that after three days underway, I need to go in for a fuel break."

"Understood. This should be resolved by then. There's one more thing." He looked at Ben. "I'd like to take Ben with me to serve as an advisor."

"You're joking!" Sam said with astonishment. "Do you realize what you're asking? What if we end up tangling with the Russians or the TCO thugs? You want me to risk going into a fight without my GQ OOD?"

"Hear me out." Simmons held up his hand. "It's a lot to ask, but consider the risks if I have to decide about your role without your knowledge or experience. No one on my team understands *Kauai*'s capabilities and limitations. I could easily put your guys, my guys, or both at unnecessary risk through sheer ignorance. Wouldn't it be better to avoid a jam than to fight our way out of one?"

Sam shook his head. "Even if I were to agree to that view, even if I believed I could assume that risk for my crew and ship, what about Ben? He's not trained for this kind of work. You cavalierly hung his ass out before without a by-your-leave or apology."

"Captain, I take exception to your characterization of that event. We had the risk under control. Now we have three teams available in support instead of one. And that's just my guys. I've heard the FBI, DEA, and ATF are moving in now that we've got terrorists, drugs, and bombs in play. We're covered far better than before." He paused, glancing at Ben. "I understand what I'm asking of you, and I wouldn't just throw you in the blades. Too much has happened on this trip,"

Sam stared at Simmons without speaking. After half a minute, Sam turned to Ben. "What do you think, honestly?"

Ben felt an icy ball forming in his stomach, the memory of his fear in the car chase still fresh. After a brief pause, he replied, "I'll go along with whatever you decide, Captain."

"Not good enough, dammit!" Sam shook his head. "I need to know if you can do this. If not, it's your duty to tell me here and now. This plan is way above and beyond the call. If you aren't confident in success, I'll put a stop to it, and nothing more will be said." He looked at Simmons. "By anyone!"

Ben blinked and swallowed. He glanced at Simmons, then back at Sam. "I'm in, sir. Let's finish this thing right. But I have one request before we commit."

"Name it."

"Chief Drake is already on to something out of whack on this patrol, and Hoppy will cover for me while ashore. They need to be read in to do it right. And, Captain, you need the job done right. That's what it will take to make me confident."

"Agree a hundred percent." Sam nodded and turned to Simmons. "There you go, Doctor. That's our *sine qua non*. Take it or leave it."

Simmons's mouth opened and closed, and his face hardened. "All right. But those two are it, agreed? I'm already way over my quota on this."

"Agreed. Now you get how I feel."

"Do you want me to read them in or be in the room?"

"No. I know my people and how much I can share. I want them to be able to ask questions and speak frankly without you fidgeting in the room." He looked at Ben. "We'll brief them in the sector's SCIF after securing from mooring stations. Are you going to be OK taking her in? Remember, you're still 'under oath' here."

"I can cut it, Captain. Hell, I can use the distraction at this point."

Sam nodded. "Fine. I guess there's nothing else to say, except, God help us all." He stood and offered his hand to Simmons.

Surprised, Simmons stood and shook Sam's hand firmly. "Thank you, sir."

Trumbo Point Annex, Naval Air Station Key West, Florida
20:41 EST, 17 January

Ben

Sam and Ben walked over to the sector building after preparations for another sortie. Drake and Hopkins had preceded them, having completed the refueling and setting up the charts for the departure, respectively. Ben was used to periods with little banter when hanging around with Sam—friendly as he was, no one would call him talkative—but this silence was thunderous. Ben was sure his CO was having second thoughts about this decision. Finally, Ben couldn't take it anymore. "It will be OK, sir. We've plenty of backup, and we have to see it through."

Sam continued staring straight ahead as he walked on through the darkness. "Do we? Why us? If this were real, it should be the biggest deal ever. All Hands on Deck. Yet, it's just us and an unknown number of men in black. We depend on a man who lies for a living. You heard the captain. She as much as said, 'Yeah, it's BS.

Just follow your damn orders.' Now I will have to sell the mission to Chief and Hoppy without letting on that deep down, I think it's a load of crap." He glanced over at Ben as they passed under one of the pier lights, noted the grim expression, then smiled, put an arm around his shoulder, and shook it gently. "Sorry, XO, this is new for me, and I needed to vent a little. Odds are we'll come through this with the bosses scratching their heads and the rest of us laughing our asses off that a looney-toon Ph.D. bamboozled them." Both men smiled as they arrived at the sector building.

Drake and Hopkins, already waiting in the SCIF, stood up when the two officers entered. "Sit down, please," Sam said as he closed the door, and both complied while Sam and Ben joined them at the table.

As Sam opened his mouth to speak, Drake interrupted. "Captain, you're here to tell Hoppy and me that the ops we've been on for the past few days are not a space rock hunt. Also, we've somehow gotten mixed up with dangerous people, and the worst is yet to come." Seeing the two officers glance at each other, he continued, looking straight at Ben. "XO, you need to stay away from spying, politics, and poker tables. You can't even be in the room with someone bullshitting without breaking out in tells."

Ben blushed, and Sam chuckled out loud. "Now, Chief, while we ponder whether that is a virtue or a shortcoming for our brave XO, why don't you tell us what you think you know."

Drake turned to Sam. "We come across a drug boat with a kind of damage I've never run into before. Next thing, we're diverted from our patrol, and some IC-type drops out of the sky and takes over. XO goes with him to check something out and comes back as shook up as anyone I've ever seen. The next day we stop a yacht with stealth tech being run by a no-shit evil villain lady and set to blow itself up. The finale was that session on the mess deck. Dr. Spook spun this bullshit story about a goldilocks meteor—big enough to smash the hell out of that boat, but not so big that anybody would notice." He looked at Ben. "Sir, you couldn't handle sitting there while you knew that dude was lying to me. And that *is* a virtue in my mind, by the way."

"Right, Chief," Sam began. "We've had to keep the crew in the dark because the information is sensitive. Well, the situation has changed. We need to read you and Hoppy in if we are going to complete this mission. But before that, you need to accept what I'm going to tell you is as classified as it gets. If you disclose this information ever, you, and likely Mr. W and me, get thrown into Leavenworth. Chief, Hoppy, what do you say?"

"Yes, sir," Drake responded. "Let's have it."

"Understood, Captain." Hopkins nodded.

"OK," Sam began and then related the story behind the mission, including the possibility they were dealing with a loose nuclear weapon. Drake and Hopkins listened throughout with rapt attention, Drake nodding periodically, and Hopkins, silent and still with eyes growing wide at the big revelation of the hunt for the nuke. He withheld his and Ben's doubts about the truth of the worst assumption—sharing those would do more harm than good. "So, here we are. Any questions?"

Drake leaned back in his chair and shook his head. "Captain, if anyone else had told me that tale, I would've thrown the bullshit flag, and that would be that. Sorry to put you on the spot, but do *you* believe there's a loose nuke out there?"

So much for holding back. "Chief, I honestly don't know. If I had to lay a bet, it would be no. But I think it's at least possible with all the weird stuff going on here. We must run down that possibility. Regardless of what I believe, we have lawful orders, and we will carry them out."

"Thanks for the straight talk, sir. I'm with you." Drake nodded. He paused, turning to Ben. "Besides, I have the human truth detector here backing you up."

Sam turned to Hopkins. "Hoppy?"

Hopkins looked back and forth at the two officers. "OK, Captain. This takes getting used to, but your word will do for me. My question is, why tell us now? What's changed that we suddenly need to know?"

"The investigation has shifted from sea-based to shore-based. Dr. Simmons will continue processing the imagery data obtained on the UAV flights. He will work with his own team members to follow up on leads on the ground the UAVs couldn't pick up. We'll remain in the vicinity to provide support since the vehicle, however it's armed, landed in the water." Sam looked at Ben. "We'll also provide a liaison to Dr. Simmons to keep us in the loop and offer expertise on what a one-ten can do and what it can't. Mr. Wyporek has volunteered, so I'll be leaning on you two a lot more while he's ashore. Hoppy, you will take over the XO's operational duties. We will stand easy in terms of LE patrolling because we're short-handed and have to stay on station if needed. Chief, you get the admin burden. I need you to look after the crew even closer since I'm down a set of eyes."

Drake turned to Ben. "XO, haven't you been around long enough to learn not to volunteer for stuff?"

Ben mustered his best smile. "C'mon, Chief, good sleep, hotel showers. What could go wrong?"

"Permission to speak freely, sir?" Hopkins interjected, and Ben did not need a psychology degree to tell she was furious.

"That's why we're here." Sam nodded.

Hopkins turned to Ben. "Sir, with all due respect, are you out of your damn mind? Pardon my French."

"Take it easy, Hoppy." Ben appreciated her feelings but was surprised by her vehemence. "I'll be going in eyes open, and we'll have plenty of backup."

Hopkins wasn't backing down. "Sir, you're not trained for this. It's not Russians that scare me. Frankly, I think that part's pure BS. It's that lying piece of crap Simmons and his drug gangs. You've just told me he dragged you into what could have been a firefight. He did it with no notification and probably no more thought than he gave to if he wanted OJ with his eggs. You weren't in the room staring down that bitch for two hours, like Shelley and me. And I wouldn't trust

Simmons any more than I would trust her. Don't do this! Please, Captain!"

Ben was about to speak, but remained quiet when Sam held up his hand and leaned forward. "Emilia, can you do this job?"

Her mouth opened and closed, and then she looked down. "Yes, sir. You know I can."

"Very well. Your concerns are well-founded. Please believe that Mr. Wyporek and I have discussed them and others at length. Bottom line: the mission and many lives could depend on clear and correct language at the right place and time." He turned to Drake. "What about you, Chief? Let's have it, no holding back."

Drake shook his head. "Sorry, Captain, but I'm with Hoppy. I don't trust anyone who lies right to my face. Ever. Are you sure you want to gamble Mr. Wyporek's life with this guy, not to mention ours?"

A slight smile softened Sam's expression. "OK, I'll admit that I'm not the good doctor's biggest fan. But recent experience has moved this decision from the gamble column to the one labeled 'calculated risk.' I can assure you I'll be reassessing that risk constantly as we go along, and the XO will too. We're done if either of us sees anything that changes the game. You've *my* word on that."

Drake's grim face did not change, but he nodded. "OK, sir. I can do the job for you."

Sam relaxed and leaned back. "OK, guys. Mr. Wyporek always gives it to me straight, even when he knows I won't like it. I depend on him for that, and I'll depend on you to do the same, please. Anybody got anything else? No? Let's get'r done then."

They all rose together and stood awkwardly until Drake broke the tension. "Captain's the last one on and the first one off the boat, sir," he said with a smile and a motion toward the door with his right arm.

****

Ben changed into casual civilian clothes and picked up a weapon "Go Bag." It contained an M4 Carbine, Sig pistol, several ammunition magazines for each, body armor, and a combat first aid kit Bryant had put together at Sam's request. He turned the keys to the locked files over to Sam and then met Simmons on the mess deck. The agent gazed at the ship's crest mounted on a plaque on the forward bulkhead. *Kauai's* crest comprised the escutcheon of the Kingdom of Hawaii over a fouled anchor with the ship's motto, *Fortiter et Fideliter*, across the bottom.

"Ready, friend?" Simmons asked as he approached. At Ben's nod, he glanced once more at the plaque. "'Bravely and Faithfully.' That's a damn good sentiment for a unit that has your back."

Ben stared at the plaque and was slightly embarrassed that he had never looked up the Latin phrase. "Yes, I suppose it is. Shall we?"

Sam, Drake, and Hopkins were waiting on the pier by the entry port when the two men approached. Sam shook Simmons's hand and nodded. "Good luck, Doctor."

Receiving a blank expression from Drake, an icy glare from Hopkins, and no offer of a handshake from either, Simmons said to Ben, "I'll meet you over at the car." He turned and walked off along the dock.

Ben turned back to his shipmates and shook first Sam's, then Drake's hand. Sam's grip was firm and prolonged, and he smiled sadly on letting go. Drake's was equally strong, and he held Ben's eyes and nodded as he looked down on the young officer.

At her turn, Hopkins pushed his hand aside and hugged him hard, whispering, "Be careful, sir."

"Um, I will," came his stunned reply.

After she released him and stood back with the others, Ben picked up his bag, faced Sam at attention, received a nod in return, and turned to leave the boat.

After watching Ben get in the car with Simmons and drive off, Sam turned to Drake and Hopkins. "Ready for sea, Hoppy?"

"Yes, sir."

"Chief?"

"Ready for sea, Captain."

"Very well. Let's set mooring stations and get going." Sam returned their salutes and turned toward the ladder to the Bridge, followed by Hopkins as Drake turned toward the Main Space hatch.

9

Introductions

U.S. Route 1, six miles West of Marathon, Florida
22:13 EST, 17 January

Ben

One of Simmons's teammates provided the car they rode in from Key West. In it, they found the car keys, directions, and a key for a room at an off-brand hotel in the Key town of Marathon. The two men shared little conversation while Ben drove through the darkness. He was still processing his two enlisted shipmates' astonishing reaction to his acceptance of the mission while Simmons engaged in cryptic mobile phone communications. Simmons broke the silence about fifteen minutes before their arrival.

"That was some sendoff. For you, I mean, not me. Although it surprised me that your captain's farewell to me was the warmest."

"The bomb-defusing operation gave him cause to recalibrate. He sees the best in people, even those who give him ample reason not to. The other two think you're playing us and are uptight about my going off with you."

"And this surprises you?"

"The being played part or the other?"

"The latter."

"Kinda. I'm the XO. The arrangement I have with the skipper is that he's the smiling backslapper, and I'm the crabby nitpicker. I don't seek opportunities to be a dick. But I will do it when the hair or uniform pushes outside the regs or spaces need policing."

"You often get on Hopkins or Drake about that stuff?"

"Are you kidding? Never."

"So, you're not there to keep them toeing the line. Do you offer expertise to them to help them do their jobs?"

"It's usually the reverse."

"Really? It doesn't bother you on some level to ask your inferiors for help?"

Ben glanced over at him and then returned to the road. "Are you trying to pick a fight with me right now?"

"Why would you say that?"

"They are not my *inferiors*; they're my subordinates. I have authority over them because I'm the XO, not because I'm *better* than them. Shit, I've learned plenty from both of them."

"Do all Coast Guard officers think like you?"

"No, not all of them."

"So, let's continue down your path a bit. You think the world of your CO, correct?"

"He's the finest officer and man I've ever known."

"Would it surprise you to learn he feels the same about you?"

Ben was at a loss for words and just glanced again briefly at Simmons.

"Well?" Simmons pressed.

"There's no way he told *you* that!"

"Friend, I remind you he was about to rip my head off for putting you in danger the other day. I've been poking him regularly since I arrived. The only time he went beyond a contemptuous brush-off was when I said unkind stuff about you. Given your regard for him and his regard for you, is it that surprising the people who work for you feel the same?"

Ben continued to stare forward. "Are we there yet?"

Simmons chuckled. "Ben, I'm sorry to put the microscope on you, but we will be mixing up with real out-of-the-box stuff soon. I won't have time for explanations or pep talks when things get weird. I know your background pretty well—my outfit has access to that kind of information. You don't have any tactical experience other than your car ride with me the other day. The point of all this psychobabble is you will do OK, whatever happens, get me? A bunch of top-shelf people not only like you but trust you. That means something."

"You should keep in mind that car chase scared the shit out of me."

"I congratulate you on your sanity. Fear in those situations is normal, and fear is always useful when it informs your decisions. Fear's only a problem when it *dictates* your actions."

"Right. Thanks for the pep talk, Obi-Wan. Are we there yet?"

"Almost there, young padawan." Simmons chuckled. "You'll need to know a few things about my team before we arrive; it'll make things smoother in the introduction."

"Shoot." Ben was relieved his psyche was finally out of the spotlight.

"Besides the processing team, we have specialists for dealing with our TCO opponents and any new Russian 'friends.' Once we knew the other side was in the game, they deployed forward to cover the analysts. Art Frankle is the lead. He's an old agency hand, *my* mentor, or 'Obi-Wan,' as you put it. Lashon Bell is his partner, not much on conversation, but one of the best tactics guys you'll run into. Now, on the processing team, we have Steve Newsome, who keeps comms up and is quite a code monkey. He also takes care of our resident genius, Victoria Carpenter, who's amazing at pattern recognition and math. She can glance at a full-page matrix and not only tell you the determinant, but any notable quirks in the data. Also, she has a mild form of what used to be called Asperger's Syndrome but is now more kindly referred to as being 'neuro-diverse.' She does not have OCD, but her frankness is jarring at first."

Great, Ben thought. *I'll bet she looks like Velma from the Scooby-Doo cartoons, only geekier and neurotic to boot.* Aloud, he asked, "Um, I never met anyone like that. Any triggers or issues I need to worry about?"

"Nope. Just roll with it and don't take anything she says too personally—she calls it *precisely* as she sees it, no sugar-coating. Oh, and if she has anything arranged in her workspace, don't mess with it. It won't set her off or anything; it'll just distract her."

"Right," Ben said, thinking, *you just can't make this shit up.*

Conch Inn, Room 118, Marathon, Florida
23:23 EST, 17 January

Ben

The agents working with Simmons had booked three adjacent rooms, and Lashon and Steve had swept them thoroughly for microphones and cameras. The hotel was mostly vacant in the offseason and a little shabby. However, its single floor and row of rooms made it ideal for security. Ben and Simmons occupied the center room, which doubled as the command center for the group since the rooms on either side provided a screen against any would-be eavesdroppers.

Simmons's team had gathered in the center room on the notification he and Ben were a few minutes out. He gave the prearranged knock sequence, opened the door, and led Ben inside. The greetings were led by Victoria, who was, to Ben's great surprise, a beautiful, petite young woman with pulled-back auburn hair and large aquamarine eyes in a heart-shaped face. She hugged

Simmons and said in a surprisingly husky voice with a midwestern accent, "Hello, Peter! I am very happy to see you." She turned to Ben with a smile. "You are Lieutenant Junior Grade Wyporek?"

Holy crap! Even her voice is incredible. Breathe, boy! Ben took a breath and played it as cool as he could. "Yes, I am. I am very pleased to meet you. You can call me Ben if you like."

"Why would I like to do that when your name is Benjamin?" Her smile faded.

"Some people like to call me Ben because it's shorter to say, but I like how you say 'Benjamin,' so I would be happy if you called me that."

A slight smile lit up her face, which Ben thought was one of the loveliest he'd ever seen. "Good. We have been working all day and ordered pizza. Mine is a thin crust with pepperoni and green peppers. Would you like some as well?"

"Victoria, I can't think of anything I would rather do more right now."

"That's good." She then abruptly turned and walked behind one table, sat, and began typing, gazing at the screen.

OK, there it is. Ben directed a puzzled glance at Simmons and got a shrug in return. He then turned and greeted the rest of the team. The pizza arrived about fifteen minutes later. Ben sat back and munched a piece of Victoria's favorite while he listened to the team update each other on the events of the past days, sneaking glances at the lovely young analyst whenever he could.

Frankle, the senior member and coordinator of the team, led the discussion. He was the oldest and presumably the most experienced of the group, with graying, close-cropped hair and a pair of reading glasses perched down on his nose.

"You did well setting up out here. We're out of sight, but still in the loop," Frankle said as he sipped a bottle of Heineken. "FBI, DEA, ATF, seems like half the DoJ has descended 'covertly' on Key West to assess the threat. So far, they're all focused on the drugs and bombs, nothing going on regarding either that stealth kit your folks found or the 'other thing.'" He glanced at Ben.

"He's read in." Simmons nodded. "Has the usual turf war kicked off yet?"

"Boy, howdy. Our guy says the leads for the FBI and the DEA almost came to blows. Bottom line is that the word is out, though not officially, that we bagged two narco-terrorist boats. Also, they are turning over every rock in Miami and Key West, looking for contacts and accessories. With the spotlight on those places, we believe we are in a clear spot between them.

"The bad news: that operative you guys nailed on the sailboat got away."

"What?" Ben nearly choked on a mouthful of pizza.

"Yep. She got a call off before you put her in the bag. Anyway, the marshals taking her to lockup got bushwhacked shortly after leaving the Coast Guard base. One dead, one fifty-fifty. They may have killed or wounded an attacker, but nobody was left behind. We got a hit on the biometrics and this gal's real bad news, an assassin, actual name Valentina Petrova, drummed out of the Russian SVR because she was too psycho even for them. Our 252 opponents attract cross-wired types like her."

Simmons saw Ben's face and interrupted, "Don't panic, friend. Now that she's graduated to federal cop killer, her face will be everywhere. She knows her only chance to stay alive is to exit this country as fast as possible."

Frankle nodded. "True. Hell, her own people might have grabbed her just so they can knock her off before she makes any deals. A man can hope, anyway."

Simmons weighed in again. "She's connected with that first boat. Any Intel why they took a chance running a load that big? Seems like a big gamble. I mean, that loss has to hurt, even for them."

Frankle nodded. "Yeah, it has people scratching their heads. It may be a rogue element in the organization, or they thought they had the juice in place to keep people quiet."

Ben piped up, "They may have tested it in dry runs or smaller loads. I'm sure you guys know how lean our coverage in the Deep Caribbean is these days. The hardest part's getting through the passages, but they can hide in the commercial traffic if they're radar-masked. It's hard enough to see them when they aren't masked."

Frankle nodded. "Makes sense. But drugs are you guys' problem, you and DEA. Anyway, they're on it, so we're standing off the boat investigation unless there's overseas work to do."

"Have they done any testing on the radar masker we found on the second boat?" Simmons asked.

"A little. So far, it's invisible to the Coast Guard surface and aircraft radars. They plan to run it against high-end DoD models when they start serious testing. It's spooky. Drugs are nasty, but it's the other stuff they're running that scares me."

"No kidding. OK, let's talk about our little caper here. Victoria, can you come here, please? We need you to talk about what you found."

"Yes, Peter," she said, pushing back from her console and moving to join the group.

"Ben and I went ashore on Resolution Key because of evidence of human activity. There was no joy on the warhead, although I think the 252s looked in there. As far as I can tell, the rest of our aerial surveys have shown nothing positive in the areas we believe the missile could have crashed. We're handicapped because we don't have any baseline imagery for comparison."

"That's not true, Peter," Victoria interrupted. "Besides Resolution Key, there were vehicle tracks on seven other islands among those surveyed. The imagery revealed the tracks were likely from the same vehicle that explored Resolution Key."

"Interesting," Simmons said with a slight, contemplative pause. "What does that suggest to you, Art?"

"Our 252 friends are as clueless about where their boat got hit as we are. Do you think they were playing this on the fly? Why do that when they can just push aside anyone they run into? It's what they always do."

"Yes, in the Balkans and South America, where nobody gives a shit about a few more bodies. Here, if they knock off innocents, the heat comes quickly and heavily. There isn't enough bribe money to make *that* go away. Better to avoid trouble—check on their pre-scouted spots and, when they find one that's clear, call in once they anchored." He paused briefly. "That's too bad. My hopes that the 252s will lead us to the landing site are fading."

"Mmmm, yeah," Frankle said, peering over his glasses between Simmons and Bell. "So, what's the plan?"

"Maybe we'll be fortunate, and Victoria's work will produce a definitive answer." Simmons glanced at the woman and received a nod in return. "However, we have to assume it's up to legwork again. Art, please tell me you got hold of the National Park Service stuff."

"Yes and no. We have the digital form of the most recent survey maps for the area. Many are PDFs, so image comparison won't give us much. Back to ground-pounding for us."

"About what I figured. At least the maritime constraint bounds our problem a bit. I suggest we split the load. Tomorrow, Art, you and Lashon take the easternmost four areas here." He pointed at the larger scale chart. "And our young coastguardsman and I will take the western areas. We'll be looking for signs of unusual shore erosion, recently flipped wood, or anything that points to a micro-tsunami that the impact might have generated. And we'll have the ground sensors."

"Long shot finding anything," Bell said, entering the conversation.

"Agreed. But we'll be down to that if Victoria's efforts don't bear fruit. Speaking of which, Victoria, once your runs are complete and you wrap up your initial analysis, I want you and Steve to pack up your gear and head back to Maryland. We're done with the UAV surveys, and we're spread too thin here to provide you two with adequate cover with all the bad guys running around. We'll hook up again once you're plugged in back in Bethesda."

"I understand, Peter," Victoria replied somewhat sadly. She turned to Ben. "I wish we had more time to work together, Benjamin."

Ben's heart jumped. "Well, Victoria, we have a few hours, don't we? Can I pitch in?"

"No." Victoria glanced back at the computer work area. "Everything is batch processing right now. However, I read your paper on the SAROPS project that provided the basis of your search strategy. There were several flaws and shortcomings. Would you like me to tell you about them?"

Ben blinked and opened his mouth in surprise, then noticed over her shoulder that Simmons was watching him with a slight smile. He consciously dialed down his ego. "Of course, Victoria. I'm always looking for ways to make progress."

"Oh, good." For the next five minutes, she explained everything from a suboptimal choice of prior probabilities to grammar and punctuation errors. When she finished, she asked, "Do you see how you could have improved this?"

"Yes, I do, Victoria," Ben said, trying to recover from the intellectual beating he had just taken. "I hope you aren't disappointed in me, considering I'm not the mathematician you are. Also, there were many demands on my time when I wrote that." He had to admit to himself that he was heartily sick of school and just going for "good enough" on the project at that point in his Academy tenure. He never dreamed it could come back to bite him with an attractive woman.

"I'm not disappointed." She nodded. "Very few people are as intelligent as I am. I hope you are not sad. Sometimes, it is hard for me to tell."

"On the contrary." He smiled warmly. "You can never go wrong being honest with me."

"Oh, good. In that case, I like you. Very much."

"Despite my inferior scholarship compared to you?" Ben teased with a smile.

"I am not bothered by that. You are very handsome and a hero." She nodded.

"Oh, ah, thank you," Ben blushed and stammered. "I'm not a hero."

"I do not understand." Victoria's smile disappeared. "You received the Coast Guard Commendation Medal for saving three lives last year, and you just arrested a dangerous criminal."

Ben had started stammering again when he saw Simmons over Victoria's shoulder, giving a thumb's up and mouthing silently, "Take the win."

"No, Victoria, it's my mistake. I just never thought of myself as a hero."

"Well, you are." Her subtle smile returned. "Will you tell me about your life as a Coast Guard officer, please? All I know is what I could read in the official records."

"Certainly. Is there any place, in particular, you would like me to begin?"

"Yes. Please tell me the story of how you saved the mother and her two children. It was noted in your citation for the Coast Guard Commendation Medal."

"How do you know about that?"

"When Peter learned he would be working with *Kauai*, he was curious about the officers in command and asked me to pull your records."

Ben glanced at Simmons with a raised eyebrow. "That explains some things." After receiving a wry smile and shrug in return, he turned back to Victoria. "It was a matter of being in the right place and time, I guess. I was driving down from Virginia to my new job on *Kauai*, and the weather was pretty bad with icy roads. A jerk in a pickup truck nearly ran me off the road when he passed me and did run that family off. The woman lost control and punched through a guardrail right in front of me. You should have seen it—their minivan was hanging half off the embankment with a sheer forty-foot drop. I came up and stood on the rear bumper to keep it from going over until help could get there. It was freezing cold, and the emergency services were two-blocked with calls."

"Sorry to interrupt, Benjamin, but what does 'two-blocked' mean?"

"Oops. Sorry about the jargon. It means they were super busy. It would have been more than an hour before they could get to us. I was pretty worried because the lady and one child were unconscious, and there was a real danger of hypothermia for everyone. Fortunately, some guys pulled up to help, and we were able to get them all out and to the hospital ourselves."

Victoria flashed the most alluring smile Ben had ever seen and said, "There must be more to it than that, Benjamin."

Ben shifted nervously and said, "I did have to enter the vehicle to pull them out."

"You climbed into a wrecked vehicle hanging over a cliff to save people you did not even know? Why would you do that?"

"It was a calculated risk. With the other three guys hanging on the back, there was more than enough weight to balance mine when I went inside. Besides, I was talking to the little girl inside the whole time, and I couldn't leave her and her family to freeze to death...or worse."

"That was a courageous thing to do, Benjamin. Does it make you uncomfortable to talk about it?"

Ben smiled back. "Normally, it would. But it seems OK when I'm talking about it with you."

"Oh, good! Please tell me more about your life."

"You might find it boring from here—you've just heard my most exciting story."

"No, no, no. What you do is so different from everyone else, and everything about your work is new and interesting to me. Please continue."

Ben plunged into a lively discussion, answering detailed questions for the better part of an hour. Although he enjoyed himself in the conversation with the beautiful, attentive analyst, the effort of ensuring everything he said was logically consistent and idiom-free was more fatiguing than he realized. Eventually, even Victoria noticed Ben was flagging.

"You look exhausted, Benjamin. I am tired too. I think it is time we went to bed."

"What?" Ben sputtered, eyes wide. Victoria pulled back in alarm at Ben's apparent shock.

"You're right, Victoria," Simmons intervened with a grin. "Why don't we head to our rooms, and we'll pick it up again in the morning."

Nice going, dumbass! Ben thought tiredly. *You've managed to scare off the nicest girl you've ever met. Did you really think she would invite you into the sack after a couple of hours of conversation?*

Steve stood up and shuffled to the door, with Frankle and Bell close behind. Victoria stood up and checked the monitor for the model's progress. Then she walked over and hugged Ben, which he happily returned in kind.

"I am glad we had time together, Benjamin." She smiled with a warmth that made Ben's heart jump again. "Good night."

Ben stared briefly at the closed door and turned to Simmons. "Holy shit, Doc! I did not see *that* coming."

Simmons patted the young man on the shoulder. "A sudden bold and unexpected question doth many times surprise a man and lay him open."

Ben tilted his head. "Doc, I can't even guess where that bit of poetry came from."

Simmons smiled. "Not poetry, Francis Bacon. You know, you're alright, coastguardsman. Get some sleep. We roll at dawn!"

U.S. Route 1, twelve miles west of Marathon, Florida 06:47 EST, 18 January

Ben

Ben and Simmons were en route to their first investigation scene, the former driving while the latter confirmed overwatch with *Kauai* on Simmons's radio. The image parsing runs had yielded no definitive insights. As Simmons suspected, success in finding their lost warhead would come down to close inspection on the ground in the locations rated the most probable.

Steve and Victoria had packed up quickly, and the goodbyes were brief and heartfelt. It delighted Ben to find Victoria even more beautiful in the morning.

"Will you come and visit me in Bethesda?" she said to Ben as he placed her case in the car.

"Yes, I'd like that very much. But it might be some time. I can't leave the area while *Kauai* is operational or in readiness, you understand."

"Yes, I know," she said wistfully, and then kissed him on the cheek before getting in the car and driving off. Frankle and Bell followed a minute later—with no word on the escaped assassin or any of her associates, Simmons took no chances. They would follow at a discreet distance to Homestead, where the technician and analyst would board an agency plane for the flight to Montgomery County Airpark in Gaithersburg, Maryland, and home. The two agents would then hit their search areas on the return trip.

Observing his young companion lost in thought as they drove to their first destination, Simmons asked, "She's quite a girl, isn't she?"

"Victoria? Yes, I have to say, I've never met anyone like her. Is she, I mean, are she and Steve?" He paused.

"No, Steve has a partner, and even if he didn't, he'd probably be more interested in you than her."

"Oh. So, she's unattached?"

"Correct. As you might expect, a relationship with someone like her is an enormous challenge. She's had a few, and none ended well." Simmons gazed hard at him. "Hmmm, I feel compelled at this point to ask you your intentions."

"Yeah, right."

"No, I am totally serious here."

Ben glanced over, one eyebrow raised over the sunglasses. "You're totally serious, eh? What are you, her father?"

"*In loco parentis*. Just think of me as a kind of big brother with a loaded Uzi."

"You've got to be kidding. She is an adult, after all."

"Yes, but a very unusual adult. She struggles to read people and can't pick up on malicious intent. Hence, she's the perfect mark for whatever slick operator comes along. She's also a beautiful young woman with access to highly classified stuff. It means she needs looking after."

"Excuse me for saying so, but isn't 'slick operator' part of your job description? How did someone like this fall under your protection? You don't seem the type."

"Fair question." Simmons nodded. "I met her when she was a very precocious thirteen-year-old. She was the younger sister of my fiancée. Their parents were dead, and Julie, my fiancée, was raising her. Her condition was just starting to be noticeable then, and she was in an accelerated special needs program."

"Was? You two break up?"

"No, unfortunately, she died just before we were to be married."

"Oh, I'm sorry."

"Yeah, me too. Anyway, I regarded Victoria as my little sister by then. So, I took care of her until she graduated, and when I went with the agency, I snagged an analyst position for her. She's been invaluable with analysis work across the board. So, there's plenty of us watching after her now, but I'm the principal."

"I see. So, you and your buddies will beat me up and send me to Guantanamo if I have the nerve to call on her?"

"If you intend to get in a quick lay and hit the road, you can depend on the beat down. I don't think you'd do anything that low, but I've only known you a couple of days."

"I don't know how to respond to that."

"Right. Unlike her, I'm super good at reading people. I wouldn't be alive now if I weren't. I can see you are falling for her, and that's not surprising, given her looks and how disarming her personality is. In case you're wondering, her attraction to you is not an act—she's incapable of guile. To her, you are a handsome, intelligent, and kindly hero around her age, someone she would naturally be drawn to. If she comes to believe you reciprocate that admiration, she *will* fall for you. Hard."

"That'd be bad because...?" Ben was getting a little annoyed at the implied slight of his character.

"Because being with her takes work. How did you feel last night, just talking to her?"

"It was nice. At first, I felt like I did in the speech lab when I was trying to learn German in high school, but I was getting in the rhythm toward the end. This morning, it felt natural, not a big lift."

"Yet, it was a lift."

"What do you want from me, Doc? I like her, and I want to get to know her. She's different, I get that, and the usual rules don't apply. I've had relationships before, and the ones where I got dumped were because

I couldn't read the code. Now, here's a wonderful woman who is unencrypted. I want to try that. How do I avoid an 'extraordinary rendition'?"

Simmons chuckled. "That's a good one. Hey, from what I've seen, you're one of the good guys. The quality of your associates and their high regard for you do you credit. My belief that your near-pathological honesty would make you a failure in my line of work strengthens that assessment. I believe you'd be great for each other. But she is neuro-diverse. She is now what she will be forever—she won't be 'getting better.' So, while you discover whether that's what *you* want, and what you want *is* important, I just want you to be careful with her. Because if she develops a strong attachment and you end up dumping her, it'll be traumatic. All finer feelings aside, it'll disable her for quite a while, and our team can ill-afford that these days. What I ask is, to use your term, be unencrypted—explain the process and don't 'woo' her until you're sure she's the one."

"OK, I get it. You've got my word that I'll take it slow. I won't have much opportunity before this PB tour is over, anyway."

Simmons nodded. "Time and distance can work for you. Email her. None of us use social media for obvious reasons, and she relishes getting personal messages."

Ben smiled. "Doc, I can't tell if I'm being encouraged or discouraged here."

"You two together would be a great thing. You two passing in the night would be status quo—not great, but

OK. You two breaking up is a tragedy to be avoided. That clear enough?"

"Crystal. It looks like we're coming up on the exit."

"Right." Simmons pulled out his radio. "X-ray One Delta, Uniform Two India. Over."

"Uniform Two India, X-ray One Delta, go ahead," Deffler's voice replied.

"X-ray One Delta, arriving at the first site now. Over."

"Two India, roger, completed a perimeter sweep with negative contacts. Over."

"One Delta, roger, please assume overwatch, will advise when we're complete. Over."

"Two India, WILCO. Out."

Simmons placed the radio back in his pocket and glanced at his laptop. "OK, there's a place to park about a half-mile down. The anchorage you ID'd is a quarter-mile from there."

"Roger that." Ben kept the car on the hard-packed sand path. A minute later, he sighted the clearing and pulled the car over to park.

Simmons looked at the laptop and said, "OK, there are a few spots we need to check out, but a general sweep of about two-hundred-fifty yards north and south of the potential anchorage." He closed the laptop and climbed out. He grabbed a long cloth bag out of the trunk and followed Ben through a gap in the foliage to the long, vacant beach.

The two men started at the south end, spread out about five yards, and strolled northward, turning over any driftwood they found to see if the top weathering was as expected. Simmons took a four-foot-long sensor pole out of the bag every twenty yards, drove it about six inches into the sand, and punched some buttons on a touchscreen on the side of the box atop the pole. When they reached the northern extent of the beach adjoining the anchorage, Simmons sat down on a larger log and pulled two Gatorades out of a cooler in the bag. "Have a seat for a few minutes." He handed a bottle to Ben.

"Really?" Ben was grateful for the cold drink. Even in the relatively mild temperatures of mid-morning, the sun and long trudge through the soft sand had left him rather hot and thirsty.

"Yup, take a load off. I need it quiet while we take the measurement."

Ben sat down while Simmons clicked some buttons on the laptop. Within a few minutes, he heard the dreaded buzzing heralding the inevitable mosquito swarm and began brushing at his ears quietly. After a few more minutes, Simmons clicked some more keys, then said, "OK, that's it."

"What's the purpose of that?"

"The poles have audio sensors, laser seismometers, and GPS. We added pingers to our nukes so we could find them quickly in a Broken Arrow scenario. There's no reason to believe the Russians wouldn't do that too. If anything, they're more accident-prone than we are, as the current situation proves. We record a few minutes of data stream pairs from the sensors in each place. I'll upload those to the cloud now, and Victoria can pull them when she gets back. If she finds any uncorrelated tremors, particularly rhythmic ones, they may be from a nearby audio homing signal. The difference in time between arriving surface vibrations and audio can tell us the source's distance to each sensor pole. We then use True Range Multilateration of multiple sensors to discover the source's estimated location."

"Oh, I see." Ben had learned about True Range Multilateration—using distance to multiple fixed points to fix a position—in his coastal navigation classes at the academy. "I'm glad you're not just dragging me around kicking crabs."

"Oh, come on, friend. I told you we would not see anything the Puma's can't. Let's get going. We've got three more beaches to visit. Oh, and there's a can of DEET spray in the bag."

Ben gratefully pulled it out and started spraying. "You guys carry bug spray with you?"

"Don't leave home without it. You can't be slapping and scratching when you're staking out bad guys." He continued typing, packaging, and uploading the data to the unseen high-altitude UAV, which passed it at a reduced rate into the DIA "cloud" via SATCOM. Finally, he closed his laptop and stood up. The two men retraced their steps, picking up the sensor probes on the way. By the time they returned to the car, more than an hour had passed since they arrived.

10

Reconnaissance—Land

USCG Cutter *Kauai*, Gulf of Mexico, twenty nautical miles northeast of Key West, Florida
07:28 EST, 18 January

Sam

With *Kauai* down one of her OODs, Sam took the 0400–0800 Morning Watch to give the other duty standers a break. Although it meant rousting up about a quarter past three in the morning, the 'Four-to-Eight' was Sam's favorite. He never tired of seeing the sunrise at sea. He couldn't put his finger on exactly why, but the gradual lightening of the eastern horizon and the first stab of bright fire were rejuvenating, regardless of how tired he was. It also provided the opportunity to practice the ancient art of celestial navigation in the pre-dawn twilight. He loved the challenge of measuring the altitude of several stars using his treasured Cooke Kingston sextant Bobby Moore had given him as an

OCS graduation gift. After his relief, he planned to break out the nautical almanac and trig tables to "reduce" the star sights he recorded to a celestial "fix" he could compare to the GPS readings. Although unneeded in the GPS age, the activity provided Sam with a stimulating connection to the past.

Around 07:30, Deffler appeared on the Bridge and walked over to Sam. After saluting, he said, "You wanted to see me, Captain?"

Sam returned the salute. "Yes, Fritz. I heard from Mr. Wyporek that he and Dr. Simmons, and another team of agents, will do land surveys in the Keys today. Can both birds be in the air with Dr. Simmons ashore?"

"Yes, sir." Deffler nodded. "I can bring Mike Morgan up here to help monitor after the second launch. We'll need to stagger the launches by at least thirty minutes for setup and to avoid a crunch at the end."

"That would work out pretty well. The teams' work start times are about three hours apart, and it'll be standard overwatch flights for both."

"Good to go, sir. When do you want us airborne?"

"Plan on a 08:30 launch for the first bird. Work out a sortie plan with Hopkins—she has the survey schedule—but get up with comms with the land teams to confirm around 08:00 that it's still a go."

"Yes, sir." The airman smiled.

Sam noted the spring in the tall airman's step and voice. "You're pretty chipper for someone on his fourth day of patrol boat austerity."

"Like I said, sir." Deffler held up both hands and, looking at one, said, "Back home, I have snow and cold."

Holding up the other, he continued, "Here, I've got sun, warmth, excellent food, and great company. I can hack sea showers for that any day of the week."

"Great company? Anyone in particular?"

"Um..." The petty officer looked down at his feet.

"Ah, I see. Disregard the question," Sam said, thinking *I need to keep an eye on my OS1—good for her!* "OK, let me know if you run into any problems."

"Will do, sir." Deffler saluted.

Watching him go, Sam noted Lee's arrival and her preparations to relieve him as OOD at 07:45. After a few minutes of very diligent effort—she was relieving her CO, after all—she offered relief to Sam, who accepted with a smile and returned her salute. He had to admit he was starving, and he knew Hebert stood by to toss on a Western Omelet for him. His thoughts moved inward as he stepped off the sunlit Bridge to head below for his meal.

Although he only decided last night, Sam grew increasingly uncertain about the mission on which he had signed up his crew. He then chided himself for his irrationality. The discovery of the smuggling enterprise had drawn in a host of agents, and that was a vast pool of resources available for surveillance and backup. Yet, this advantage could be lost by the reckless approaches the DIA agent seemed inclined to take. Bobby Moore had told him many sanitized accounts of being dropped in the middle of a shit storm by an eager-beaver intel weenie back in his days on the teams. Simmons fit the general description, except he seemed to drop himself into a shit storm rather than send others to get chewed up. Sam didn't care that much about the man's safety. He did, after all, pick Sam's sorest spot to hit. What worried him was his influence on Ben.

He had no doubts about Ben's courage or tactical skills. What troubled him was the young man's lack of experience with this sort of operation. Hoppy had nailed it, as usual, "*you aren't trained for this.*" Anyway, not in the soft skills of situational awareness or, more importantly, recognizing when matters were getting out of hand and taking a stand. Particularly with Simmons. Sam shook his head to clear these evil thoughts. The comforting routine of the cutter underway helped, but did not vanquish the lingering undercurrent of worry he felt for his young friend and protégé. *A couple more days, then we'll be done*, he thought. By then, someone in authority would wake up to this nonsense, and they could return to their regular job.

U.S. Route 1, near Resolution Key, Florida
14:28 EST, 18 January

Frankle

Frankle and Bell had seen the analyst team safely to Homestead Air Reserve Base south of Miami and onboard an agency plane for the flight back to Maryland. After watching the plane takeoff and climb out, the two agents grabbed a quick bite at a local Burger King and then headed down toward their first survey point of Resolution Key. Their casual clothes and

National Marine Fishery Service badges and hats would offer cover for their activities in the survey areas. These would come in handy if they ran into tourists or the elderly beachcomber Simmons encountered during his earlier visit.

Frankle loved being in the field, especially when the assignment was within the United States. Here, he did not have to worry constantly about running afoul of foreign law enforcement or counterintelligence. In his late fifties, he was pushing on the edge of retirement, at least from field ops. Even he had to agree it might be time to size up a less "kinetic" assignment. Not today, though. He was in the field with a partner he liked and trusted.

Bell was fifteen years younger than his partner, an able performer, and a very cool customer. He was not a college graduate, unusual for a DIA man. Bell was a good athlete but didn't have enough talent to draw a sports scholarship and wasn't interested enough in academics to compete there. He found his stride in three enlistments in the Marines, the last ending as a Team Leader in the 2nd Recon. After several successful joint missions during Southwest Asia deployments, his tactics and intel talents were well-known enough to draw agency recruiters. Bell took the jump to the better-paying but more hazardous career as a DIA field agent.

Bell was an enigma to his contemporaries. He was more comfortable listening than jumping in on office discussions on sports and entertainment and rarely indulged in the usual banter when in the field. Although valued for his professional skills, he ran through several partners who could not get on with such a reticent wingman. When Frankle's name came up for a partner, the word around the team was "an afternoon with Lashon Bell is like an afternoon alone."

Frankle enjoyed having younger partners, both because he liked their relatively unjaded outlook compared to his contemporaries, and he relished the role of mentor. Several junior agents, including Simmons, had matured under his tutelage and went on to success in the agency. Frankle had a knack for finding common ground with his charges, and Bell was no exception. A former Marine himself, Frankle had a ready lexicon and "carousing protocol." He used these to fix a bond with the younger man, and they soon formed a solid and enduring partnership founded on mutual respect and complementary skill sets.

As suited both men, Bell drove while Frankle navigated and kept the conversation going. Both felt relief the analysis team had departed, if only because it allowed them to shift from defense to offense. They each had affection for Victoria, but neither thought it a good idea to bring her into the field. It was another point of dispute between Frankle and Simmons on this op.

The fact was, Frankle thought his former mentee had lost a step with this idea of recovering a lost nuke. The veteran agent wondered how Simmons convinced their superiors to go in as deep as they had. He saw nothing conclusive in any of the evidence the junior agent presented. *Well, it's above my paygrade*, Frankle thought. *But at least it's drawn out the bad guys.* If nothing else, this mission had uncovered a major U.S. smuggling axis for the association known as the 252s. They weren't the only TCO, but its nameless, ruthless pervasiveness in Europe and South America put it in a class by itself. *We should be running down leads and kicking in doors, rather than pounding stakes into a beach hoping to hear Russian beepers,* he concluded to himself.

He looked at his partner. He suspected Bell thought the same, but twelve years as a Marine Recon Specialist does not leave one questioning or bitching about lawful orders. Frankle had learned before you couldn't wind Bell up—he'd just draw up in silence like a stolid turtle and await the storm's passing. Finally, he broke the silence. "About two miles to go. Keep an eye out on the right. It's not well-marked, apparently."

"Roger that."

"What did you think about our new Coast Guard friend?"

"Young and green, but I get a good vibe from him. I think he'll be one of the better ones if Pete doesn't get him killed."

"Better one what?" Frankle was glad this line of questioning had connected.

"Officer. Most of them aren't worth a shit before they make O-3, some even then. This guy thinks, and he listens. He also has balls—you saw his file, right? But he doesn't let them overrule his head. I'd work with him once he got over being green."

"Yeah, kids today, whattaya gonna do, eh?"

Bell glanced over and gave a rare hint of a smile. "He'd make an excellent candidate for your next partner."

"Two things wrong with that, partner." Frankle smiled back. "First, I'm not searching for a new wingman. Second, it will be a few more years before he works through his obligated service and gets into the itchy feet stage. By then, I'll be sitting in my cabin down on the Santee, drinkin' beer, shootin' ducks, and waiting for that pension check from Uncle each and every month."

"That'll be the day. OK, here's the turnoff."

He slowed for the turnoff, and Frankle turned away with a slight smile and radioed, "X-ray One Delta, Foxtrot Six Echo. Over."

"Foxtrot Six Echo, X-ray One Delta, go ahead. Over," Morgan's voice replied. He had relieved Deffler of communications.

"One Delta, Six Echo, arriving on-scene area one, request status. Over."

"Six Echo, One Delta, roger, overflight complete. One low-risk contact in sight, stationary on the island's northern tip. No other activity. Over."

"One Delta, Six Echo, roger, maintain overwatch. Over."

"Six Echo, roger out."

Frankle secured the radio in his pocket and turned to Bell. "Sounds like the old geezer Pete ran into is still hanging around. Just for grins, let's keep the pistols in the sensor bag."

"Roger that."

"OK, let's follow the trail. It leads through the middle to a spit on the northern tip. That's where we'll take the readings."

"Copy." Bell concentrated on keeping the car on the trail and clear of the trees. "Maybe you and the old geezer can swap Viagra tips while we're waiting."

"Hey, that's hilarious, junior. You're getting mighty smartassy to the guy who signs your evaluation!"

"I like to live dangerously."

Bell pulled the car over a quarter-mile south of the shack. The old gentleman sat in his chair, fishing, and turned when the agents stepped out of the car. Shading his eyes, he watched until they planted the first sensor stake, after which he got up and went inside the shack.

"What's got into him?" Bell asked while they paced out the distance for the next sensor insert.

"Probably hiding his catch. We are NMFS agents, you know."

"Oh, right, like we're on the lookout for beach poachers." Bell shook his head.

Frankle smiled. "Hey, he's Canadian. He doesn't know any better. Maybe he thinks he'll have to pay us off. Suits me. I'm not interested in a conversation." He glanced at his partner. "Even if it means I miss some Viagra tips."

Bell grinned as he drove in another sensor stake and flipped on the switch. The process continued until all twelve sensors were in place. While the two agents waited for enough time to pass, Frankle's cell phone buzzed with an incoming text message. He put on his reading glasses to read the message, and as he read, his eyebrows raised appreciatively.

"Well?" Bell said somewhat impatiently after several seconds. Frankle didn't reply; he just handed him the phone with a smile.

"Hot Damn!" the younger agent continued in a whisper, handing Frankle back his phone.

"Yep, something to look forward to." He glanced at his watch. "OK, that's long enough. Let's go." After uploading the sensor data collected, he turned and glanced toward the shack while Bell moved forward on the sensor line. Frankle wondered if he shouldn't walk over and ask a question or two as a genuine NMFS agent might. It was a passing thought. He turned to follow the other agent as he gathered the sensors and moved to the car.

Lantern Key, Florida
15:27 EST, 18 January

Ben

Ben had just parked the car, and they were both stepping out on their final survey run when Simmons's phone gave an incoming IM tone. He read the message and smiled at Ben. "Good news! It seems like they have a strong lead on our evil lady villain." He paused and glanced up at Ben. "I'm allowed to use such terms for *her*, right?" Receiving a "Give me a break!" look in return, he continued. "It seems 'other technical means'—you can read that as the NSA—have localized her on Little Pine Key. I imagine one of her flying monkeys forgot to turn off his cell phone. Our third team is on the way to set up surveillance. Frankle and Bell will head over as soon as they wrap up their last beach. When Team Three gets eyes on, they'll call the Justice folks in to keep it legit and disengage once they are relieved."

"What about us?" Ben asked hopefully. The fact was, their activities that day had left him very bored.

"Sorry, young padawan. It's heads down on data and charts for the likes of us tonight. Someone has to stay on the mission. Besides, as my friend Matt Kemper would say, 'you couldn't swing a dead cat down there without hitting a Fed.' Soon they'd be asking who you are and why you're there."

"Oh, I guess you're right," Ben said with obvious disappointment.

"Buck up, friend! While they're tangling with Eurothugs, we could save the world! 'And gentlemen in England, now a-bed, shall think themselves accurs'd, they were not here, and hold their manhoods cheap, whiles any speaks, that fought with us upon Saint Crispin's day!'"

"Now, that's from Shakespeare's *Henry V.* I know that much," Ben said with resignation.

"I should hope so. Once more unto the beach, dear friend, and then we can go for a beer."

USCG Cutter *Kauai*, Gulf of Mexico, twenty-one nautical miles northeast of Key West, Florida 19:56 EST, 18 January

Hopkins

Hopkins came off the 16:00–20:00 OOD watch and swung by the mess deck for soda and chips from the community snack storage. She was pleasantly surprised to see Deffler with a tub of parts she presumed were UAV components. He stood and smiled on seeing her, and she decided to sit with him. Hopkins had grown to like the tall flier over the few days they had worked together. She admired his quiet professionalism and intelligence and enjoyed his sense of humor. And he was damned good-looking.

"Mind if I join you?" she asked, pouring a cup of coffee instead of soda.

"Please do," He gestured at the seat across the table.

"I won't interfere?"

"No, no. Routine checks for water intrusion. I take from Pile A," He selected a small part. "Inspect for any signs of water, plug it in the tester, all green, good to go, and deposit in Pile B."

"I thought you said they're water-sealed."

"I did indeed, but water always finds a way, particularly when it's especially salty and going after airplanes produced by the low bidder, we're deliberately crashing into the water. No worries here, just preventive maintenance."

"Hmm."

"Can I ask you a question?" Deffler inquired after a minute of silence and two more completed components.

"Sure."

"Can I help you with something? It seems like you've got the burden, as my old grandpa used to say."

"Yeah, I do, actually. It's this mission. Is it me, or is the world coming unglued?"

Deffler replaced the part he had just picked up on the "to do" pile and sat back. "What do you mean?"

Hopkins took a sip of coffee, then set down the cup. She started small, carefully weighing what she could say in the openness of the mess deck. "What's your read on Simmons?"

"He's a force of nature." Deffler smiled. "I only know him from a brief meet and then working alongside him here. It's like working with the eggheads from the R and D Center, but the secret agent shit brings in a whole 'nother dimension. He seems to know his stuff, but he's deep and dark. What of it?"

"Do you trust him? I mean, would you trust him with your life?"

"You mean, would I be worried he'd have my back if the shit hit the fan? Honestly, I'd be OK with him. I talked with one of his tech buddies while we were waiting around at Homestead, and he implied the guy is a James Bond-type legend. He's really put a twist on the other side's ops. And he's all about putting as wicked bad a twist on them as humanly possible. He doesn't worry about getting promoted or anything like that."

Hopkins relaxed a little. "So, you feel safe with him?"

"Oh, hell no, I didn't say that." He shook his head. "He *is* the go-to guy when the shit hits the fan. The problem is, if he can't find a handy shit-fan collision, he'll do his best to create one." When Hopkins's eyes widened, he quickly added, "Whoa, what's with this? He's gone, right?"

"Yes, but he's got the XO with him."

"It seems to me the XO's got a good head on his shoulders. He'll be OK. I don't know what's going on here, but I don't think the bad guys are interested in Doc's science project. They're trying to get their boat back. Hey, I can see the CO and XO are pretty good guys, but they're still officers. What's worth getting so worked up about?"

Hopkins's eyes narrowed, and she sat back. "Fritz, you wouldn't be asking that question if you'd been here a year ago when they came in to replace the old command."

Deffler could tell from the body language and tone he had stepped into it, but he pushed forward. "I've heard a few people mention problems with the last CO, but nothing specific. Feel like telling me about it?"

Hopkins felt the anger that had cropped up subsiding. *How could he know? Looking at us today, you could not believe it.* "Okay, you found a sore spot. Sorry about that. No need to unload this on you." Deffler reached across the table and touched her hand. Oddly enough, she didn't flinch or pull away.

"No shit. If you don't mind telling me, I'd like to hear the story."

"There's a short but very exciting story behind it. Have you ever had a bad CO, a really bad one?"

"I've had some I didn't care for, but I wouldn't consider them as 'bad.' Seen a few bad officers in my time, but they usually get sorted out or shit-canned by the end of their first tour. I can't imagine one of them making it to Commander, much less CO of an air station."

Hopkins nodded. "Yeah, I couldn't imagine it either. Like you, I've seen good and bad officers, but the COs are a cut above. When I got here eighteen months ago, the CO had been for here six. Fritz, I've never seen a boat as messed up as this one. People were just plain *scared.* The CO had two settings—uptight and detonate. If he was around, you would get screamed at or talked down to."

"What about the XO or the chief? I can't figure Drake putting up with that."

"Chief Drake wasn't here yet. The chief that was here was 'retired on active duty.' He just did what he needed to avoid getting chewed up. The XO? He was broken by then. He was OK before, not a hard-charger, but did the job. He was as scared as the rest of us, trying to get by until he completed his tour. The CO was even harder on him."

Deffler rolled his eyes. "I don't get guys like that. I heard they relieved him. What did him in?"

Hopkins closed her eyes briefly as she remembered the day. "It was right after Chief Drake got here. We were working on that last big Alien Migrant

Interdiction Operation from Cuba. Ever done an AMIO patrol?" Deffler shook his head, and she continued. "They're heartbreakers at the best of times, but this one was terrible. We were headed to Bahia de Cabañas with a couple of dozen migrants for repatriation when something stirred them up. The ICE guy and translator were handling it, but the CO decided to rip them a new one in front of the prisoners. That kicked off a no-shit riot. When we finally got things under control, we had to MEDEVAC the XO and BM1, and two of the Cubans were dead."

Deffler gaped in astonishment. "My God, 'we got things under control'? What did you do?"

"Let's just say some creative, complex rudder maneuvers on my part, combined with a fire hose team led by Chief Drake, did the trick and leave it there. After that, we couldn't continue the mission, so the Command and Control cutter took off the migrants, and we headed back to Miami. The Sector Commander and the Coast Guard Investigative Service were waiting at the dock for us, and they took the CO off as soon as we moored. They brought in a squad of agents who put everyone on board through a hard-core interrogation. At least the CO was gone. So was the XO. I'm sorry he got hurt, but his leaving was for the best.

"So, there we were, low as you get, wondering what's next. I was in the deepest funk I can ever remember, but Chief held us together. Lieutenant Powell showed up the next day, took command, and started turning things around. A couple of weeks later, Mr. Wyporek arrived and dropped right in like an old hand. I've never seen anything like it. I don't know how they did it, but they got rid of the loafers and whiners. They brought in John, Shelley, and Lope, and we're back in the game and far better than before, even considering the CO."

"That's quite a story." Deffler smiled. "I see why you like them. You have an impressive team here, and if they made it happen, they deserve a lot of credit. But I'm still not getting why you're so wound up about Wyporek. Surely, he can handle a simple shore detail."

"Look, you said yourself that Simmons is a loose cannon. He says he has backup, but I wouldn't trust him as far as I can throw him. I see him running straight into a buzzsaw without a care in the world, and guess what? I couldn't give a damn. My problem is that my XO, who I happen to think is one of the best men I've ever known, has a big blind spot when he thinks duty calls. Did you know Simmons almost dragged him into a shootout in Key West?"

"What?"

"Yep, the first hint the XO had that trouble was brewing was when Simmons asked him out-of-the-blue if he could do stunt driving. Next thing he knows, they're speeding through Key West with a carload of armed psychos on their tail. Simmons did have backup. His guys staged a car wreck—no shit, a car wreck, I'm not making this up—to take out the bad guys, but our guy was a sitting duck the whole time. If he'd been chewed up, I'm sure Simmons would have just said '*C'est le Guerre*' and moved on. And yet, when that creep says 'I need a PB expert,' off he goes, with the CO's blessing. Dammit!" She paused when she saw the concerned look on Deffler's face. "Sorry, I'm a little loony when it comes to stuff like this."

"Don't worry about it. I'm glad to take the heat for you. I would be a little careful about going on full afterburner in front of Chief or one of the O's, though." Deffler tilted his head.

"Too late." Hopkins shook her head sadly. "I sort of lit them up during the brief. *Respectfully*, of course."

"Of course." Deffler smiled, relieved the tension in the conversation was subsiding. "I take it from the fact you're here and not locked in the brig means the Old Man has a soft spot for you."

"No. Well, maybe a little, but not like you think. He knows this is déjà vu for me."

"How so?"

"Um, you know I lost my husband, right?"

"Yes, I heard that. I'm very sorry."

"Thanks. the XO reminds me of him, is all."

"Really?" Deffler asked with a sly smile, and his left eyebrow raised.

Hopkins chuckled. "Not like that, you idiot!" Her smile disappeared when she continued. "He charged off on a SAR case he shouldn't have taken and didn't come back."

"He was in the Guard?"

"Yeah, a BM2 coxswain. We were stationed together in Oregon. My younger son Jamie was just a year old. I was thinking hard about getting out, and we were trying to figure out how to swing it financially when it happened. The surf was up, too high, but he went anyway. It took out him and his crew."

"Geez, I'm sorry. It must have been hard."

"It was hell. But the station really helped. We worked around it until my mom got there, and she, the boys, and I have been together since. I'm still mad at him for taking that mission." She brushed away a tear. "And I miss him every day."

"I wish there's something I could say, but I know there isn't." He gave her hand a brief, soft squeeze.

"Thanks. Enough wailing by me. What's your story? I hope I'm not crying on a married man's shoulder here." She had noticed he didn't wear a ring, but operational people seldom did in the field because of the risk of injury.

"Nope. Tried it, but it didn't work out."

"Oh, now I'm sorry. Her fault or yours?"

"I think it's shared between us and the detailer," Deffler replied, referring to the chief petty officer in charge of enlisted assignments at the Coast Guard Personnel Command. "My first tour was at Barbers Point, and I fell for and married a local Hawaiian gal. Any place after Hawaii would have been a step-down, but they sent us to Elizabeth City."

"Ouch," Hopkins imagined the culture shock of moving from Oahu's western shore to rural North Carolina.

"Yeah, we had two little girls by then, and she was missing her family, but at least it wasn't *too* cold in the winter. The next tour did us in, though. I asked for

Barbers Point, St. Petersburg, or Sacramento, and I got, wait for it, Kodiak."

"You're kidding!"

"Nope. I was paying back for that tour in paradise in the detailer's mind. The CO and XO tried to help, but that just made the detailer dig in harder. I get it; everybody's got a sad story. The system would blow up if they got down in the weeds all the time, yadda, yadda. So we went. She did her best, but she just couldn't take it anymore after a year, and neither could I. So, we broke up, and she moved back home to Oahu with the girls, and I stayed on."

"Wow, it's hard enough to be away from my boys for patrols. I can't even think about *living* apart from them."

"Could be worse. I'm still friends with the ex, and she makes sure I get Skype time with the girls every day I'm not deployed. Plus, every visit I have with them is a treasure. Would you like to see them?"

"Heck, ya," Hopkins replied with a smile.

As she looked through his smartphone pictures of the two young girls, clearly Hawaiian, but with some of the angular features of Deffler's face and large blue eyes, Hopkins gushed, "My God, they're beautiful! Oh, I'm so sorry you're apart, Fritz."

"Yeah, hopefully, I can build enough brownie points and get back there. If I work it out right, I can get there on my twilight tour and see them through high school."

"Sometimes, hope is the only strategy you have." Hopkins nodded.

"Don't I know it. So, what's your hopeful strategy?"

Hopkins looked up. "I'm above the cut for chief. I'll have to rotate off the boat to pin it on. My hope is to get a nice quiet sector job in someplace that's not crazy expensive to live in. I love my mom, and she's my hero for taking care of the boys when I'm out, but I need a house with some space, if you know what I mean."

"Yeah, I get it. Sounds like you're not so happy about moving on."

"Believe it or not, I considered turning it down. I really like the crew, and the captain has practically made me an operations officer. Wouldn't happen anywhere else, even as a chief." She looked down and shook her head. "But we need the money, and the captain said staying's not an option."

"I thought he liked you."

"He does. A lot, and that's why he said no way."

Deffler nodded. "Powell is something special. He knows losing you will hurt, no matter who they get in behind you."

"Thanks." She glanced awkwardly at her watch. "It's been real, but I need to do some XO stuff and hit the rack. Anything I can do to help?"

"You already have." He smiled, then looked down. "Nah, just doing a little extra to pass the time. I'll be checking out soon."

"OK, I'll see you in the morning." She gave his hand a quick squeeze back as she got up.

11

Preliminaries

4601 Bryant Ave, Little Pine Key, Florida
20:18 EST, 18 January

Frankle

Frankle and Bell approached the surveillance position occupied by the two agents from Team Three, Gerard and Kelly. The last of the twilight faded an hour ago, and the first quarter moon would soon follow. The Team Two men had parked their vehicle about a quarter-mile away to avoid revealing their presence. They walked carefully through the brush using low-light field goggles, the receding moon and stars providing plenty of illumination for the latest night vision devices. Both teams were equipped with Blue Force Trackers feeding position information for "friendlies" into a heads-up display integrated into their goggle lenses. These made elaborate verbal challenges and countersigns unnecessary. The incoming agents were silent until

Frankle kneeled beside the seated Gerard and took off his goggles.

"Long time, no see, Billy," Frankle whispered. "How come you guys are staking out the rear? Didn't you get here first?"

"True, old man," Gerard replied, drawing a good-natured cuff on the back of his head. "Turns out the Feebs are bringing in their primo breach team from Miami and didn't want us in the way. I can't argue with that, honestly. Those guys trained up together. We stand an excellent chance of crossing wires during the big push if we're mixed in with them. They'll be here in a couple of hours, and then we go live. Plan is to wear 'em down for a few hours to get them punchy, then breach at 05:15."

Frankle gave a non-committal grunt. His experiences working with the FBI had been unsatisfactory. He did not like the rigidity of their tactics. Also, he had never met a situation lead that was not a first-class asshat. The house was a large ranch-style, with a screened porch. A path led from the house to a dock hosting a large speedboat. Like many on the Keys, the house was raised as a hedge against the storm surge accompanying hurricanes. Two sets of stairs led down off the front and back porches. The underside of the house was open except for two bathroom-sized enclosures. "Hmmm. Defensible, but it kinda commits you to a last stand." Frankle returned his view to the house proper and noted some lights, but no sign of movement. "They on to the stakeout, you think?" he asked.

"No question. Haven't seen a sliver of a silhouette since sunset."

Frankle turned his view to the dock and fixed on the RHIB. "That's plenty of boat. What do you think, thirty knots?"

"Forty at least would be my guess."

"The big chief didn't think that is a good egress option?"

"Nope. She's got that covered with a CBP Blackhawk. One door, easy to pick them off coming down. Figures they'll see they're sitting ducks on the run, even if they make it to the boat and either give up or shoot it out."

"Won't work," Bell interjected as he took off his goggles.

"I don't know, partner," Frankle responded. "I'm not the biggest fan of the Bureau, but it sounds reasonable to me."

"They can't cover the back with a helo when there's fog."

Both senior agents turned toward Bell. After a few seconds of astonished silence, Frankle said, "Fog? You've got to be kidding, son. This is the Florida Keys, not Monterey, California."

Bell shook his head in the dark. "Don't you guys check the weather before an op? Stable air mass, warm water, and a weak cold front is moving through around 01:00—no wind, just enough to cool down to the dewpoint. Twenty bucks says that we'll be socked-in by

03:00," he said. "If I were them, I'd wait until I could barely see that dock, then I'd kick off a firefight in front. Or wait until we try to breach and throw us off-stride. Once the rearguard has the DOJ occupied, I think we'll see Valentina squirt out the back with cover fire and haul ass in that boat. She can scoot across Florida Bay and be on the mainland in an hour. With nothing in the air, our chances of running her down or even tracking her to a landing onshore are on the 'none' side of slim-to-none."

"Kind of a long shot, don't you think?" Gerard asked.

"Better than no shot, which is what she'll have trying to plow through the front. Just sayin', we might want to scope out a blocking position on that path from the house."

Frankle considered the possibilities. He knew that, although very rare, fog was not unknown in the Florida Keys, particularly in the winter. He also knew Bell was an old hand at planning ops on unfamiliar ground, and including weather in the planning could be the difference between success and failure. The deciding factor was the man's certainty. He wouldn't have brought it up, much less pushed hard, if he wasn't confident in his prediction. Frankle turned to Gerard. "If he thinks we'll have fog, we'd better plan for it. That's the worst case. It couldn't hurt to set up for it." He handed his partner the low-light camera. "OK, mister science guy, find us a good setup to cover that dock and a covert route."

"On it." Bell took the camera and crept off.

Frankle turned back to Gerard. "Are you sure she's in there? It doesn't figure her going to ground here when she probably could have made it to the mainland in the initial breakout."

"No doubt. We got an excellent shot of her looking out the window, and facial rec kicked back a ninety-seven percent match. But I'm with you. Something's wrong. She's making a lot of mistakes for someone who's supposed to be a shit-hot operator."

Frankle frowned. "Maybe that jolt the Coasties gave her tumbled her gyros a bit. I'll take 'em any way I can get 'em, but we'd better stay sharp and assume they're up to something."

"Like?"

"Like everybody with a federal badge is gathering here. It's the kiddie soccer scenario—everybody runs to the ball. Meanwhile…"

"Yeah, I get what you mean. You want to check with the boss?"

"Can't hurt. At least we see it gets passed to Pete that he's on his own until morning." After a pause, Frankle looked around and continued, "We'll set up a defense in depth. You guys take it close and cover the stairs, and we Marines will dig in by the boat."

"Roger that." Gerard nodded. "What do I tell the Head Fed if she wants to talk to you?"

Frankle snorted. "Tell her I'm out taking a piss or a nap or something. Remind her of my 'advanced age.' Should be enough to convince her to go elsewhere for castle stormers."

Gerard grinned. "Roger that."

Conch Inn, Room 118, Marathon, Florida
20:47 EST, 18 January

Ben

They had ordered dinner via GrubHub to avoid the open exposure in a restaurant. Simmons used a new credit card under one of his aliases, and Ben had the only contact with the delivery driver. The food was decent, Ben was glad not to deal with fast food again, and the beer was excellent. The conversation was light, with Ben sharing details of his upbringing in Northern Illinois, his academy experience, and his first tour on *Dependable*. His efforts to elicit similar information from his DIA companion were politely rebuffed, which did not come as a surprise. He got Simmons to admit the "pretty grad student," for whom he had gained his literary knowledge, and his late fiancée was the same person. However, he cut off further inquiry along that line, and even Ben could see through the agent's carefully preserved bonhomie that her death was still very painful for him.

Simmons wiped his hands after a long pull on his beer and said, "You know, that cooking on *Kauai* spoiled me. You can keep the close quarters and sea showers, but man, take out just won't measure up anymore."

"You can always head to a swanky restaurant and live it up." Ben smiled in return.

"Um, yeah, let me run down the 'list of swankies' in Marathon. Putting aside that we need to reduce public presence to a minimum when we're in the field, any

236

notions you have of DIA agents running around high-class venues in tuxes are in error." He noticed Ben grinning at him. "What?"

"Sorry, trying to picture you stepping out of an Aston Martin in black tie, and someone hands you a martini. Yup, you're right. Does not compute."

Simmons feigned a severely insulted expression. "I take deep umbrage at your implication, sir! I'll have you know that I've masqueraded as some of the finest people in the social register on many occasions!"

"You have my most sincere apologies, your lordship." Ben joined in the game. "I hope this will circumvent the need to demand satisfaction or any other regrettable social rituals."

"Very well." The agent nodded with mock solemnity. "The lack of ready cape-holders compels me to accept your apology, but do not think for a minute you can expect treats like this in the future!" Both shared a hearty laugh, cut short by an incoming call on Simmons's encrypted cell phone. He smiled when he saw the originating number and hit the speaker button before laying it on the table between them. "Hello, Victoria! You're on speaker with Benjamin and me. How was your trip?"

"Hello, Peter and Benjamin. My flight was three hours, twenty-seven minutes..., um, I mean, my trip was fine, thank you, Peter." Her voice dipped slightly at the end. "I have finished processing your surface sensor data. Would you like me to tell you the results?"

"Yes, very much, thank you, Victoria. Can you give us a summary, please?" the agent replied carefully, winking at Ben.

"All sensor arrays showed many transients congruent with natural background vibrations in the area. Three sets showed unusual readings not consistent with the natural phenomena of the area, but none of these were persistent or rhythmic."

"It's OK if you can't answer this, Victoria, but can you speculate on what could've made the transient vibrations?"

"I have put the signatures through a comparative database we have assembled. Some are consistent with metal-on-metal collisions, and others are plastic rubbing on plastic. A few are classified as 'relay closing.' However, our comparative database is sparse because the technology is new. Those classifications, particularly the last one, are low probability matches compared to the others."

"That is very useful information, Victoria. Can you tell me which locations' data included those unusual readings? Also, were the readings stronger in any location compared to others?"

"Yes," the analyst replied with more animation. "Lantern Key, Johnston Key, and Resolution Key all had the unusual readings. Resolution Key was significantly stronger than the others, almost an order of magnitude stronger."

Ben perked up. "Do you think..." He stopped when Simmons raised his hand.

"Victoria, could the presence of the old beachcomber on Resolution account for the high transients you noted?" Simmons asked.

"Yes, Peter. It would suggest a problem with the sensor array had it not read an increase when a human is active in the vicinity."

Simmons nodded. "Yes, I thought as much. I was hoping the stronger signal was not on Resolution—that would have been a 'man bites dog' story."

"Peter, I do not understand why a man would bite a dog or how that is relevant."

"Sorry, Victoria." The agent smiled. "I was using a journalistic aphorism. The point is that a man biting a dog would be a significant news story."

"Oh, yes, I see now. That is clever."

"OK, if there's nothing else to report, I'll let Benjamin say hello."

"No, Peter, nothing else."

Simmons took the phone off the speaker and handed it to Ben. He then retired to another room.

Grateful for the privacy, Ben said, "Hello, Victoria. We are off speaker, and I'm alone here."

"Hello, Benjamin. It is good to hear your voice. I hope you had a pleasant day."

"Far better if I could have spent it with you, but I would say that it's been an enjoyable day." He imagined her smile at the other end. "Peter provided your email address, and I'd like to send you a letter occasionally if that would be OK."

"Yes, I would like that, thank you. I know it will have to wait until you return to your ship, perhaps longer if you have communication restrictions."

It encouraged Ben she knew and understood operational security. One of his earlier relationships had foundered on that very issue. "Yes, or even after we return home when I can access my personal email. I just wanted you to know that I was thinking about you and looking forward to seeing you again."

"Oh, that's very sweet of you. I am also looking forward to your visit. There is much to do and see."

"Yes, I'm sure there is. Victoria, I really like the sound of your voice. I appreciate that Peter had to short-stop you, but would you mind telling me more about your trip and whatever else you would like to share?"

"No, I don't mind at all!" Ben was content to let the conversational roles of the previous night reverse. He enjoyed listening to the plummy sound of her voice and the intricate detail in her language. Ben regretted bringing the session to an end when Simmons returned to the room about ten minutes later and pointed at his watch.

"I'm sorry, Victoria. Peter is reminding me we have more work to do."

"I understand. I enjoyed our conversation and hope we can have another one soon, Benjamin. Goodbye."

"Me too, Victoria. Goodbye." Ben disconnected and handed the phone back to Simmons. "Not complaining here, but I'm surprised you allowed that on a government phone."

"Ah, young padawan, we buy burner phones and use adapters to put the sim cards in our encrypted gear. Now that you're done sweet-talking my little sister, I can switch out the sim." He winked. "It's a practice bordering on paranoid, perhaps over the border.

"I admit to being more than a little disappointed at the results today," he continued. "I was hoping the ground sensors would tell us something more than they did."

"So, what do we do now? *Kauai* heads out for refueling at the end of the day after tomorrow at the latest." He hoped Simmons would tell him of a deadline for ending the ET hunt.

"We hit the imagery tonight for a couple of hours, then head back to Lantern, Johnston, and Resolution tomorrow. We plant and leave the sensors in place for hours instead of minutes this time." He rubbed his temples absentmindedly. "Something will break tomorrow. I can feel it." He moved to hook the laptop up to the room's TV with an HDMI cable. "Ready for some genuine intel work?"

Ben groaned. "Can I have my job application back, please? The IC is not for me."

Simmons chuckled and pulled up the Park Service and UAV composite image files. "Alas, once you have strayed into the Dark Side, forever will it dominate your destiny!"

4601 Bryant Ave, Little Pine Key, Florida
05:12 EST, 19 January

Frankle

Bell was off by half an hour, but the rest of his weather forecast was spot-on. A light mist had crept in about half past midnight, and it had blanketed the entire area within an hour. Frankle could barely make out the few lights showing at the house from his position near the dock. The FBI had formally announced their presence at midnight, with negotiations ongoing since. Government agents closed off any egress, but they lacked any alternative for a clean takedown other than an exposed assault "uphill" on the stairs. Fog prevented any use of helicopters, as Bell predicted. The plan was for a simultaneous push from the front and underside of the house. After breaching through the floor and tossing in flash-bangs, the main assault would push through the front, with sharpshooters clearing the windows and explosive charges on the door. With no hostages to worry about, anybody not lying prone with arms outstretched after entry would draw kill shots. Except for Valentina Petrova. She was a High-Value Target or HVT. Everyone wanted her alive, if practicable.

Although Frankle couldn't see him through the fog and concealment, Bell hunkered down on the left side of the path, deadly still. The Blue Force tracker in his goggles showed Gerard and Kelly closer to the house. Their position covered the back door and stairs. The assault teams were getting into position. Negotiations, if you could call them that, cut off at 05:00. The deal offered was, essentially, surrender or die. Their reply was an Eastern European version of "Screw you!" *So much the better.* Frankle had seen and read enough about the 252s that he had no issue with snuffing out them all.

Frankle shivered. It wasn't cold, but the light chill and the dampness of fog, combined with lying still for an extended period, cut right through him. *Cold in the goddamn Florida Keys—you are getting on, old man!*

"Two minutes, team leads call ready," the Scene Lead called on the tactical net. "Alpha Ready,"; "Bravo Ready,"; "Charlie Ready," replies followed, the last from Gerard up near the house.

"Delta ready," Frankle sent. He shifted in his position and thumbed the selector of his M4 from "safe" to "burst," then gave his Glock a touch check. While the seconds counted down and he stared into the fog, he could see in his mind's eye a dozen other agents tensely shifting, grasping weapons and equipment, coiled to spring.

His headset came alive. "Standby, ten seconds, five seconds, three, two, BRAVO GO." At the last word, a loud boom sounded from the house, and almost simultaneously, his headset shrieked briefly and went silent, and his goggles flashed a blinding light and immediately darkened.

"What the hell?" Frankle said to himself, then keyed the radio. "Any station, Delta, over." No reply—the headset and goggles were dead. He tore them off and tried to blink away the afterimage of the flash. After a few seconds, the sounds of flash-bangs arrived from the direction of the house, followed at once by a continuous overlapping staccato of automatic gunfire. Whatever shit the targets just pulled, the assault teams had recovered quickly and pressed the attack, he thought. His night vision was slowly returning when he heard Bell shout the fallback verbal challenge and receive two streams of shots in return. Frankle aimed in the general direction of the gunfire and fired bursts with his M4, hearing a cry suggesting at least one round had struck home. He stood up and swept his sights, ready to fire again, when a figure flashed past.

He spun around and raised the carbine for another burst when Bell shouted, "Check fire!" The thuds of running feet followed shortly afterward. A second later, a loud crash on the dock, with the yells from Bell and a woman, set Frankle into a run. A few steps later, he could make out two figures struggling on the dock. The larger figure grasped the smaller by the leg with one arm, the other dragging behind while the smaller figure reached forward. Frankle immediately stepped on the smaller figure's hand, drawing a female cry of pain, and kicked away the object he presumed was a handgun. He pressed the muzzle of the M4 into the prone figure's temple and shouted, "Enough!" When she stopped struggling, he continued, "Right hand back!"

"Fuck you!" was the muffled reply.

"Go ahead, give me a reason, bitch!" Frankle spat. "Right hand back! Do it now!"

As her right hand came back, Frankle grabbed her thumb, laid down the M4, and snapped and tightened a handcuff on the woman's right wrist to another yelp of pain. He then seized her left arm, took his foot off her hand, drew the other wrist back, and applied the other handcuff. He reached into his pocket, drew out a syrette, popped the cap, and jammed it into his prisoner's thigh. Within about ten seconds, the woman's body went limp. Frankle checked her pulse and then turned to Bell, gently helping him over onto his back. "Talk to me, partner!" he said, noticing the gunfire from the house had ceased.

"Shit." Bell groaned, gasping for breath while trying feebly to raise his head. "Took one...in the arm...the other in...the vest. Tasting blood...busted rib, lung."

"Okay, Okay. Lay back; I've got you." Frankle grabbed another syrette holding a morphine dose and jammed it into the younger man's unwounded arm. "Just gave you a dose of the good stuff. Hang in there." He pulled out a handkerchief, found and applied direct pressure to the arm wound, feeling Bell tighten in pain at first and then go slack as the morphine took effect. "Billy! You there?"

"Yo!"

"Lashon's hit! Get the medics back here; my comms are down!"

"Shit, Art! Everybody's comms are down! Kelly's running to get someone! I'm coming back. Hold your fire!"

"Come ahead, hurry, I need a hand. Follow the path!" Frankle drew his Glock with his free hand. In the dark and fog, he was taking no risks.

"On the way!" After a few seconds, a figure appeared in the fog.

"Beagle!" Frankle challenged, his Glock at the ready.

"Baron!" came Gerard's reply. Both agents, who had scoffed at spoken passwords in the digital age, gave silent thanks for the resilience of the old habits. Gerard approached and kneeled beside Bell. "How is he?" he asked with deep concern.

"Not good. Besides this, he took one in the chest. Looks like he cracked a rib and punctured a lung. I gave him a shot, so at least he's out of it. I don't want to move him without a stretcher." Frankle nodded toward the woman. "Help me watch that piece of shit. I gave her a thirty-minute amp, but you can never tell with them."

"Damn, you still got it, old man."

"Not hardly. Bell tackled her after getting shot to hell. I just cuffed and scuffed her."

"Okay. Man, this was one shit sandwich. I heard at least two 'Agent Downs' from up front." Gerard continued staring at the woman. "I don't get it. We nailed the only one coming out the rear door, and there's no way in hell anyone else got by us."

"When it gets light, I'll bet we'll find a bolt hole between here and your position. Gotta give 'em credit— that might have worked. If it wasn't for this hardhead." Frankle gazed hard at his stricken partner. "Where the hell is that medic? Billy, run over there and tell them we have an agent down, critical. I don't want to hear that they're up there patching up bad guys. Bring back a litter by yourself if you have to. And tell her nibs we have the HVT. That should produce some attention."

"On it," Gerard jumped up and trotted forward.

After the junior agent disappeared into the dark and fog, Frankle turned back to his friend. "It will be OK. Hang in there, partner." *Goddammit! I AM getting too damn old for this crap!*

12

Realization

Conch Inn, Room 118, Marathon, Florida
06:18 EST, 19 January

Ben

"Holy shit!" Ben bolted awake. Simmons rolled out of his bed with a thud and grabbed for his gun. "Wait, wait, it's OK," Ben blurted.

"Dammit, friend, you'd better find a more peaceful way of rousing yourself!" Simmons exclaimed. "What the hell is going on?"

"I think I may know where it is." Ben opened the laptop on the table. After a brief boot period and logon, he opened two files they were looking at last night. "Something was bothering me, like I was missing something, but I couldn't put my finger on what. I guess I was too tired to think straight. OK, here—Resolution Key, the Park Service comparison set from three months ago." He turned the screen to Simmons.

"OK. Same thing I looked at a dozen times. I don't see anything," Simmons said with irritation.

"Exactly! The dog that didn't bark! Where's the shack?"

Simmons leaned down, and after a second, a broad smile opened on his face. "Where indeed! Well done, Sir! That crafty little bastard was the lookout. I'll bet they found the impact point right off the island. He's keeping watch until things cool down and they can get some heavy recovery stuff in there. Nothing to see here— move along, folks!" He clapped Ben on the back and then turned and grabbed his cell phone.

Ben had folded up the laptop and finished dressing when he noted a concerned expression on Simmons's face. "What's wrong?"

"I can't get Frankle or Bell or anyone on Team Three," Simmons replied with concern. He turned back to his phone. "Hello, Gypsy-1 here. I need Gypsy-2 and Gypsy-3's status now." He covered the microphone and glanced at Ben. "They're pinging them now. Get ready to go—we may have to bolt." Turning back to the phone, he answered, "For how long? OK, OK, pull your heads out of your asses and get everything else moving! Target is Resolution Key—north end of the island. We're on our way, ETA in thirty-five. Right." He punched off the phone and turned back to Ben. "Leave it! They've been down for at least sixty-five minutes, and they can't raise or even ping them. At last comms, they were moving in to assault, and then everything went dark. They've sent a unit down to investigate, but somehow it didn't occur to them to tell the guy the two teams were covering! If they're down, the odds are good the opposition has eyes on us, and they're calling in the heavies. Move!"

Grabbing the weapons bags and leaving the rest, both men darted to the car. With Simmons driving, they sped out of the parking lot onto U.S. 1 westbound, heading for Resolution Key.

****

A minute later, a second car pulled out from across the highway and started following Ben and Simmons. The driver and his companion had taken heed of their predecessors' mistake—they would not show themselves. A tiny tracking transmitter they had attached to the rear bumper earlier that morning allowed them to track the Americans' vehicle while following out of sight in the foggy twilight.

The car's passenger called in to alert the assault team the targets were moving. With luck, they were following the lures to the prepared ambush point. The two men would call in the new position if their destination were elsewhere and keep watch until the assault team arrived.

The coordinated operation to the west had worked perfectly. Dozens of federal agents who could have provided support were now out of play. Simmons was on his own except for his military companion, who was not even special forces, given his grooming. The Organization had a positive lock on the nettlesome agent's position and an overwhelming advantage in

250

force for the first time. Simmons was the prize, perhaps even worth the cost of the shipment lost through his interference.

U.S. Route 1, two miles west of Marathon, Florida
06:26 EST, 19 January

Ben

It was misty on the U.S. 1 bridge with fog in either direction. Ben worried about the impact on air surveillance and surface support if they ran into trouble before it burned off. He pulled out the handheld radio to make contact, hoping the fog was a localized issue today.

"*Kauai*, Shore-One, radio check in the green, over." Ben released the press-to-talk switch. After a brief pause with no response, he tried again. "*Kauai*, Shore-One, radio check in the green, over."

"Shore-One, *Kauai*, read you lima charlie in the green, how me, over?" Bondurant's voice replied.

Ben was relieved their high-altitude UAV still provided a communications relay. "*Kauai*, Shore-One, have you the same. Need to talk to Charlie Oscar in private, please, over."

"Standby One," Bondurant replied. Within a minute, Sam's voice came on the radio.

"Shore-One, *Kauai* Actual, on the headphones with speaker off."

"*Kauai*, Shore-One, we believe we have a lead. We are on U.S. 1, en route to Resolution Key. The target is the shack we saw on the spit on the island's northern tip; estimate possible contact in twenty-five minutes."

"Shore-One, we are about fifteen west right now in moderate fog. We'll make the best low-vis speed toward you, but it will be an hour and a half before we can get to you. Can you hold on making contact until then? Over."

Ben looked over at Simmons, who shook his head. "We can't wait. By now, the other guys may be en route, and we can't allow them to get to that warhead. This is a no-shit national security priority. Tell them to hurry because we're committed."

Ben nodded. "Negative, sir. It's a race between us and the other side. We've lost comms with Simmons's teams about an hour and a half ago, and he's sure the opposition is on to us. We have to beat them to it, over."

After about half a minute, Sam replied, "Shore-One, *Kauai*, roger, proceed at discretion. National Defense ROE now active, acknowledge, over."

Ben noted the stress in Sam's voice, understandable, given he had just approved Ben to use deadly force at discretion. "*Kauai*, Shore-One, acknowledge National Defense ROE, over."

"Shore-One, *Kauai*, maintain contact, if practicable. We will transmit situation reports in the blind every fifteen minutes, starting on the hour. Godspeed Ben, over."

"*Kauai*, Shore-One, roger, thank you, sir, out."

"Just to be clear," Simmons began. "We'll be going in with weapons drawn and rounds in the chamber. We don't want to shoot, but we take him out if it looks like him or us, OK?"

"Yes, Doc," Ben tried to keep his voice even. "That's what National Defense Rules of Engagement means. You'd better be right about this. My CO's and my asses are really hanging out right now."

"Same as all the rest of us, friend."

Ben pressed the point. "Doc, are you sure there's a nuke there?"

"What?" Simmons replied in astonishment.

"Look, the evidence is all circumstantial. There are some fearsome assumptions behind the conclusion there's a loose nuke. What if you're wrong?"

Simmons continued staring ahead and took a deep breath before answering. "OK. Am I one hundred percent sure this is a Broken Arrow? No, obviously not. But it's the best theory I have to explain everything. You need to approach this from a risk management perspective rather than a criminal justice, 'beyond a reasonable doubt' view."

"I don't follow."

"If there's no nuke and we waste our time, what's the harm? Negligible. If there is, and we let the 252s get to it, it'll be a catastrophe."

"And if we get bottled up by the 252s before *Kauai* or your guys show up to support us?"

After a slight pause, Simmons replied, "OK, I guess 'negligible' wasn't the best word to use, but the risk calculus is still the same."

The excitement of his discovery disappeared. Between Sam's response and Simmons's cold reasoning,

Ben felt like he was being carried along by events he was powerless to control. It was the car chase all over again, and he hated it. But after a few more seconds, the rational part of his brain won out, and Ben conceded. "OK, I guess I can see the logic of that point."

"See, good news! Hey, I get this is scary—remember what I told you about fear? This is one of those times when you hang it out there, trust your colleagues, and hope the breaks come your way."

"Right," Ben concluded, staring forward as they drove through the fog.

****

Twenty minutes later, they reached the turnoff of the highway on Resolution Key. Ben's head had been on a swivel throughout the trip, scanning for trailers while Simmons drove. Nothing. He hoped that was a good sign, and they weren't waiting to pounce when they arrived at the shack. Time for one last check-in. "*Kauai*, Shore-One, over."

"Shore-One, *Kauai*, go ahead, over," Sam's voice answered almost at once.

"*Kauai*, Shore-One, turning on to Resolution now. Estimate contact in one-zero minutes, over."

"Copy. We're still in fog here. Our ETA is one hour, fifteen minutes, over."

"Roger that, sir. We'll look forward to seeing you then, over."

"Take care, Ben. Out."

Simmons nodded and said, "Now, what we will do is pull up next to the shed and step out with our guns drawn and held behind us. If he's outside, we'll try to get close enough to keep him from getting inside before we make our move, but if he goes for the door, we jump him. Clear?"

"Clear."

"If he's not outside, we'll just play it on the fly. It will be hard, but don't shoot if you have a choice."

"Thanks, Dad."

"OK, that *was* a little condescending, sorry." Simmons smiled sadly. "Just stay cool and keep your head in the present."

After about six minutes, the car rounded a dense patch of bush and coconut palms. Once clear of the vegetation, the ground formed a natural causeway leading to the spit on the island's northern tip. The fishing shack lay near a copse of palm trees, invisible in the light fog. A minute later, Ben could see the shack a quarter-mile away, the view becoming clearer as they approached. When the car pulled up to the structure, no one was in sight, and the two men quietly got out, drawn pistols held behind them.

"Should we split up and flank him?" Ben whispered as he walked carefully through the soft sand.

Simmons shook his head, whispering back, "Too much chance of getting into each other's line of fire. Let's move about five feet apart and advance in line abreast." Simmons glanced at Ben and received a thumbs-up in return.

As the two rounded the shack, they suddenly faced the old Newfoundlander. All three men stopped in their tracks about twenty feet apart, and Simmons said, "Hello again, friend. We have more questions for you."

After a brief instant, the man dropped the pail and fishing rod he held and bolted toward the door. Ben reacted on instinct, holstering his weapon as he ran in pursuit. "Stop, Federal Officer!" Simmons followed just a step behind.

The squatter was stepping through the door when Ben leaped for a flying tackle and crashed into the man. The two rolled several times past the shack, and Ben's attempt to get his arms around the man drew a blow to his solar plexus that knocked the wind out of him. As he rolled clear and laid gasping for breath, Simmons jumped on the man. Ben watched in complete astonishment as the two men traded blows in rapid succession in a martial arts display that would have put Donnie Yen to shame.

Finally, Simmons got the upper hand and shouted, "Tase him, dammit!"

Ben snapped out of his awed paralysis, quickly drew and activated his taser, and fired it into the squatter's chest. As the man began convulsing, Simmons disengaged and shouted breathlessly, "Cuffs! Cuff him!"

Ben dropped the taser, grabbed a pair of flex cuffs out of his belt pouch, pulled the stunned man's arms behind him, and cinched the loops over both wrists.

"Legs too, then search him carefully," Simmons said, bent over and panting.

Ben took out another pair and attached them below the man's ankles. Then he carried out a laborious search that netted a box cutter, combat knife, and what looked like a penknife. He turned to Simmons and said, "That's it."

Simmons had finished panting and stood upright, glaring at the bound man. "Stand off to my left, pull and charge your sidearm. If he breaks loose, shoot him. Try for a leg if you can."

Ben nodded, eyes wide, took a couple of steps to the side, and drew and charged his Sig pistol. The man on the ground rolled onto his back and then sat upright, his legs to the front. He shook his head briefly, then glanced back and forth between Ben and Simmons, finally settling on the latter.

"CIA?" the man asked.

"*Please.*" Simmons shook his head in disgust. "My compliments, friend. For a minute there, I thought you would get the better of both of us. I don't suppose you'd care to tell us who and what you are."

"As you said—*please.*" The man smiled slightly.

"While you and I trade unenlightening pleasantries, my colleague here will have a look in your little hovel over there. Before that, we need to reach a mutual understanding to behave in a civilized fashion from here on out. I have absolutely no problem ending you, nor doing so in an excruciating and gruesome way. Given that, are there any booby traps waiting for him in there?"

The man smiled. "No, you got the drop on me."

Simmons smiled back, drew and charged his pistol, pointed it at the man, then turned to Ben. "Peek in the door, do not enter. If you see a phone or any other hand-helds within reach, check them for tripwires before picking them up."

"Roger that," Ben said, holstering his pistol. As he walked toward the shack, his fear grew, with his heart pounding, and he started looking down to make sure he wasn't stepping on anything that could maim or kill him. Ben reached the doorway, drew and turned on his flashlight, and began a close examination around the perimeter of the opening. He could hear Simmons and the squatter talking, but couldn't make anything out as he concentrated on his check.

Once the doorway examination was complete, Ben shined the flashlight in the doorway in a systematic search of the floor and walls of the shack. Nothing was visible inside other than a low, bamboo-framed bunk and a small table with a wallet, cellphone, and an opened pack of cigarettes on top. Ben drew and extended his 16-inch expandable baton and poked the cellphone and wallet. No tripwires. He reached in and carefully lifted the phone and then the wallet, then turned and walked back to Simmons and the squatter.

"Lieutenant, I think we have found our target, or at least the caretaker. My money is on there being a nuclear warhead somewhere in the water just north of here, and we can do a grid search once my people show up."

Ben opened his mouth to reply, but remained silent when the cellphone emitted two beeps, three seconds apart.

"Looks like your backup has arrived," the squatter said with a rueful smile.

Ben glanced at Simmons, who shook his head at the squatter and said, "Not us. Are you expecting anyone?"

The man stopped smiling and replied, "No."

Simmons looked over at Ben, who asked, "The 252s?"

Simmons nodded and looked back at the squatter. "You heard of the 252 Syndicate?" After the man nodded grimly, Simmons added, "Well, they are headed straight for us. I presume you'll suffer the same fate as us if they grab you."

"Worse, probably. The signal indicates two vehicles, just clearing the highway," the man replied.

"That gives us about ten minutes. Ben, check on *Kauai*. This group won't be rookies—they'll be combat-ready, probably with armored vehicles."

Ben donned his headset and keyed the radio. "*Kauai*, Shore-One, over."

After about five seconds, Sam's relieved voice replied over the channel, "Shore-One, *Kauai*, read you loud and clear."

Ben moved the selector to the voice-activated position. "*Kauai*, Shore-One, you need to go off-speaker again."

After a few seconds, Sam replied, "Shore-One, *Kauai*, the speaker is off. I'm on the headset."

"*Kauai*, Shore-One, we've made contact and confirmed. We have one in custody, believe he is with

259

the Russians. The bad news is the TCO is headed this way. Two confirmed vehicles, expect hostile action in ten minutes, and Doc tells me this will be their A-Team. They'll have plenty of firepower and armored vehicles."

"Roger Ben, is there any way you guys can dodge them?"

"Negative, sir. The only clear route is a narrow path in the center of the island and just a causeway in the north, leading to the spit. If we left now, we would run right into them and be sitting ducks."

"What about Simmons's people? Over."

Simmons shook his head. "They're at least thirty minutes out."

"Negative, sir. They're at least thirty minutes out," Ben repeated.

"Roger." Sam's voice was low and even, but Ben could still hear the concern, even over the radio. "We are seven miles away. I'm ordering emergency speed; fog be damned. Do whatever you need to do to stay alive, clear?"

"Roger that, sir. See you soon, out." Ben took the transmit switch back to off.

"How long before they get to us?" Simmons asked, slamming a magazine into his Uzi.

Ben paused. *Seven nautical miles, twenty-eight knots.* "Fifteen minutes, give or take, but they will need a visual target to engage." He glanced offshore at the fog with concern. "I doubt this fog will clear off by then."

"I don't suppose he can fire high to scare them off."

"No way. A stray shot could reach down to U.S. 1. He won't take that risk, even for me."

"Right." Simmons finished the readying of his firearms. "I guess we'll just have to hold until they can get in the fight."

"Pretty much."

"Right, go grab the guns."

Ben trotted to the back of the car, opened the trunk, and took out his and Simmons's weapon bags. When he came back around the shack, he almost dropped both when he saw the squatter uncuffed and helping Simmons drag a log over to the shack. "What the hell, Pete?"

"We have reached an understanding," Simmons replied. "Don't just stand there! We're screwed without cover!"

Ben dropped the bags by the shack and got to work, dragging logs and driftwood to the shack. The frantic effort of building up the makeshift barrier out of driftwood and hand-shoveling sand to fill in the gaps kept Ben's mind off the fact that they had been in a fight to the death with the man working next to him just minutes ago.

****

It surprised the 252 scouts that Simmons and his companion had not taken the bait but departed the highway on Resolution instead. It was a pleasant surprise: they considered using Resolution for the trap, but its geography was so ripe for an ambush that no one believed the American agent would fall for it. And yet, here he was. According to the tracking instrument, he was stopped on the island's northern tip, and it was the least defensible spot on the least defensible island in the group. Amazing.

When the assault team arrived, the scout lead passed on orders that the two Americans were to be taken alive at all costs, and no explosives were to be used in the capture. Something brought Simmons to Resolution—they decided to find out what it was. After the assault team passed, the scouts repositioned off the highway within the scrub beyond the tree line. They would watch the escape route until the assault team completed their work and departed.

13

Engagement

USCG Cutter *Kauai*, Gulf of Mexico, seven nautical miles west of Resolution Key, Florida 07:13 EST, 19 January

Sam

"Green Deck! I need eyes on scene—get that bird airborne and screw the regulations!" Sam shouted across the Bridge. "OOD, what's the bearing from here to the north tip of Resolution?"

"A moment, Captain. OK, zero-eight-three magnetic at six-point-eight," Hopkins replied.

"Deffler, initial heading zero-eight-three, set altitude at five hundred, fast as she'll go!"

"Right, Captain. Airborne at 12:14 Zulu, heading zero-eight-three, passing seventy-five for five hundred." After a minute, he continued, "Level at five hundred feet, max thrust selected, operations normal, checking the optical package now. OK, eyes working, speed of advance forty-seven knots."

Despite Deffler's objection about unmanned aircraft operating regulations in restricted visibility, Sam was kicking himself for not launching earlier. "Very well, when you are a quarter-mile from the scene, throttle back, and activate Ghost. And get that second bird up in case they splash number one—green deck. Keep it a half-mile dead in front of us for now with wide-angle on the camera. If you see ANYTHING, shout it out. You're our advanced lookout."

"Yes, sir!"

Sam stared at the display screen. He could barely make out the waves on the water passing below as the Puma sped through the mist at fifty-five mph. "OOD, get us there. I want everything the old girl has."

"Yes, sir!" Hopkins contacted Main Control on the Ship's Service Telephone. "Chief, OOD, we need every knot you can give us. It's what we were afraid of. Roger, take the engines. We're heading into shoal water, so you can expect a crash back order as soon as we get a target lock. Yeah, thanks, Chief." She turned to Sam as she hung up the phone. "Chief's got engine control now and is pulling out the stops, Captain."

"Thank you." Sam turned and grabbed the microphone for the PA system. "All hands, Captain speaking, we're heading for Resolution Key at full speed to back up Mr. Wyporek. He and Dr. Simmons are pinned down by a heavily armed criminal force. Set General Quarters Condition One. This is not a drill." He hung up the microphone and pulled the switch on the GQ alarm box, starting the twenty-second alarm gong.

Sam grabbed one of the spare handheld radios, stepped outside, turned up to the Flying Bridge, and shouted, "Lookout!"

Seaman Pickins appeared at the rail. "Yes, sir!"

"Get down here!"

Pickins grabbed the ladder and slid down, hands and feet on the outside, landing with a thud. He pulled up to attention in front of Sam. "Yes, Captain!"

"Pickins, take this radio...." Sam handed it to the young seaman. "And get down on the bow. We're hauling ass in fog, and you're our last line of defense against a collision. You see or hear anything that we can hit; you call it in on the radio and then run like hell. Got it?"

"Yes, sir!"

"You might hear shooting off in the distance. Ignore it. Keep your sweep thirty degrees on either side of the bow, understand?"

"Yes, sir! Sweep from three-three-zero to zero-three-zero!"

"Right on! I'll call you if I can, but don't wait for any orders when you feel us doing a crash stop. Just beat feet back to the boat deck and report to Bondurant, clear?"

"Yes, sir!"

"Well done, son." Sam clapped the young man on the arm. "Good luck. Off you go!"

"Yes, sir!" Pickins said, saluted, and then ran off to his post on *Kauai*'s bow.

Sam turned to glance forward. Repositioning the lookout to the bow would only buy them a few extra seconds of warning at twenty-eight knots, but Sam was banking every second he could.

Drake

Machinery Technician Third Class Brown was assisting Drake in running his routine morning checks in Main Control when the phone rang. Drake lifted the phone with concern—if the Bridge was calling, it couldn't be good. "Main Control, Drake."

"Chief, OOD, we need every knot you can give us. It's what we were afraid of."

"He's jammed up, isn't he? Okay, Hoppy, if you can pass me engine control, I'll pull the topping stops. I think I can squeeze a few extra knots from the old lady."

"Roger, take the engines. We're heading into shoal water, so you can expect a crash back order as soon as we get a target lock."

"Right then, I need you to give me a heads up about a minute before so I can replace the stops and slam in back full without blowing us up. On it now."

"Yeah, thanks, Chief."

He slammed down the phone, grabbed a set of pliers out of the box, and turned to Brown. "Dave, take the throttles and hold at ninety-eight percent until I give you the signal and then edge it up. We'll start with Number One!"

Drake laid down between the engines, carefully reached the pliers in, and gripped the topping button on the fuel control, extracting it and putting it into his pocket. He glanced at Brown and held up one finger, and the junior petty officer put his hand on the right-hand throttle. Drake gave an exaggerated nod and then fixed his gaze on the fuel control, providing a repeating pinching signal with his fingers for Brown to advance the throttle. When the control arm reached the point Drake couldn't risk anymore, he held up a fist and looked at Brown, who held both hands. They then repeated the process on the number two engine. He got up, moved to the control station, glanced at the digital reading for the cutter's speed through the water—thirty knots—and let loose with a "Hot damn! Payback time— hold together, baby!" The engine instrument readings were a nightmare scenario for any engineer, but Drake knew the engines could take it for a brief time.

Brown, wide-eyed after the procedure and aghast at the readings, turned and shouted over the noise of the engines, "How long will they take this Chief?!"

"As long as they need to!" Drake shouted back.

"What should I do if one lets go?!"

"If parts start flying, we hit the fuel shutoff and get out!"

"What do I do then?!"

"You damn well better catch up to me, son!"

Sam

After a minute, the engines were running at maximum, and Sam felt they were running faster than any full-power run they had before. "OOD, ETA, please."

Hopkins was not freaked-out, exactly, but a full-power run in low visibility was very high-risk, bordering on reckless. A collision was likely if another vessel appeared directly ahead of them out of the fog, ending this mission, if not the patrol boat herself. Hopkins had dropped the scale on the search radar to two miles when Sam ordered full speed to achieve the highest resolution and probability of detection. And she stayed bolted to the screen. She glanced at the SeaWatch panel and replied, "Captain, speed of advance is twenty-nine. I make it... twelve minutes now, maybe eleven and a half."

Sam was impressed. *Twenty-nine knots and thirty through the water. Well done, Chief!* "Very well. Any shoaling to worry about?"

"Captain, if it was low tide right now, I'd be pissing my pants, but we'll be OK all the way. It will be close at the end. And, by the way, we're violating the wake limits in the Great White Heron National Wildlife Refuge," she added with a slight grin.

Sam returned a sad smile. "Book me. When this is over, the Department of Interior guys will be the least of my worries." According to the book, Sam should connect with the District Command and seek a Statement of No Objection for use of force. Of course, there wasn't a hope of getting an SNO in time to help Ben. He shared a look with Hopkins. Sam would do whatever it takes to save his friend and shipmate, even if that violates standing orders. Calling now would only risk the more severe charge of disobeying a direct order.

The look they shared made clear both knew this truth, and neither would say it. After a few seconds, Hopkins looked down at the radar screen, and Sam turned back to the fire control station.

The crew scrambled to their GQ stations, donning vests and helmets. Sam fastened his vest and stepped over to the Fire Control Station, where Williams had activated his console and worked through the warm-up of the main gun. "Williams, load with armor-piercing when you get online. How will the infrared sight do in this fog?"

Williams pressed a few buttons and moved the joystick to check the infrared gun sight's operation. "Better than visual with the long-wave camera, maybe seven hundred yards, sir." He made another selection, and with a series of "clanks," the chain mechanism loaded the first Armor Piercing Discarding Sabot-Tracer round into the twenty-five-millimeter main gun. "APDS-T loaded, gun ready."

Sam turned back to Deffler, who was just putting on his helmet. "Deffler, reposition over here at fire control, please. I may need your eyes for shot spotting."

"Yes, sir." He activated the internal antenna of his laptop and then pulled it out of the docking port to cross the Bridge. "Hi, sailor!" He winked and kneeled next to Williams.

"Don't start," Williams growled back.

Sam grabbed his binoculars and went out onto the starboard bridge wing. He need not have bothered with binoculars—visibility was a quarter-mile in the fog—but he needed something to steady his hands. Hebert was already in battle gear and was preparing his machine gun for action. "Whattaya say, Chef?" Sam said with a forced grin.

"Same as always, sir," Hebert replied with a tight smile. "You catch 'em, and I'll cook 'em."

Sam patted him on the back and continued to the end of the walkway. He gazed astern and briefly watched the "rooster tail" produced by thrust from the propellers. *Kauai*'s creamy white wake stretched straight back and spread out behind on the smooth water until fading from sight in the fog. He then turned his gaze inward and took in the sounds: the muffled roar of the diesel engines; the bumping and clanging as the crew prepared for battle; the snapping of the U.S. flag and Coast Guard ensign in the stiff wind high on the mast; the rush of the water passing at thirty knots and the intermittent thumping from the hull hitting the small waves. Through all this, the captain of the Coast Guard Cutter *Kauai* bowed his head and prayed. "Please, God, keep him and us safe for just ten more minutes."

Resolution Key, Florida
07:25 EST, 19 January

Ben

"I can see them," Ben said when he could make out the black shape of the large SUV coming through the mist. His "barricade," if it could be called that, was barely

270

two-and-a-half feet high. "They don't seem too worried about us."

"Not much to fear from small arms. You don't happen to have an anti-tank rocket on you, by any chance? No? No." Simmons's face was expressionless as he stared at the approaching SUVs.

Their new companion, who still held to his assumed name of Bill, crouched to Simmons's left, staring at the approaching SUVs with Simmons's Glock in his hand. The two men had agreed on a temporary alliance against the impending threat, with the understanding that Simmons and Ben would look the other way afterward when the man fled, assuming they were still alive. Ben was not at all happy about this, trying not to think about how easy it would be for Bill to shoot both of them in the back.

Ben couldn't remember ever being so scared and swallowed hard as he watched the vehicles' slow approach. "Shouldn't we spread out? I mean, one shot with an RPG can take out all of us."

Simmons shook his head. "No, we need to keep close to the shack. They won't risk an explosive shot this close to the target, at least, until they figure out what it is. We move off, and they'll blow us away for sure."

"OK. Just a reminder. It's my first firefight."

Simmons shot Ben a glance and smiled. "Yeah, I remember. Don't worry, Ben, you'll be fine. Keep your head down, and other than that, it's just like the gun range."

Ben selected the voice-activated position on his radio. "*Kauai*, Shore-One, hostiles in sight and approaching, over."

"Roger One, we're almost there, and we have eyes on scene. Where are you? Over," Sam's voice replied.

The sound of Sam's voice and the knowledge a Puma was providing him situational awareness provided some relief from the gnawing fear. "We are all barricaded by the shed, sir, within fifteen feet. Everything moving is hostile, over."

"Roger that. Hang in there! Out."

"Hell is empty and all the devils are here," Simmons quipped.

"Shakespeare, *The Tempest*," Ben responded.

"Well played, sir. We'll set you up with a pretty Lit major yet." Simmons smiled grimly with his eyes fixed on the approaching vehicles.

The line brought the thought of the lovely young analyst he had met a mere day and a half ago to mind. "If I don't make it back, would you tell Victoria... Well, you know what to tell her."

"You will make it back," Simmons snapped. "Just keep your head in the game!"

"Perhaps you should have considered a more experienced wingman," Bill said snidely.

"He'll do. Why don't you give us a break and shut up!" Simmons replied.

The two SUVs split apart and continued their slow approach. Simmons noticed the rear window of the left one coming down and put two Uzi bursts toward it. The window quickly raised. "Stand by for dismounts. They'll be using the vehicles for cover. You take the one on the right. Shoot at anything you see outside the vehicle, but don't take a lot of time aiming. We need a steady fire on them, or they'll rush us. Remember, stay low!"

Ben's vehicle slowed, and a head appeared around the back. Ben raised his carbine, firing a three-round burst, and the head disappeared. The SUV stopped, and two more heads popped up over the hood and fired automatic weapons. Rounds slammed into the wood barrier and ground, throwing up sand and wood splinters. Ben returned quick bursts in the general direction, noting Simmons and Bill were doing the same toward their vehicle. "*Kauai*, Shore-One, we are taking fire; repeat, we are taking fire. Request immediate assistance!" Ben discarded the radio and laid down a quick set of bursts, and one black-clad figure tumbled from behind his vehicle. *Steady fire, stay low, steady fire, stay low.* Ben drilled his mind to the task at hand.

USCG Cutter *Kauai*, one nautical mile west of Resolution Key, Florida
07:27 EST, 19 January

Sam

"Conn, Mount 51, sound of gunshots zero-four-zero relative, no visual target!" Hebert shouted through the bridge door from his position on the starboard machine gun.

"Conn, aye!" Hopkins replied.

Sam watched the scene ashore unfold in real-time in the video feed from the orbiting Puma. His heart pounded, and he felt rising nausea as he watched the SUVs split apart and then stop. Figures emerged from both vehicles.

"*Kauai*, Shore-One, we are taking fire; repeat, we are taking fire. Request immediate assistance!" Ben's voice burst from the radio.

"Conn, Mount 51, sound of continuous gunfire zero-five-zero relative, no visual target!" came the redundant report.

"Conn, aye! Captain, one point seven miles to shoal water."

Hopkins had called down to Drake at the two-mile point, and Sam saw the engine speed back down slightly to "normal" emergency ahead in response.

"Very well, prepare for crash back. Williams?"

"Nothing yet, Captain, sorry," Williams said, shifting in his seat.

Hopkins announced, "Captain, one and a half miles to shoal water." Into the telephone, she said, "Chief, stand by for crash back."

"Very well, stand by," Sam responded.

On the Puma's video display, Sam saw Bill take the fatal hit and fall back dead. His heart was in his throat until he leaned forward to peer at the screen, then a wave of relief when he saw the long hair and beach clothing, apparent even in the low-resolution image. It must be the prisoner. He noted a pause in the action and saw the figures behind the westernmost vehicle aim a mortar-like device and fire it. The camera picked up a flash of a small object, then a burst overhead Ben and Simmons's redoubt. Either Ben or Simmons—from the camera aspect and mist, he couldn't tell which—fast-crawled to the other briefly, then returning to his position. Sam was unconsciously pounding his right fist on his thigh as the scene played out before him.

"Getting something," Williams said. "Yes! Two targets on long-wave IR."

Sam leaned in. "Surface action starboard, train on the target on the far left and standby. Deffler, illuminate the hostile vehicle farthest west." Standing up, he shouted, "OOD, Crash Back Now!" He keyed his handheld radio. "Pickins, haul ass back to the boat deck now!"

Hopkins shouted into the telephone, "Main Control, Conn, Crash Back, all back full!"

"Unmasked," Deffler piped up. "Target illuminated."

Sam held on to the safety rail as the patrol boat pitched down and violently shuddered while shedding speed quickly in the emergency stop. He watched the firing resume on the screen, and the figures started moving from behind the vehicles and closing on Ben and Simmons's position.

"Main Control, Conn, All Stop!" Hopkins shouted into the phone when the speed dropped to zero. The roar of the engines immediately died away.

"Conn, Mount 51, more continuous gunfire bearing zero-six-zero relative, no visual target!"

"Conn, aye!"

"Target identified, target confirmed, on target and tracking!"

"Batteries release. Commence fire!"

Drake

Drake held the phone to one ear and his finger in the other to hear Hopkins's orders over the engine noise. Sweat poured down his face as he stared at the instruments—the engine room was sweltering during normal cruise conditions. After ten minutes at extreme speed, it was like an oven.

Hopkins held the line open. When Drake heard Sam shout the initial crash back order, he did not wait for Hopkins to repeat it—he just dropped the phone and smoothly but quickly closed the engine throttles. When the RPMs had died down enough, he declutched the engines from the propeller shafts, shifted to reverse drive, and reclutched. After a short spine-tingling shriek from the clutches, the propellers showed reverse turns, and Drake advanced the throttles. The propellers bit against the cutter's forward speed and sent a fearsome vibration through the hull. The engine room was a cacophony of roaring engines, rattling tools, and the sharp pings of propeller cavitations. Holding the phone to his ear again while gripping a stanchion to stay upright, Drake watched the ship's speed readout drop to zero. He retarded the throttles to idle and declutched when Hopkins's "all stop" order came. He switched the engine control selector back to the Bridge, picked up the phone, and reported, "Conn, Main Control, engines at all stop. Returning engine control to Conn."

Main Control seemed almost quiet compared to the last few minutes with the engines at idle. Brown had just started to relax when a series of loud thuds and sharp vibrations startled him. He looked frantically between the engines and instrument panel and shouted, "Shit, Chief! What now?"

"Relax, son." Drake wiped the sweat from his forehead while staring forward with a worried expression. "It's the main gun."

Resolution Key, Florida
07:20 EST, 19 January

Ben

Ben had already spent one magazine and slammed another into the carbine, resuming fire. His pistol was also charged and ready. Suddenly, there was a pause in the firing, and all the targets were out of sight. Ben glanced left along the barrier and froze in shock. Bill was sprawled out face up behind Simmons, eyes open and blood leaking from a hole in his forehead.

"Eyes front!" Simmons whispered urgently.

Ben whirled back to peer at the SUVs and whispered, "What are they doing?"

"Retasking," Simmons said, pulling a small package out of one of his pockets. "They'll try to take us now for interrogation."

"What do we do?"

"Don't get taken."

"Thanks."

"No, I mean, whatever you have to do, DO NOT get taken by these guys." He looked Ben in the eyes. "Nothing would be worse, believe me."

"Right."

Some activity behind his SUV attracted Ben's attention. There was a "whump" sound, and a grapefruit-sized object sailed over their position.

"FACE DOWN!" Simmons shouted.

Ben turned and buried his face in the sand when a loud "pop" sounded overhead, followed by a "whir" and a stabbing pain in the back of his right leg. A severe muscle cramp-like pain spread over his body within seconds, and he could not move. He tried to shout in terror, but all he heard was, "Ahhhhhh!" He felt another prick in his neck, and the pain subsided, although he still could not seem to get his muscles to work.

"It was a micro-flechette with a tetrodotoxin derivative. I've given you the antidote, but it'll be about thirty seconds before it's fully effective," Simmons whispered as he pulled the now empty syrette out of Ben's neck. "Fight it! They'll be rushing us in a few seconds—you need to be shooting."

The pain subsided, but the world moved in slow motion. Ben sensed time was passing, perhaps while the enemy waited for their chemical attack to take effect. Finally, he saw movement again near the vehicles. Ben's hand closed on the grip of his pistol, and it felt like it weighed a hundred pounds as he raised it off the ground. He squeezed off first one and then several rounds in quick-fire. Simmons fired his Uzi in full automatic, and two of the approaching figures fell to the ground. Another burst of automatic fire from the SUVs threw up more sand, and Simmons grunted and crumpled with a hit.

Suddenly, the SUV on the right lurched and leaned to the left, its tires flattened. The windows of the stricken vehicle shattered, and the fuel tank exploded, engulfing it in flames as a series of loud thump sounds arrived from offshore. The two dismounts still standing darted toward the remaining SUV.

Holding his wounded left arm, Simmons grimaced. "What the hell?"

Ben recognized the sound of a twenty-five-millimeter gun and croaked, "It's *Kauai*!" He laboriously brought his pistol to bear on the other SUV.

A black-clad gunman next to the SUV blind-fired a rocket-propelled grenade to seaward in the general direction of the incoming tracer fire. He then piled with the other survivors into the vehicle, its rear tires spinning and throwing up sand and dust.

USCG Cutter *Kauai*, six hundred yards off Resolution Key, Florida
07:30 EST, 19 January

Sam

"Check fire, check fire, shift target right. Deffler, illuminate the other vehicle." Sam struggled to keep his voice low and even.

"Check fire, aye, shifting right," said Williams, punching "Lock/Unlock" and moving the console's trackball to the right until the reticle sited on the other glowing object and flashed green. The Puma's illumination dot now appeared on the image.

"Target illuminated," Deffler said.

"Target identified, target confirmed, on target and tracking," Williams punched the "Lock/Unlock" button again. The artificial intelligence in the gun sight fixed on the signature of the selected "hot" object. It noted the need to realign and signaled the main gun's traversing system, slewing it a few degrees to the right.

"Incoming rocket!" Deffler shouted. The warhead flashed just clear of the cutter's stern with a hiss and self-detonated a second later.

"Commence fire!"

Another series of loud bangs with the rattle of spent cartridges hitting the deck meant more quarter-pound twenty-five millimeter rounds were on the way. The penetrators shed their sabot jackets on leaving the barrel, and their tracer tails made them look like red glowing streaks as they vanished into the mist at almost four times the speed of sound. At slightly under six hundred meters to target, flight time for each round was a little under half a second. The SUV driver started turning to return to the causeway immediately instead of building up speed first. It was his last mistake. The aspect change increased the image size, and the low speed allowed Williams to target it expertly. The brief flight time meant lead and windage were not a factor. He came on target at once. The first hit severed the right front wheel, and the second punched through the door armor, spewing lethal fragments in the cabin. The last hit shattered the fuel tank, igniting the scattering gasoline with its tracer tail. Soon, the infrared picture on Williams's gun sight was again washed out with heat from another wrecked and burning SUV.

"Check fire. Standby." Sam gazed at the UAV display. Two SUVs were burning, with three motionless human figures strewn between them, and it appeared several more lay near the second vehicle. He waited impatiently while the Puma continued its orbit in slow flight, finally clearing the drifting smoke. "Zoom in on that." Sam pointed at a figure crouching beside another near the hut and jammed the transmit button on his radio. "Shore-One, this is *Kauai*." No response. "Shore-One, this is *Kauai*, respond!" Turning, he said, "Deffler, can you get his attention?"

"Yes, sir," While he slewed and zoomed the image, Deffler goosed the engine to full and switched off the Ghost system. The kneeling figure looked up and around. He fixed on the aircraft, exaggeratedly touched his ear, and gave a thumbs-down. He then held his right arm straight up with his left pointing horizontally into it, giving the "Send Litter" signal—a general call for medical aid. Deffler zoomed in on the scene, and it became clear Ben was the one signaling. Simmons was prone and not moving, and both were very bloody.

"Ceasefire. Secure the twenty-five." Sam grabbed the PA microphone. "Stand Easy General Quarters, Away Rescue and Assistance Detail, Health Services Technician, contact the Bridge." Sam leaned down and gripped Williams's and Deffler's shoulders with each hand and gave them a soft shake. "Thank you, guys." Williams and Deffler shook hands firmly as Sam crossed the Bridge. "OOD, in this calm, any course works for the boat launch. Let's try minimum steerageway to the northwest, please."

"Very good, sir," Hopkins replied, blinking away tears. She looked across at Deffler, nodding when he looked up at her and received a nod in return. The ship's telephone buzzed, and she picked it up. "Bridge, OOD. Right, standby. Captain, it's Doc."

Sam nodded and took the phone. "Doc, Captain."

"Yes, sir," Bryant replied.

"The UAV has eyes-on. The suspects are down, but the XO and Simmons both appear wounded. XO is ambulatory and hand-signaling for a litter. Comms are down, so I can't tell the severity."

"Understood, sir. I've got the full kit with me, and we'll bring the litter in case we need it."

"Good. Now listen carefully, Simmons's people are on the way, and they'll probably have EMTs along.

However, unless *you* are convinced he really needs a hospital, you get the XO away from those people and back to the boat. I'll back whatever decision you make."

"Understood, Captain," Bryant replied.

"Right, good luck." Sam hung up the phone and keyed his radio. "Boat Deck, Captain."

"Captain, Boat Deck, go ahead, sir," Bondurant replied.

"Boat Deck, how soon before you can launch?"

"The boat's at the rail and ready, sir. They'll be off thirty seconds after Doc boards. Lee and the boat seaman have sidearms, and I put Jenkins in with a shotgun. Hold, sir. Doc's here and onboard. Request permission to launch the boat."

Sam was going to order the boat crew to be armed. *I should have known Bondurant would cover that.* "Standby," Sam said and turned to Hopkins. "OOD, the boat is ready. How's our course?"

"Steady on two-nine-zero, bare steerageway, sir," she replied.

"Very well, hold that." He keyed the radio again. "Boats, you're cleared to launch. Good call on the weapons. Tell Lee to head zero-eight-zero until she sees the shoreline, then continue to land as close to the scene as possible."

"Yes, sir!"

Sam touched Hopkins gently on the shoulder and quietly said, "Thank you, Hoppy." Then he stepped outside to wipe his own eyes. He tried to work a painful cramp out of his right hand while watching the RHIB dropping into the water for launch. When the RHIB was away, he stepped back inside. "Williams, start a secure chat with OPC, please."

"Yes, sir," Williams replied, shifting to the SeaWatch station.

"Sir?" Hopkins asked Sam when he stepped behind Williams.

"OOD, I'm about to put what my H65-flying brother-in-law Eddie calls the 'Aviator Approach' to the test." Sam smiled sadly.

"What's that, sir?"

"It's easier to obtain forgiveness than permission."

14

Aftermath

**Resolution Key, Florida
08:01 EST, 19 January**

Ben

Bryant had just finished initial treatment on Simmons's arm wound when several agency SUVs arrived, and three well-equipped EMTs stepped out and ran over. "Through and through in the upper left arm, bone seems OK, no bleeds," Bryant said to his counterpart.

"Right, we've got it."

"OK, XO, that was a four-point-oh job with the first aid. Let's have a look at you now." Bryant pulled on fresh gloves.

"I'm fine, Doc." With an expressionless face, Bryant reached up and touched the right side of Ben's head and showed him the blood on his glove. "OK, except for the hole in my head."

"You'll live, XO. Just let me get this patch on to keep the rest of your brains from leaking out, and I'll sew you up when we get back to the boat." After cleaning and applying a bandage to the wound, Bryant took Ben's arm. "OK, sir, let's move along."

"Give me a few minutes, Doc."

Bryant started to protest, then pointed at his wristwatch. "I'll give you one hundred twenty seconds, sir."

"For sure, thanks." Ben glanced over at Bill's body—his head and torso were covered by a blanket he had retrieved from the shack. He kneeled beside Simmons. "It seems we're shipmates no more."

Simmons smiled as the EMT worked to prepare him for the stretcher. "I'm sorry about that. You did real good today, and I'd like to keep you around."

"Bull. I was scared shitless and damn near blew the whole deal by getting myself speared."

Simmons frowned and grabbed Ben's arm gently with his right hand. "Don't kid yourself. Everybody's scared shitless in a gunfight, present company included. Do you think you 'blew it' by getting hit? Guess what? I took one too. I juiced up before the shooting started just in case, but I was hoping to spare you the hangover—it's a bug we're still working on with the antidote.

"Think what would have happened had those goons gotten to our 'friends' before they could jump. No, you and your crew were really something today." He smiled warmly. He noticed Ben staring at the two covered bodies. "You bothered by that?"

"I don't know. It was righteous then, but I haven't killed anyone before."

"That's the downside. You might have issues later because you're a good man. If it comes to that, remember that those animals would have blown up *Kauai* and murdered any survivors if it weren't for the fog. If you need something to keep you going beyond the fact that you saved your family out there, call me. We have people who're good at that sort of thing."

"Thanks." He turned again to look at Bill's body. "I was afraid he was going to cap us both."

"He might have, but I doubt it. There is a certain threshold of honor in this business, and we'll treat him right."

"You think the Russians will claim him?"

"If they don't, we'll give him a good burial under the tricolor."

"Sir, we need to get him to a hospital," the EMT interjected.

"Sorry, carry on, please." Ben shook Simmons's hand and then stood up. "Seeya, spook."

"Sooner than you think." He then looked past Ben and cried, "Art!"

Ben turned to see Frankle trotting up to them. He kneeled down with a look of concern upon arriving and took Simmons's right hand. "Pete! Damn glad to see you're still with us."

"Yea, verily, brother. What the hell happened? Where's Bell?"

"They pulled another of their surprises. Suckered us into an assault and then activated some kind of EMP generator. Radios, cellphones, and vehicles were all knocked out. Hell, they even brought down the overwatch UAV. It was back to 'charge up the hill,' but we got them. Bell took one in the arm and one in the vest that broke a couple of ribs. He'll be OK, but he'll be out of action for a while. He took down the Dragon Lady with an open-field tackle, though. That was *after* they had shot him, the tough bastard!"

"She dead?"

"Nope. She's knocked out in the back of a CPB Blackhawk, flying to Homestead."

"Nice one. They decide what they will do with her?"

"The Frankle Plan would be either tell us everything you know and live out your life in the safety of a Supermax or don't, and we'll announce that you did and leave you to your fate in the system. Those making the call are unlikely to seek my keen insights." The agent chuckled.

"Gentlemen," a clearly annoyed EMT said. "We need to move this man now!"

"Sorry." Frankle smiled. "Please go ahead. Pete, I'll see you at the hospital." While two EMTs carried off the litter, he turned to Ben and offered his hand. "Thanks for bringing him through this, Coast Guard."

Ben shook it readily. "It was more the other way around, but you're welcome."

"No, we really owe you on this one. I hope we'll have a chance to work with you guys again—I love folks who bring cannons to a gunfight!"

They all turned when the other EMT standing by cleared his throat. "Your officer has been exposed to a classified nerve agent," he said to Bryant. "He's had the counteragent, and no further treatment is required. He needs to be kept under close observation for forty-eight hours, and," he glanced at *Kauai* offshore, glistening white in the emerging sun. "No operating motor vehicles." He turned to Ben. "You'll have a hell of a headache in about three hours. I recommend acetaminophen—no aspirin—and plenty of water." He turned to Bryant again. "You know, it wouldn't hurt to let us take him to the hospital, just in case."

Bryant shook his head, remembering the direct order from his CO before he boarded the RHIB. "Thanks, but I've got this."

"That OK with you, Lieutenant?" the EMT asked somewhat rudely.

"Petty Officer Bryant's medical judgment will always do for me," Ben replied coldly.

"Suit yourself." The EMT walked off to catch up with his comrades and Simmons.

Frankle flashed Ben a mock salute. "Be seein' ya, Coast Guard!" He then turned and followed the others.

As Ben turned to Bryant, the latter's face spread into an evil Grinch-like grin. "Looks like we'll be roomies for the next couple of days, sir."

"Yeah. You're enjoying this, aren't you, Doc?"

Bryant took Ben's arm to steady him, and they walked through the soft sand toward the RHIB. "XO, you have NO idea."

****

Simmons's compatriots had taken over the battle scene for cleanup. No evidence of the encounter, not even the ersatz beachcomber shack, would remain in a few hours. However, there was still a Russian warhead, probably nuclear, in the vicinity. That meant *Kauai* had to stay on security watch while other federal forces closed off access to the island on the land side. A flotilla of recovery vessels was en route for extensive surveys of the area.

Lee threaded the needle between the need for speed and a smooth ride in the RHIB as she transported Ben and Bryant back to *Kauai*. She maintained a calm, professional exterior despite the shock of seeing her XO with his head bandaged and covered with blood. Lee smoothly slewed the boat alongside the cutter, grabbed the fall, and slammed it in place on the lift frame in a single swift maneuver. Looking up, she gave a thumbs-up to Bondurant. "Ready for pickup!"

Seeing Ben was still a little shaky climbing out of the RHIB, Sam came down from the Bridge to meet him. He was concerned at the sight of all the blood, but relieved at his young friend's smile and mock salute. He gripped Ben's right hand and shoulder and feigned his best "angry dad" expression. "Mister, you scared the shit out of me back there!"

Ben replied with mock solemnity, "No excuse, sir. Shall I retire to the captain's cabin for the requisite flogging?"

"No, too much paperwork. Say fifteen 'Hail Marys' and contemplate your many inadequacies."

"About that, sir. I'm ready to give you a hand on the reports...."

"Like hell," Sam interrupted. "Doc gave me the picture on you, and your rack is your duty station until further notice."

"Sir, I can still...."

"Enough. That's an order, discussion over."

"Yes, sir. What are our orders, sir?"

Sam smiled. "When the fireworks ended, I started a SIPRNET chat to report in. I got as far as reporting we had taken out two vehicles and a mess of bad guys when I got a 'Shut the Hell Up!' order. We're holding on here for now. They're establishing a maritime security zone and aviation Prohibited Area over the island and out to two miles offshore until further notice. They've diverted *Mohawk* from her Yucatan patrol, and she should be here to relieve us in about twenty-four hours. It'll be close on the fuel, but we'll head straight back to Miami when relieved."

"How do they expect to keep this under wraps, sir? You can see that smoke plume down in Key West, and all the feds crawling over this place are bound to cause questions."

"Ah." Sam smiled. "Haven't you heard? It's already on commercial radio that an F-22 out of Tyndall Air Force Base crashed on Resolution during a training flight. Happily, the pilot ejected and is safe. But the island is closed to the public until the mishap investigation and cleanup is complete."

Ben nodded and turned to see Drake approaching. The big chief petty officer said nothing, just stepped up, gripped the young man's shoulders firmly, and gazed into his eyes, beaming. After a few seconds, he released Ben and turned to Sam. "Captain, I respectfully request that you put this young man in hack until we get back to Miami. I've got plenty of shit on my hands without any more emergency power runs and crash stops."

"Already done, Chief. How do things look?" Sam smiled.

"We'll get home all right. I will need a butt-load of parts when we get there, though. We overstressed, over-torqued, over-temped, and over-sped almost every damn thing in the hull. I would be obliged if we could limit her to twenty knots on the trip back. Also, for planning, we'll be hard down when the mooring lines go over."

"I hear ya, Chief. I need to hold down the fuel consumption, anyway. Should I worry about you finding the parts?"

"Naw, I know some guys." Drake saluted, then sauntered off.

Sam pointed at Ben. "Rack, mister, now!"

"Aye, aye, sir." He glanced up at the Bridge to see Hopkins looking down with a slight smile. They exchanged nods, and Ben turned and retired to his room.

The prognosis from the agency medic was accurate—the headache that came on three hours later was blinding and debilitating. The Tylenol Bryant administered was only just enough to keep Ben from wanting to blow his brains out. Fortunately, after about four hours, the pain passed as quickly as it started, and he fell into a deep and sound sleep under Bryant's watchful eye.

Six hours later, rested but still slightly wobbly, Ben submitted to a going over by Bryant, who refused to sign him off for duty. He reluctantly consented to Ben walking accompanied up to talk to Sam. Seeing Ben walking unsteadily across the darkened Bridge, Sam stood up from his seat and motioned for him to sit down. "No, I'll be all right, sir," Ben said.

"Do as you're told, sir." Ben sat down, and Sam leaned over and continued softly. "We got a follow-up SIPRNET message while you were out. We are officially quarantined until further notice—no one leaves the ship and no comms of any kind. When *Mohawk* arrives on station and assumes the watch, they will flash us their callsign, and we are to reply 'Tango' by signal light only and depart. We are to send the RHIB over to the island in about ten minutes to pick up a special medical crew. They'll check all of us for radiation exposure on the way. When we arrive in Miami, the crew will be confined to the boat incommunicado. You and I are to report to the District Office at 02:30."

"Zero-Two-Thirty? What's happening at 02:30 on a Wednesday, sir?"

"Our interrogation, apparently. The orders are to secure all logs and present ourselves in a conference room over there."

"Shit, Skipper!" Ben felt an icy ball forming in his stomach. "What can we do?"

"Shave, put on a fresh tropical blue uniform, and hope for the best. Same as always. OK, you've put in an appearance. Why not head below? I'll be down in an hour or so, and we can chat about your little adventure." Seeing Ben hesitate, Sam continued with a warm smile, "Number One, you're in my seat. Kindly retire below to your own, please."

"Very good, sir." Ben stood unsteadily. Bryant moved quickly from the opposite side of the Bridge to help and, taking Ben's arm, helped him down the ladder to his room. About an hour and a half later, Sam appeared at Ben's door, holding a chair.

"Doc, I need the room," Sam said as Bryant stood. "I want you to stake out the forward end of the passageway. No one, and I mean no one, is to pass until I come out and tell you otherwise, clear?"

"Yes, sir," Bryant replied crisply, taking the chair from Sam and stepping out of the room. As Bryant sat, he saw Lopez at the other end, and they nodded at each other and sat in watchful silence as Sam shut the door.

****

Ben sat on his bunk, and Sam sat on Ben's chair, putting a box of tissues on his desk. Noting Ben looking at the box, Sam said, "Just in case." When Ben looked back at him, Sam continued. "Ok, it's not a SCIF, but it's as close as possible. Ben, I need you to take me through your experience, the full monty, from the moment you got into the car with Simmons in Key West until you stepped back aboard. We're completely off the record here, absolutely between you and me, no rank, friend to friend, so don't hold back. Be as detailed as possible in describing how you felt during the events. I understand that's hard because it's so unnatural for us, so I'll prompt you if that's needed." Seeing Ben staring at him in astonishment with his mouth half-open, Sam continued. "I want you to trust me on this. You need to talk about everything now. It will make an enormous difference to you later."

At Sam's prompting, Ben went through the chronology of his off-cutter actions, beginning with the arrival at the hotel and meeting with Simmons's team. Ben saw the slight twinkle in Sam's eye at his description of his conversation with Victoria, despite the latter's silence and diligent effort to keep his face expressionless. Ben described the relative boredom of the next day, the excitement of discovering that Resolution was the target site, and the encounter with the Russian agent that followed.

When he revisited the battle with the TCO gunmen, the fear inside returned to the surface, and he trimmed down the detail in his description. Sam leaned forward and insisted Ben dig in and describe his feelings completely and accurately, prompting him when he hesitated. The full range of emotions returned while he completed the story. Ben again felt the gnawing, escalating fear of watching as the vehicles moved in slowly. Then, the stark terror of the chemical attack and Simmons's wounding. Last was the intense elation and relief when *Kauai* could finally engage. Sam handed him the box of tissues at that point, and Ben was astounded to realize he was crying.

What seemed like minutes passed, and Sam reached across and gently gripped his shoulder. With the worst over, Ben steadied down. He looked up at Sam, who smiled back, released his hold, and sat back. Eventually, Ben could ask, "How did you know?"

Sam shook his head. "I didn't. But *I* damn near lost it on the Bridge just watching you go through that ordeal. I thought you had to be carrying a lot more inside, and knowing you, you'd just let it sit and fester. I figured I would drag it out of you now. It's better than risking it popping up tomorrow when we're not among friends."

Ben nodded. It embarrassed him to break down before his CO and friend, and doing so in an interrogation would be infinitely worse. He looked across at a grinning Sam. "What?"

"You know, lad," his friend said as he stood. "They should use you for a template for the next Jack Bauer. Let's see, you find a lost Russian nuke and capture one of their spies. Check. You step from there into a firefight outnumbered five-to-one by a bunch of murdering sociopaths and win. Check. And, naturally, hook up with a beautiful girl. Check." He stepped out the door and told Bryant and Lopez, "That's all, guys, thanks." He looked back in and finished with a slight smile. "Please hold off on doing anything like that again until after I'm tour complete! Will you be OK, or do I need to call Doc back?"

"I'm awesome, sir," Ben replied, drawing a broad smile from his friend. "Isn't there anything I can do to help, sir? Doc has me pinned down, and I'm going bat-shit crazy here."

Sam nodded. "If you feel up to it, can you draft a memo from me to the CO of Air Station Cape Cod? I want to give Fritz and Mike cover on the flights yesterday. Keep it unclassified. Just say Fritz called out the regs against flying in fog. I overruled him because of national security and safety-of-life and now take full responsibility for the decision. You know what I need. That would take a big rock out of my backpack."

"Consider it done, sir, and thank you. I already thanked him for saving my life, and it feels good to pitch in something tangible."

Sam didn't reply, just gave a thumbs-up.

****

Coast Guard Cutter *Mohawk* arrived the following morning and anchored a comfortable distance offshore of Resolution Key. Sam had ordered the main engines restarted when the large cutter appeared on the horizon, and *Kauai* weighed anchor as *Mohawk* set hers. After about ten minutes, during which her underway routine was secured and anchor watch set, *Mohawk* signaled "NRUF" by flashing light, to which Hopkins replied simply "T" using the hand-held signal lamp. Within a minute, *Kauai* was cruising for home at the stately speed of twenty knots.

After the warhead discovery, firefight, and cathartic debriefing session, Ben found himself at loose ends. He was desperate to get his mind off what he assumed would be a thorough grilling on their return to Miami. He completed and polished the memo Sam had requested. Ben tried to resume OOD duties, but Bryant put that to rest after running a weird procedure he called a "Mini-BES-Test." An appeal to Sam was equally futile, and Ben resigned himself to catching up on the paperwork that had languished in his absence and convalescence. He was surprised to find the stack of paperwork he had left in his inbox completed and filed. In its place was a handwritten note: "You're Welcome. Never do it again! With Respect, J. Drake, MKC; E. Hopkins, OS1." Reflecting on the similarity to Sam's enjoinder earlier, Ben placed the note in a document protector and stiff folder and put it carefully with the other personal items in his bag.

He thought about composing a draft of his first email to Victoria for when they came off lockdown and even laid out a few sheets of paper before deciding he was in the wrong mood. He was putting them away when he spotted Hopkins walking by in the passageway. "Hoppy?"

"Yes, sir," she replied, stopping in the doorway.

"Thanks for taking care of, well, everything."

"That's my job, sir."

"I think it went well above and beyond your normal job. You were right back in the session in Key West, and

I don't want to think about what could have happened if you guys hadn't got there when you did."

She looked back at him coolly, stepped into his room, and dropped her voice so what she said next would be private. "*Do* think about that, sir. You guys walked straight into a blind alley without backup. Why do a damned fool thing like that? You know the captain had to throw away the book to save your ass, and he stands a good chance of getting relieved of his command over his decisions yesterday. You could have avoided putting him in that position by saying 'enough' at any stage of the game to that crazy spook. Remember *that* when you two are standing tall downtown tonight, *sir*."

Ben hung his head. "Yes, I definitely will."

After a moment, her expression softened. "XO?"

"Yes?" He looked up dejectedly.

"On and off the record, I'm really glad you've come back to us, sir." She gave him a warm smile.

"Thank you," Ben replied with a slightly quavering voice. Hopkins nodded and turned to leave him to digest this latest lesson in leadership.

A few hours later, Ben was on the Bridge with Sam, overseeing Hopkins as she brought *Kauai* back into port in Miami. After an uneventful transit and quick maneuver dockside, Hopkins turned to Sam. "Ship is moored, Captain. Request secure main engines and set Charlie status."

"Very well. Outstanding job, as usual. We will miss you, Chief-select."

"Thank you, sir," she replied, then turned to issue the orders to snug the vessel down for a dockside stay.

Sam turned, and Ben noticed he looked exhausted and old, with the lines around his eyes and mouth visible even in the low lighting on the Bridge. "I guess we might as well get squared away for tonight's festivities, XO."

"Yes, sir," Ben replied with concern. "Is there anything else I can do for you, sir?"

"Nope," his friend replied, and, seeing Ben's expression, he smiled and patted him on the shoulder. "Don't worry, Ben, we'll be OK." He then turned and headed off to his cabin.

15

Verdict

Brickell Plaza Federal Building, Miami, Florida
02:25 EST, 21 January

Ben

Ben hated the Federal Building. A lot. Nothing good happened when you visited the Federal Building—the best you could hope for was to break even. That was true for visits during a typical working day. And when they summon you and your CO here to explain yourselves at two o'clock in the morning with your crew locked-down incommunicado awaiting the results? Well, my friend, you can be sure you're facing one *hell* of a climb to "break even."

The fun started the moment they arrived. The guards at the entrance took advantage of the absence of a lengthy queue of irate federal employees at this hour to give Ben and Sam a thorough examination. Then, the two men passed through a similar screening by two

301

cold-as-ice defense counterintelligence special agents
outside the secure conference space on the eighth floor.
After checking their IDs, scanning their fingerprints,
and confiscating their cell phones and anything else
electronic, the agents ushered the two officers into an
anteroom. Before leaving and locking the door, the lead
special agent said a curt, "Wait here until they call you."

Ben was desperately worried. Nothing in his
training or experience prepared him for the events he
faced over the last week. Hell, before a week ago, he
couldn't even *conceive* of them. Sam's expression did not
help. Also deep in thought, he was apprehensive, and
rightfully so: Sam bore the entire responsibility for
everything within his command. After a brief time, Sam
glanced over, and, seeing Ben's worried look, his face
softened into a sad smile. He put his hand on Ben's
shoulder and gave it a soft shake. "Take it easy, Ben.
We'll come through this OK."

Ben and Sam's decisions and actions seemed right in
the heat of action, but many violated Coast Guard
regulations, perhaps even the law. In the cold light of
day, the achievements of bringing their crew through
the ordeal alive and succeeding in their mission may not
be enough. It was time to pay the piper. That potential
payment ranged from a "slap on the wrist" in his next
fitness report to dismissal from the service and
imprisonment. Ben was anxious about what they faced,
both for himself and his best friend.

A muffled conversation outside the entry door made
him turn. The door opened, and Simmons came in,

unusually dressed in a suit and tie, with his left arm in a sling. When the door closed, Ben stepped forward with his right hand outstretched. "Hi, Doc. Guess I'm glad to see you here. How's the arm?"

"Still hurts like hell. How's your head?" Simmons replied, eyeing the small bandage on Ben's head while he shook the young officer's hand.

"Been better, but OK now. Did they find it?"

"Nope, but they haven't deployed in force yet. It's there, alright—our erstwhile *tovarisch* confirmed it. It's just a matter of time."

"And what then?"

"Cooler heads are prevailing at this point, but once we have physical evidence that a Russian nuke landed on U.S. territory, all to satisfy Platov's ego, some changes will have to be made over there. I'm trying not to think about the alternative."

Ben noticed that Sam had watched the exchange with open hostility and knew that, in Sam's view, Simmons was a reckless fool who nearly got his best friend killed and forced Sam to risk his crew and ship to save him. Thanks to the agent's appalling judgment, Sam and Ben's professional life might come to an ignominious end in the next few minutes. Simmons's smug expression obviously infuriated him under the circumstances. Sam's folded arms and icy glare squashed any notion the agent had about a cordial handshake when he offered his hand.

Simmons turned to continue his chatter with Ben when the inside door opened, and Captain Mercier entered. The two junior officers snapped to attention, and Mercier quickly said, "Carry on. Mr. Powell, Mr. Wyporek, and Dr. Simmons. We are ready for you now. Please come with me."

The men filed past Mercier into the conference room, and she closed the door behind them. Three men and two women, by appearance and dress, senior government people, already sat on the far side of a large table across the room, and Mercier sat down with them. A third, much younger woman sat at the end. An elderly man in the center spoke. "Please be seated, gentlemen." He motioned to three empty chairs in the center of the room, about five feet away from and facing the table.

The sight severely rattled Ben. The setup of the three chairs in a brightly lit area of what was otherwise a moderately darkened room screamed "inquisition" to him. *Shit, they will rip us to shreds,* Ben thought as he approached the chair on the far left. He was grateful he wasn't going through this alone.

After the three men sat down, the elderly man nodded to the young woman seated at the end of the table, and she activated what Ben assumed was a recording device in front of her. The man continued. "For the record, this interview is conducted under Executive Order 10273, and all material discussed here is classified top secret, under codeword JUBILEE. Gentlemen, I need you to state your name and position and that you understand the security level of this discussion."

"And gents, that means if you talk about anything said here, you go away forever," Simmons intoned. "Oh, yes, Dr. Peter Simmons, SA2, DIA-5B." He turned to Sam and nodded.

"Samuel Powell, Lieutenant, United States Coast Guard, Commanding Officer, Coast Guard Cutter *Kauai*. I understand the classification and penalties for disclosure."

Ben's mind raced as he stared at the people sitting at the table, noting that none were providing their names for the record. After a few seconds, Sam nudged him with his elbow. "Um, Benjamin Wyporek, Lieutenant Junior Grade, United States Coast Guard, Executive Officer, Coast Guard Cutter *Kauai*. I acknowledge the classification of this discussion and the penalty for disclosure."

Frowning at Simmons, the elderly man resumed. "Thank you, gentlemen. We are inquiring into the events occurring in the Gulf of Mexico, Florida Straits, and the Florida Keys from the 13th through the 19th of this month. Let the record show the U.S. Coast Guard is represented in these proceedings with an observer." Turning to Mercier, he added, "Please state your name, rank, present station, and acknowledgment of classification, madam."

"Jane C. Mercier, Captain, United States Coast Guard, Chief, Office of Response, Seventh Coast Guard District. I acknowledge the classification of this discussion."

"Thank you, Captain." Turning to the three interviewees, the elderly man said, "Now, gentlemen, this is a fact-finding session, not an interrogation. We need the full picture of this operation as quickly as possible. Dr. Simmons's flippant remarks aside, we depend on your honesty and forthrightness here and discretion afterward. Now we've dispensed with the formalities, gentlemen. What the hell happened out there? Please start at the beginning of your involvement, Lieutenant Powell."

****

"Lieutenant Powell, do you have any other comments on the engagement?" the elderly man asked.

"Sir, I regret there was no alternative to the force I used, given the circumstances."

"I think we agree the decision was completely justified." He looked at his colleagues, who all nodded in agreement. "About the warhead recovery. How secure is this information within your crew?"

"Mr. Wyporek, Chief Petty Officer Drake, Petty Officer Hopkins, and I are the only ones who know anything about that. For the rest of the crew, the XO engaged a group of murderous drug smugglers, and we had to take part."

"I am glad to hear that, but please keep alert." The elderly man nodded, turning to Mercier. "Captain Mercier, your officers' actions in this incident were fully justified and consistent with the finest traditions of the military service. We will certainly convey this at the highest levels, and I encourage you to take care of them to the best of your ability, within the need for utmost discretion."

"I certainly will, sir," Mercier replied.

The weight on Ben's chest lifted. *OK, not fired or going to prison. Going to make lieutenant. Well, maybe.*

"Dr. Simmons, do we have any information on the man known as 'Bill' or how he could locate the missing warhead so quickly?" the elderly man asked.

"No to both, I'm afraid, sir," Simmons replied. "He was obviously one of their Canadian sleepers, but his cover was rock-solid, and so far, the Russians haven't owned up to him. As far as his ability to find the crash site, he was not forthcoming about this or anything else. I would speculate that the Kinzhal has a default flight profile that activated automatically after launch. Tracing that from the launch location would get them in the ballpark. I don't know what he could have used for the final search—we found nothing among his effects. He might have ditched it when he set up his watch in the area. We just don't know."

"I see. Do we have anything more on the men you engaged?" the elderly man asked.

"No, sir. Fake passports, IDs, etc. The tactics and weapons suggest it's the usual opposition. The only survivor of the firefight on Resolution suicided before any of us could reach him. We weren't able to recover anything new from the vehicles or personal effects. Our people are running through the port of entry records and videos, but we don't expect to find anything. We have the woman in custody, and she might offer some insights."

"It seems odd we could track her down so quickly," the third man commented. "Someone like her should have been able to slip away completely or, at least, evade capture for a longer period than eighteen hours."

Simmons replied with a slight smile, "I'd like to say that it resulted from a dazzling combination of our excellent forensic and cyber skills. However, I think—and this is more speculation—that we weren't as sharp as we believe. I think they caught on to JUBILEE right after they took a crack at us in Key West. They probably didn't know what it was about, but if it had a connection with their lost product, they wanted to find out. They helped her escape and then plugged her into a safe house, not so much so she could fight another day, but so they could use her as bait. When the word got out that she was there and it was confirmed, everybody we had in the area closed in on her, even my two teams. Lieutenant Wyporek and I were on our own when we went for that warhead, which is what I believe they were hoping to achieve. They came damn close to pulling off quite a neat trick by grabbing us. I would suggest the interrogators lead with the concept her comrades sold her out when they question Ms. Petrova. Not sure she'll break even with that wedge, but it's worth trying.

"The unpleasant news is this EMP weapon they cooked up to cover her escape. The possibilities are frightening. We have a hard enough time keeping the infrastructure safe and stopping the spread of man-portable, surface-to-air missiles and other nightmares. Imagine creating devices from ordinary electrical components that are small enough to hide in the back of an SUV. Park it under a departure corridor in Canarsie, flip a switch, and bring down an Airbus with three hundred people and a full load of fuel right in the middle of Queens again. They blew that one up during the breakout attempt. We need to lean hard on the FBI to give the remains to our tech guys.

"That issue aside, the good news is the radar masker we secured on Ms. Petrova's sailboat. It pulled into MacDill a few hours ago. We ran preliminary tests en route, and it seemed to be effective. Our people took a harder look at the hull of the original wreck once we discovered the device on the *Sunrise Surprise.* We found the remains of the self-destruct bomb and a pile of electronic scrap that could have been another masker. This suggests the device is in general service. Anyway, the DARPA folks and our engineers are hot to get their hands on it for reverse engineering and countermeasure development.

The elderly man nodded. "Yes, it's nice to have gotten more on them, at least. Now, I suppose that is it. Does anyone else have anything?" He scanned his associates again. "No? Very well, this inquiry is concluded. Gentlemen, I remind you this discussion and all information associated with this incident are classified at the highest level. Any disclosure will have the gravest impact on your country, not to mention yourselves. That's all. Thank you." He nodded to the door, and Ben and Sam stood up to leave. Ben turned to see Simmons still sitting.

"So long, friend," the agent said.

"Yeah, please tell Victoria I'm thinking of her, and I'll email her as soon as I get my head straight."

"Will do," Simmons whispered, offering his right hand as he smiled. "Good luck, Ben."

Ben shook his hand warmly. "You too, Pete."

Ben rejoined Sam, and they were making their way out of the room when Mercier pulled them aside. "Listen, I know you guys are tired, but let's chat down in my office," she said.

"Very good, ma'am," Sam replied.

"I'll meet you down there in about ten minutes."

"Yes, ma'am," Sam and Ben said together.

****

"I'll start by saying I'm sorry we had to keep you guys on edge for so long—it can't have been easy after the grommet you've been pulled through," Mercier said.

"We understand, ma'am," Sam led off. "Honestly, I'm feeling pretty lucky right now, still having a job after shooting up two civilian vehicles on U.S. soil without an SNO."

"The circumstances were what they were, and nobody will second guess you on that call. Changing focus, how did your crew do with all this?"

Sam leaned forward. "They could not have been better. Ben, in particular, deserves the highest praise and reward, and I'll be putting him and the Bridge crew in for personal awards."

Ben was deeply moved by the recommendation from the man he admired so highly. "Ah..." was all that he could say before Mercier interrupted.

"No, we can't have documentation referencing this mission." Seeing Sam's face darken, she added quickly, "We have that covered. You two will each be getting the Coast Guard Medal. I'm afraid all that will show up in the official record and your fitness reports are you received it for a 'Classified Action.' I presume you want individual awards for some of your crew as well?"

"Yes, for Chief Drake and Petty Officer Hopkins. Commendation Medal, at least. Deffler deserves one too, but he doesn't work for me."

"He's covered. Consider all those awards done. It's a pity no one will be able to brag about them. Hopefully, there will be more opportunities soon."

"Thank you, ma'am. They won't mind. If you don't mind, ma'am, what do you mean 'more opportunities'?"

"Yes, it goes with why you haven't chopped back to Sector Miami yet. We will hold on to you guys for a while, indefinitely, actually, and we'll be making a few changes."

"I don't understand."

"Did you think you gained all that talent by accident or good luck? *Kauai* was on our radar long before the mishap, with the negative personnel actions and equipment casualties well above the norm. We sent Drake in to relieve the previous chief to find out what was happening. I'm sure you realize by now that Drake is a 'fixer' in general rather than just the technical sense."

Sam nodded. "Yes, he has shown a scary ability to get around things to keep us operating, and Ben has leaned on him for the XO uglies."

"That's for sure," Ben agreed, realizing for the first time how timely and correct Drake's "If I were you, XO, I would..." suggestions had been.

Mercier nodded. "He let us know right away the old command had to go. We were working on doing that quietly when the mishap forced our hand. The challenge was finding people we could send in on short notice who could pull things together. Sam, you were already here, working up as an Ops Center supervisor, and had come off a very successful PB command in Hawaii. For XO, we took a hard look at the Prospective XO list and plucked Ben off *Dependable* a few months early, at Drake's suggestion."

"I hadn't met Drake before," Ben said.

"True, but he 'knew a guy' on the ships of several of the candidates, and you came up on top. As usual, he was spot-on.

"After *Kauai's* mishap, we decided to rebuild her crew wholesale. This provided an opportunity to try out a proof of concept of an elite Seventh District patrol boat that we can send into sticky situations like this one. We quietly made a few 'corrections' in the complement around your arrival. Then it was just a question of waiting for the proper test. This was it. It was pure luck you guys found that wreck; otherwise, we would have gotten you underway to take over."

"Okay, Captain, so we have a dream team, thanks to you and Chief Drake. I'm still happy but humbler." Sam half-smiled.

"Don't sell yourselves short. It took good leadership to save that boat. If we hadn't found a solid command cadre like you two, we would probably have just written her off and moved up the decommissioning. As it stands, you're a very useful asset, particularly now."

"Why now, ma'am?"

"You've been introduced to the challenge and understand our need to respond quickly, competently, and discreetly. Our experiment to set up a 'dream team,' as you say, has grown out of our hands. The National Command Authority needs an option to use quick, surgical actions in the maritime environment that don't gin up the chaos of diverting Navy destroyers or subs. The ability to act in home waters without stirring up issues with the DoD doing law enforcement is also a big plus. You and your crew proved yourselves able to provide that capability. We had a lengthy discussion before you guys showed up, and your pal Simmons had put in a real stellar assessment of you in his official report. You made a highly favorable impression on him."

"Ma'am, I can promise you he won't be as happy if I ever cross paths with him again."

Mercier frowned. "Oh, I see. Anyway, you impressed that committee with how you pulled off this one. Despite what you might have thought when you came in, the 'interrogation' was a genuine fact-finding and a chance to gauge you in person. They had already decided to move you along to 'better things,' provided you didn't blow yourselves up in there. Now, exercising that capability comes at a big jump in personal risk, as you have also seen. So much so, I can't order you to take it on."

"Ma'am, let me get this straight: doing this job is a voluntary assignment?" Ben asked.

"No, you can ask to be relieved, and we will approve it, regretfully. But consider carefully before you do that. Remember, the request and relief will be on the record."

After a thoughtful pause, Ben broke the silence. "What's to think about? I'm in, ma'am. But if we expect to take on any more murderous TCOs, I'd like more firepower and training than a P229 pistol and boarding officer school."

"Yes, we already put together a scratch tactical course for you in Quantico. You, Bondurant, Guerrero, and Lee, that is." Mercier smiled. "We'll be sending Lopez to Charleston for the next Maritime Law Enforcement Specialist class in a couple of weeks, and he'll get, um, 'extra attention' there. We'll be adding an ME3 billet to *Kauai* to hold him when he graduates."

"How did you know I would ask for... Oh, Chief Drake." Ben grinned.

"Yep, he's already felt them out about it. They're in if you are. Also, we're pulling *Kauai* out of action for an upgrade of the armory and combat systems. We'll see you'll have something to use when you return. For once, we have both official backing and enough funding. The shipyard availability will be an excellent cover for your absence at training."

She turned back to Sam. "I get this was a rough one, and you are too knocked out to give a considered answer. It's also a tough job for a man with a young family. Consult on the home front and call me as soon as you can."

"Thank you, Captain. Given everything you've told us, it's tough to ask to be relieved," Sam responded. "I think Jo will swallow hard and bless this, but it's a new ballgame, and she gets a vote."

Mercier sat back and smiled. "Thank you. I don't see how we can pull this off without you, and so I'd personally be very grateful if she could be persuaded. Let's see, what else? Oh yes, one last thing. We'll be moving you up to Canaveral. On the record, you will be the permanent Range Safety Cutter for the Space Center. There should be fewer questions about the Seventh hanging on to a one-ten that way."

"Um, ma'am, changing homeport generates a lot of paperwork for both the skipper and XO. How can I take care of that while I'm eating snakes up in Quantico?" Ben asked.

"We'll put a team together to cover you. It won't go into effect until after the shipyard work is complete. Anything else? With your stock so high, now's the time to ask."

"Ma'am, I'd sure like to hang on to Hopkins," Sam began. "We'll be rewriting the book to make the best use of our new stuff, and I need what she brings to the table. But I don't want to keep her if that means she gives up pinning on chief. Is there any way we can bump her billet up to E7 since we will take this boat 'off the books' anyway?"

Mercier nodded with satisfaction. "You continue to impress. Get a thumbs up from her that she wants to stay, and I'll make it happen. Anything else?"

"Yes, ma'am, one last thing. We'd have been dead ducks without our UAV support, and Deffler went out on a limb to fly them in that fog. Since he was technically the pilot-in-command, he'll be in a real jam if any pearl-clutchers start second-guessing. I'm sending a memo to Deffler's CO explaining and taking responsibility for the flights and recommending him for a decoration. It would carry a lot more weight if you pitched in."

"Man, you want *everything*, don't you?" Mercier grinned. "Don't give it another thought. Send me a copy of the memo, and I'll ring him up for a chat. We're academy and flight school classmates, which should provide some heft for you. Now, last call, anything else?"

"No, ma'am," both men replied.

"Great. One last order for both of you. Go home, get some rest and blow off steam. You need it. *Kauai* is offline until further notice. And don't even try sneaking back aboard to work for at least seventy-two hours—you know I have eyes there now," she said, shaking their hands.

"That we do, ma'am," Sam said as he led Ben out. They passed wordlessly through the outer office and down the hall before pausing at the elevator. Sam broke first, doubling over in laughter, and Ben was startled but quick to follow.

"Holy shit, Skipper! What the hell just happened in there?"

"You heard the captain. We saved the world, changed homeports, and became the Coast Guard's first Special Operations team." Sam chuckled as the elevator door opened. "Hooyah!"

After they entered and the doors closed, Ben asked, "Honestly, you think Jo will be OK?"

"She won't like it," Sam replied. "It will be a hard sell, given what she knows about Hoppy's personal history. I may have to lean on Hoppy to help close the deal, and it'll be a stretch, even with her help."

"Yes, sir," Ben said soberly, his thoughts going back to the infuriation Hopkins had expressed over his decisions on this operation. He was suddenly very concerned that this deal might be DOA.

"You OK?"

"Yes, sir," Ben replied. "It's just all settling in for me. I'll be fine."

16

Coda

Hopkins

When *Kauai*'s GV turned onto the dock around 05:30, Hopkins had been waiting anxiously on the Bridge with Deffler for over an hour. She looked over at him, and he smiled and reached out to take her hand. He really was a fine man—intelligent, funny, good-looking, and sensitive. He seemed to know she was terrified for the two officers and just stayed with her until they returned. They went down together to join Drake, already on the dock.

Hopkins's heart was in her throat until Ben flashed them a grin and thumbs-up when he stepped out of the GV. After returning their salutes, Sam and Ben each shook their hands. "Welcome home, Captain, XO," Drake said.

"Thanks, Chief," Sam replied. "Let's cut the crew loose for normal post-patrol liberty as soon as possible. You can hold off tearing down the mains for now. We're offline indefinitely, and we have an unscheduled shipyard period. No sense doing a lot of work that may just be undone."

"Very good, sir. Can you elaborate a bit?"

"I think you know the score already, Chief, based on Captain Mercier's very complete intel on *my* crew." Sam ended the answer with a raised eyebrow.

"What can I say, Captain? I know a gal downtown."

"Right. Remind me to discuss that with you later." He turned to Hopkins. "Hoppy, can we move on to the cabin in a minute, please? There's something I need to talk to you about." Seeing the sudden look of concern on her face, he added, "Don't worry, I'm pretty sure you'll think it is excellent news."

"Yes, sir."

He then turned to Deffler and shook his hand. "Fritz, unfortunately, this is the end of our time together. I can't find the words to tell you how grateful I am for what you and Mike have done for us on this op. I'm sending a memo to your CO singing your praises and stating that any violations of flying regulations were because I held a gun to your head. It's not much, but I'm sure it will cover you."

"I appreciate that, Captain." Deffler smiled in return. "I don't suppose you can find some ISR work for us around here until, I don't know, maybe April?"

Sam chuckled. "Sorry, Airedale, there are things even a PB skipper can't do. Good luck, stay warm, and be safe up there." He returned Deffler's salute and then turned to go inside.

Hopkins smiled at Deffler and said, "See you in a minute?"

"I'll be on the messdeck," he replied.

Hopkins ducked into the ship, and when she reached the cabin, Sam pointed at the spare chair. "Take a seat, please." He continued after she sat. "Hoppy, a bunch of people in high places are satisfied with how we carried off the last operation. So much so that they're going to invest in equipment upgrades and specialized training. We will be the go-to folks for special operations. As part of that, I asked for, and they agreed I can keep you— with a bump up to chief."

Sam paused as her eyes widened and her mouth hung open in shock.

"It's your decision, and if you decide to move on, you'll get complete support from me. I want you to stay, and we need your insight and skills, but you need to understand what this means. We will probably be committed to operations like the last one, some of which will involve serious hazards. I can promise you we'll be better-trained and smarter in the future, but the risks will still be high. I appreciate your candor on the last op, which was on the nose in the end. But I need to know you can take it when the kids have to launch out because it will happen, and we won't have the luxury of time for soul-searching when it does."

She could not believe her ears. Just a few minutes ago, she had been afraid of getting caught up in the relief for cause of the finest men she had ever known. Now, not only was that horror vanquished, but the most significant conflict she ever faced, leaving *Kauai* or turning down a promotion, had just been removed as well. She grinned and said, "Sir, I'm in if you and Mr. Wyporek are. I hope I can still point out when I have concerns, *respectfully*, of course."

"You damn well better call us out when we screw up. It's your ass too," Sam said as they both stood.

She was so delighted that she couldn't hold back and gave him a quick, warm hug.

"Dammit, Hoppy, dismissed!"

"Sorry, sir, won't happen again, sir. Thank you, sir!" she said, rushing out of the cabin. She bounded to the messdeck, Deffler standing just in time to be enveloped in another, more passionate hug.

"Things went well, I take it," he said dryly.

"You could say that," she replied with a warm smile. "I get to stay on board AND make chief!"

"Oh, Emilia, I'm so happy for you!"

"Yes, yes. Enough about that. Want to take a pre-chief out for some breakfast?"

"Let me get changed," he said with a smile.

Ben

After Sam, Hopkins, and Deffler left the dock, Drake had turned to Ben. "What's going on with Hoppy, sir?"

Ben grinned. "The skipper worked his spooky magic and found a way to keep Hoppy aboard *and* let her pin on chief." His smile faded. "If she wants to hang around."

"Seriously, sir? Why wouldn't she?"

"She ripped me a new one yesterday for my little adventure. I had it coming, too. Put a new spin on the dangers of glory-hunting for me. I'm unsure she still wants to work for me."

Drake looked at Ben in surprise and shook his head. "XO, you sure have some dense patches for a smart fella. She *loves* you, sir, you and the CO. Yes, she's mad as hell at you two for putting yourselves on the spot like that, but that doesn't mean she would want to be anywhere else." When Ben looked down and shifted nervously, he added, "Don't let it get inside your head, sir. Just keep doing what you're doing, and everything will be fine."

"Thanks, Chief."

Drake nodded, and they both crossed over onto *Kauai*, Drake aft toward the messdeck and Ben to his stateroom. After hearing Hopkins depart, Ben got up and stood in Sam's doorway, watching him type out something on his workstation, probably an email to Mercier.

Finally, Sam looked up, and Ben said, "I'm your ride this morning, Captain."

"Thanks, man, but I can make it OK."

Ben shook his head firmly. "No, sir. Remember a few days back, around the last time *you* slept, when you pointed out the fatigue in our passenger? I'm seeing the same thing in you right now. Look, you just saved my life at the risk of your job. Let me give back a little."

"OK, you win. Let's get going before I decide to crash here."

They strolled down to Ben's white Camaro, an academy graduation present from his parents, and climbed in. Sam nodded off before they even reached the base security gate. Observing his friend fast asleep, Ben activated his phone and used the voice feature to dial Sam's home number.

"Um, hello?" Jo answered groggily after four rings.

"Hi, Jo. Ben here."

"Ben?" He could hear the alarm rising in her voice. "What...?"

"It's OK. Everybody's fine," he interjected. "We're on the way there. Sam is pretty knocked out, and I think he's been up for about three days solid. He dropped off right after he got in the car."

"OK." Her relief was palpable. "I guess you had an interesting trip?"

"It was rough. I'll let Sam tell you about it. I just wanted to let you know he might not be the usual super-attentive hubby when he gets home."

"Thanks, I'll shunt him straight to bed," she replied. "What about you? Do you need to flop here? I can make up the couch for you."

"No, I'm fine. I'm a lot younger than you two, remember?"

"I'll pass on calling you a jerkwad just this once because I love you for taking care of my man."

"All part of my usual awesomeness." Ben smiled. "I'll see you soon."

"Goodbye Ben, and thank you *very much*," she said, hanging up.

The trip home was slow, but typical for Miami. Ben pulled into the driveway a little after 06:30, climbed out, and opened the passenger door. "Skipper." He shook Sam's shoulder gently. "Sam?"

Sam startled awake. "Wha... Oh, right." He climbed out of the Camaro and grabbed his bag. He turned to Ben and hugged him. "Thanks, man."

"You too, Boss. See you in a few days." Ben watched Sam walk tiredly to the front door before climbing into the Camaro. As he drove off, his thoughts returned to the beautiful analyst in Bethesda. Ben knew he shouldn't get his hopes up, as there were so many ways things could go off the rails. Yet, he was sure things were about to get as interesting in his personal life as they were in his professional one.

Sam

The relief and surprise of going from the edge of career death to being lauded and decorated had passed, and Sam was dead on his feet. If anything, the brief nap in Ben's car had rendered him dizzier than he was before. Sam fumbled with his key briefly, then unlocked and opened the door and entered the quiet house. He wondered if he might be the only one up when Jo emerged from the kitchen barefoot in her red nightshirt. *God, she's so beautiful,* was the single thought his fatigue-addled brain could form when Sam looked at her long raven hair and lovely dark eyes. "Jo, I..." He stopped when she put a finger to her lips. She stepped forward, cupped his face in her hands, gazing into his eyes for what seemed like minutes, and then tightly hugged him, all without a single word.

She released him, took his arm, led him toward the bedroom, and whispered, "It's rack time for you, my dear captain. Ben called me with a head's up while you were on the way. You can tell me all about it after you've had some sleep."

Sam nodded. "Aye, aye, my love." He paused at Robby and Danni's bedroom, as he did every morning when he was home, and peeked in to ensure they were sleeping comfortably and covered. Sam then let himself be led to the bed and undressed, practically falling onto the bed afterward. He felt a soft kiss on his lips as he drifted off to sleep.

"Platov Resigns, Naming Andreyev as Acting President," *The New York Times*, February 17th.

MOSCOW. Mikhail I. Platov shocked his nation and the world today, announcing his resignation as President of the Russian Federation and handing over power to his constitutional successor, Prime Minister Nikolai G. Andreyev. The official government announcement cited "medical concerns" as the reason for Mr. Platov's sudden resignation, but did not elaborate further.

Mr. Platov, 69, abruptly concluded his political career in high drama in contrast to his quiet assumption of power twenty years ago following what many experts believe was the last free and fair presidential election in Russia.

There was speculation in Moscow that Mr. Platov's resignation was, in fact, a *coup d'état*, led by Mr. Andreyev, with the support of the military and Russia's financial elite. Mr. Platov faced considerable internal opposition and near-worldwide condemnation following a series of nakedly aggressive moves against the Russian Federation's neighboring countries. Still, most analysts believed his hold on the Russian media and security services would indefinitely ensure his survival in the presidency.

One of Mr. Andreyev's first decrees as acting president was to call for the general election scheduled for March 25th next year to be advanced to May 15th of this year. He will continue to hold the office of Prime Minister while acting as President. Mr. Andreyev has retained most of his staff from the Prime Minister's Office and is expected to dismiss Mr. Platov's Chief of Staff and most of the former president's inner circle of advisors. There has been no announcement of grants of amnesty or immunity from criminal or administrative investigations for the former president, unlike those following the resignation of Russian Federation President Boris Yeltsin in 1999.

President Driscoll phoned Mr. Andreyev this morning, joining many world leaders in wishing the new Russian leader well. There is no official comment from the administration regarding how the change in leadership might affect U.S.-Russia relations. However, unnamed sources within the State and Defense Departments expressed a general sense of relief and indicated the recent pullback from confrontation in Eastern Europe is expected to continue under the new Russian regime.

Some Notes from the Author

None of the characters in this book represent any particular person (you got that, all you lawyers out there?). However, some of the best qualities of the fictional crew members of *Kauai* were inspired by many of the fine people with whom I had the honor and pleasure to serve while I was a part of the Coast Guard.

USCGC *Kauai* is fictional. There is no "D Class" of the 110-foot patrol boat series, and the last of those built was USCGC *Galveston Island* (WPB-1349). I created a fictitious D-Class to buy some extra margin of verisimilitude and get the nit-pickers off my back. The cutters *Poplar* and *Skua* are also fictional instantiations of the *Juniper*-class buoy tender and Marine Protector class coastal patrol boats. The medium endurance cutters *Dependable* and *Mohawk* are real and currently in service as of this writing.

The mishap referred to in the story that led to Sam's assumption of command of *Kauai* is another entirely fictitious plot device

The dialog between the Coast Guard people and in radio transmissions depicted in this story has much more "plain language" than what you would hear during actual operations. Including all the acronyms, jargon, and formal protocols vital for clarity and brevity in real life would have been more authentic. However, it would also be a great deal more tedious or confusing for the average reader. I ask all veterans and any other purists' forgiveness for this compromise for the sake of readability.

MAYDAY, MAYDAY – Request Assistance!

First of all, thank you for purchasing *Dagger Quest*! I know you could have picked any number of books to read, but you chose this book, and for that, I am incredibly grateful. I hope it gave you what you were seeking, be it a little extra enjoyment or just a chance to escape the trials and tribulations of life for a while. If so, it would be really helpful if you could share this book with your friends and family by posting a mention of it on Facebook and Twitter.

If you enjoyed this story, I'd like to hear from you and hope that you could take some time to post a review or at least a rating on your bookseller's website. Your feedback and support will help me as I work on future projects, and I am very interested in hearing your thoughts. Please visit my website when you have the time to provide your feedback, find out what is new, and grab the occasional freebie:

 https://www.edwardhochsmann.com

Very Respectfully,

Ed

Post a Review

Friends, we authors live and die by the ratings you provide on your bookseller's website and book discovery services such as Bookbub. If you liked this book, I ask you for one last service: please use one of the QRC/URL links below to give it a rating or review. Thank you so much for your attention and participation.

Bookbub:
https://www.bookbub.com/books/dagger-quest-cutter-kauai-sea-adventures-book-1-by-edward-m-hochsmann

Amazon:
http://mybook.to/DaggerQuest

Apple:
https://books.apple.com/us/book/dagger-quest/id6442839518

The Next Book in the Series

It's the deadliest nerve gas ever made, and it has fallen into the hands of a murderous Caribbean drug cult!

The criminal 252 Syndicate has developed a game-changing battlefield nerve gas in a secret lab hidden on an oil rig servicing ship. But the ship has been caught in a drug war in a Caribbean country, seized by one of the most vicious drug cartels in existence, and held for ransom.

Alerted by a defecting 252 member, the U.S. government has no good options. It cannot mount an airstrike or an armed raid on a nominally friendly country, and there is no time for diplomatic action that preserves the secret of the new weapon—the 252s will launch their own attack in five days. The best of the bad options is a covert raid led by young Coast Guard Officer Ben Wyporek and his crew aboard the newly-upgraded, stealth-equipped Cutter *Kauai*. But Ben's last lethal encounter with the 252s has cured his hunger for glory, and he has found his soulmate in the beautiful genius DIA analyst Victoria Carpenter. It is another deadly race against the 252s to save the world, and now Ben and Victoria have everything to lose.

Excerpt from *Caribbean Counterstrike*:

OSUV *Carlos Rojas*, under Tow, Isla de Barbello Harbor, Honduras
02:53 EDT, 6 April

Ben

Like Sam over on *Kauai*, Ben had to suppress the urge to jump every time lightning flashed out on the starboard side. The rain had passed entirely, and visibility was nearly perfect. Ben and Lopez had nothing to occupy their attention as the ships slowly moved out of the harbor, unlike their shipmates on the other vessel. He was thoroughly frightened and deduced Lopez was in the same state.

"So, Lope, when we were debriefing after the last one, Captain Mercier told us you would get some 'special' attention over at Law Enforcement School. Did that come to pass?"

"Oh, yeah, sir. While everyone else in my class was living the good life in Charleston every weekend, I was getting advanced small arms and personal defense training shoved up my ass!"

"I hear ya. I got the same thing up in Quantico. Like to freeze my ass off on that small arms range all day." He winced again in the darkness as a long series of lightning flashes strobed across the starboard side. It was actually quite beautiful, the bolts weaving up from the surface of the Caribbean and then winding through and lighting up the clouds from within. He wished he could enjoy the view. "Quite a show."

"No shit, sir," Lopez said in a measured voice. "I'd prefer to see this movie in the next showing, though."

Ben laughed, then looked forward in alarm as a searchlight lanced into the darkness from the promontory, followed by the sound of gunfire. "Shit!" He keyed his radio. "Alpha-Four, One, light off now!"

"Alpha-One, Four, roger, lighting off!" Brown replied.

As the first flare burst off to starboard, a muffled whirring sounded deep in the hull, followed by the rattling rumble from the smokestacks as the ship's generator fired. The main engines needed a lot more power to turn over than the batteries could provide, so step one was getting a generator running. As the generator's noise topped out, a second, louder whirring came up from the engine spaces. Ben's heart sank when the initial rumble of the large engine died away. A second main engine start sequence sounded a few seconds later, with the same result. Ben was about to key his radio, then thought better of it. An inquiry at this point would just distract Brown from his work. The sound of automatic gunfire came up from the well deck—the SEALs joined the fight with their heavy machine guns.

The fight between *Kauai* and the promontory was heating up, and Ben could hear the 'thumps' every half-second from the main gun and see the tracers streak across the water. Williams was doing a good job keeping the pressure on. So far, nothing more than small arms fire was being thrown their way. Suddenly, a flash followed by an enormous boom came from *Kauai*, and the main gun ceased firing. "Shit, shit, shit!" Ben exclaimed, pounding his fist on the helm console. After a few seconds, the rapid thumping and twenty-five-millimeter tracer streaks returned, and Ben let out an enormous sigh of relief.

Ben was about to comment on a second flare that had appeared almost overhead when an enormous blast threw him to the deck. One moment he was standing there; the next, he was flat on his face, covered in broken glass. "Lope!"

"Here, sir! I'm OK!" the young petty officer said as he got to his knees.

Ben looked behind the Bridge. The rocket had hit the port smokestack, which was now shredded. He had just gotten to his feet and pulled Lopez up when the second rocket hit the foredeck. This time, the forward windows shattered, and the two men were thrown down again. Worse, shrapnel from the explosion sliced through some outer strands of the towing hawser. Given the enormous strain the line was under, there could be only one result: the cascade of individual strand failures in milliseconds merged into one loud "Bang." The two new ends shot away from the breakpoint, one slamming into *Carlos Rojas*'s superstructure with a loud "clang" and the other falling into the water just short of *Kauai*.

Ben looked forward in shock as they got to their feet again, then keyed his tactical radio. "Alpha-Four, Alpha-One, we just lost the towline. We need main engines now, or we're dead!"

"Almost there, sir! We've fixed the problem and are closing up now!"

"For God's sake, hurry!"

"Yes, sir!"

Buy *Caribbean Counterstrike* today!

https://www.edwardhochsmann.com/books/kauaiseaadventures/caribbean-counterstrike/

Short Story—Ben Saves a Family

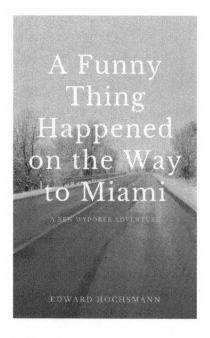

An ice storm had just passed on that frigid January morning in Southern Virginia as Lieutenant Junior Grade Ben Wyporek made his way to his new assignment aboard USCG Cutter *Kauai* in Miami. Little did he know that icy roads were about to become the least of his worries.

Read "A Funny Thing Happened on the Way to Miami" exclusively on Amazon Kindle.